ENTANGLED
LIVES

Entangled Lives

MEMOIRS OF 7 TOP EROTICA WRITERS

edited by

MARILYN JAYE LEWIS

alyson books
NEW YORK

These are true stories. Certain names and descriptions have been changed to protect the privacy of others.

Manufactured in the United States of America

This trade paperback original is published by Alyson Books
245 West 17th Street, New York, New York 10011
Distribution in the United Kingdom by Turnaround Publisher Services Ltd.
Unit 3, Olympia Trading Estate, Coburg Road, Wood Green
London N22 6TZ England

FIRST EDITION: JULY 2007

07 08 09 10 11 a 10 9 8 7 6 5 4 3 2 1

ISBN: 1-55583-998-3
ISBN-13: 978-1-55583-998-7

Library of Congress Cataloging-in-Publication data are on file.

Cover design by Victor Mingovits
Interior design by Jane Raese

Contents

Introduction

MARILYN JAYE LEWIS

"And that which hath been done
is that which shall be done;
And there is nothing new under the sun."
—ECCLESIASTES 1:9

WRITERS WHO EARN their livings, or at least subsidize their livings, by writing erotic fiction are rarely called upon to write true exposés of their own sex lives, especially these days, when erotic anthologies celebrating the most niche-marketed fetishes imaginable abound in the bookstores and so many of us have scrambled to find enough time to contribute stories to each of them. It doesn't leave a lot of room for erotic nuance in our work. And while there is almost always a kernel of truth in most fiction of any genre, it is hard to believe that erotic writers are plagued, en masse, by so many extreme fetishes in their day-to-day sex lives.

Ah, well, it's a living. And yet back in 2005, I was perusing the latest offering of adult comics over at LastGasp.com, when I happened upon the True Porn series of comic books, edited by Kelli Nelson and Robyn Chapman (Alternative Comics). I was immediately intrigued; *true* porn—it sounded so refreshing. I like adult comics specifically because the sex depicted in them goes over the top. Things happen in comics that are often physically impossible, or at the very least improbable, in actual adult sex, and for me, all that physical improbability makes the images intensely erotic. Comic-book sex is often visceral sex that is at once both shocking to look at and satisfyingly filthy; the best of all mind fucks for a rather introverted, antisocial erotic fiction writer such as myself.

However, the thought of cartoonists throwing open a perhaps cautionary door to their own intimate sexual encounters, giving us the real goods—well, as Daniel Robert Epstein of SuicideGirls.com comments in a review of True Porn, "Cartoonists have the most fucked-up sex lives." It promised to be a remarkable journey into the human sexual condition.

That's when it struck me: Why aren't erotica writers asked to openly delve into their own sex lives more often? A healthy number of the erotica writers that I personally know have rather interesting and active sex lives—to put it politely. It would make for great reading, I thought, and for a nice change of pace from the endless short-story collections of improbable fetishes that don't really allow the reader access to the writer as a human being.

Privately, I had begun making notes for my own full-length erotic memoir back in 2005. In fact, a few of the chapters were already in first draft, and I had quickly discovered while writing it that it was a simultaneously daunting, emotionally exposing, and, above all, joyful feeling of release, putting the facts of my erotic life, and not the fiction of my erotic mind, on paper at last. And not just in another essay on some particular sexual peccadillo I might be guilty of, but really taking into account the people I had been involved with, who they

2

were as living human beings and as sex partners, how I responded to my sexuality, and my regrets as well as what felt like my triumphs.

I wondered if the other erotica writers I knew, the ones who primarily wrote fiction and had been doing so for years, would share my enthusiasm for pulling back the metaphorical curtain for a change and reveal the beating hearts lurking beneath all those fictional erotic tomes.

I wondered, What about an anthology of *true erotica,* then? What might that tell us about the human sexual condition?

To my delight, the writers I queried were gung ho to find out, even though all of us were laboring under the same overloaded writing schedule already and I was asking for contributions of a somewhat hefty word count. It seemed that the lure of getting personal, of focusing on our own libidinous natures and taking center stage in our own work for a change, had an uncanny way of making room in those crammed schedules. Most of the writers said, in fact, "I know just the thing I want to write about." And every one of us was still scribbling feverishly at the already extended deadline's eleventh hour.

o   o   o

THERE IS NO SHORTAGE of erotic memoirs in Western literature, of course. In any given year, someone will be shocking us, at least here in the United States, with some steamy tell-all in hardcover. Erotic memoirs of a more literary nature, however, tend not to make it to these shores except by way of the small presses and then in trade paperback, but still, they do eventually surface, and a number of them find a healthy-sized audience. What sets *Entangled Lives* apart from the multitude of erotic memoirs, though, is that these are memoirs written by, as has already been established, popular erotic fiction authors, men and women who are published extensively in the GLBT market, and the memoirs are brief enough to be collected under one cover and thereby still fall under the currently trendy banner of "erotic anthology."

Another somewhat unusual thing for an erotic memoir is that all the writers included here are writing under their given names. You can read the unabashed accounts of our sexual insecurities as well as our overindulgences and detailed exploits. Then you can perhaps spy us in the local bar and gawk and point. We aren't camouflaged at all—except for the mysterious eighth contributor, known here as "Adam Greenway."

Adam's bio at the back of the book assures us that we are more than likely familiar with his work. That he is, in fact, "one of queerotica's most lyrical authors" and that he's a "poet, writer, and quiet enigma" who has "published work in numerous anthologies and online venues."

Adam comes to us by way of the sexually open marriage of Greg Wharton and Ian Philips. The mere title of their joint memoir, "Threeway," enlightens us as to the nature of Adam's entrance into our collective entangled lives. He came to our project almost through a side entrance and yet wound up contributing a voice, however quietly—Adam's reluctance to make so much as a groan during sex is expounded on at length in these pages by both his lovers—but still, in print he expresses the same questioning vulnerability, the same ache and unfathomable need to feel sexually satiated, to understand his own sometimes unsettling desires as the identifiable contributors here.

When Ian and Greg alerted me that their memoir would tell the story of a threeway that was currently unfolding in their marriage, and that the third man in question, who was also in publishing, had agreed to be part of the memoir under a guarantee of the strictest anonymity, I at once donned my detective's cap and tried to figure out who the mysterious "Adam Greenway" was. After all, who among us can resist the temptation to solve such a salacious puzzle? I had my suspicions and eventually learned that I had guessed right. And while I was eager to read the final *Rashomon*-type tale, where each man gives his take on what really happened while the three were courting, seducing, and then ultimately fucking one another, I wasn't prepared for how moved I was going to be reading it.

Not knowing "Adam" personally but knowing his work and his reputation in the industry, I was not only honored that he was contributing to my erotic memoir project but, while reading it, also touched by his willingness to be so candid, so matter-of-fact about his own particular vulnerabilities and desires.

Indeed, that was what struck me most profoundly about every memoir submitted here. I'm not going to be coy about it. As the deadline drew nearer and I knew everyone's contributions would soon be landing on my desk, I was more than a little voyeuristically gleeful with anticipation. After all, my colleagues, who are all known for their abilities to write intensely erotic stories, would soon be regaling me with all the prurient details of their own private lives—who wouldn't welcome an opportunity like that? The project was by far the easiest editing job I'd ever undertaken. The high level of professionalism among the writers had a lot to do with it. But more than that, I was so absorbed by each of these memoirs while reading them that it was hard to believe I was actually getting paid to essentially just sit there and read.

I had expected this particular group of writers to approach the topic of their own sex lives with sincerity and an almost brutal honesty—these were the qualities I already appreciated in their fiction. Yet I still wasn't prepared for the other key ingredient underlying each of these memoirs: trust. Each writer's trust in me as the editor to approach what they'd committed to print with a suitable level of appreciation and respect, and trust in you as the reader to risk seeing yourself reflected, to whatever extent, in each of these confessions.

Hadn't I gone on at length in various interviews over the years about how trust was, in my opinion, the most erotic element of sex? That without trust, sex is merely sex, or perhaps even a stymied—or even a mortifying—emotional experience? And still the truth of it struck me anew while reading these memoirs. The details in these pieces are often not only sexually graphic but also emotionally raw. I felt nothing less than honored by the high level of trust my colleagues had placed in me by opening the door to the inner workings of their hearts and minds, not to mention their libidos, as wide as they did.

Lest I gloss over it, I should mention that I also contributed a memoir to this collection. I wrote it expressly to be included here; it wasn't one of those chapters from my full-length memoir that was already in first draft back in 2005. This piece, I knew, would have to be a final draft, that it was going to print. So I knew from experience what the mental processes were, what the potential stumbling blocks might be, in exposing the intimate details of one's private sexual world to the faceless world-at-large. Two of the primary thoughts that played devil's advocate with me were: *Do people really want to know this stuff about me?* and *Once this is in print, people are going to* know *this stuff about me.*

I have my own vulnerabilities and insecurities. I'm still not completely convinced anyone does want to know the secret machinations underlying my intimate relationships, my sexual fetishes, or my exhausting erotic obsessions. I pushed on, though, until I had finished my piece, at least convinced, as I always am when writing something sexual, that somebody somewhere will relate to it in a positive way, that readers might read what I've written and find a reason to rejoice in their own sexual identity, flawed and inexplicable as our sexual identities might sometimes seem.

The truth of my conviction stared me in the face again and again while I read these collected memoirs. I can't say for certain if my own contribution achieved its goal of inalienable validity for readers; I can't really be impartial about my own work. But I can testify with confidence that my fellow contributors achieved the goal in spades. Time and again, I felt as if what was being said by another writer could have easily come from my own insecure (often rambling) inner erotic monologue, and the fact that the given writer sallied forth, regardless of the insecurities, into the tumultuous fray of his or her own "sex life"—well, perhaps you get the picture. As I quoted from Ecclesiastes at the opening of this introduction, "There is nothing new under the sun." But I take that idea as a joyful, unifying element of all humanity. At our cores, we are unique, but are we really that different?

How we do differ is what excites me most about our uniqueness: our voices, what we choose to experience, and then how we express it. I like to think of these writers here as my comrades. Most of us have met at various professional functions, or even gone out and gotten a little too drunk together. We are familiar with one another's work and careers.

And it still didn't fully prepare me for the stories each of these writers would choose to tell.

A case in point being Rob Stephenson, a writer I first knew as TruDeviant. It was a moniker that served him well and gave the reader fair warning about what type of erotic story they would soon be encountering. I have now known Rob for several years. I was half expecting his memoir to be a disquieting affair, perhaps a sadistic account of some hapless Chelsea boy forced into the face paint of a clown and a degrading piece of women's lingerie. . . . I couldn't have been more wrong. I learned more about Rob Stephenson from his piece included here than I'd ever learned from going to lunch or dinner with him, or out to some bar in Chelsea, or in various conversations we've had over the phone. I didn't know him when he was young. He was already forty years old when we met. But suddenly I saw him as a young man, vulnerable, questioning, and searching, undertaking his first serious gay relationship, staking out his sexual identity through frequently unsatisfying trial and error.

It's his story to be sure, but so many parts of it are my story, and I suspect, if you're old enough, parts of it are your story as well.

I knew beforehand that Bill Brent's piece would take us to some dark places. I knew a bit about what he'd been experiencing over the last few years, hooked on meth and caught in that stranglehold of constant tweaking and extreme sex. Not everyone comes back from that trip, although so many people these days have embarked on it.

I was very familiar with Bill's strength as a writer, though. I knew he would be relentless in his mission to record his experiences as accurately as possible. The honesty and the anguish come together here to paint a picture we all have a place in:

where it is that our insecurities lead us, and how we learn from that place and find our way back.

It's interesting to note that the three women contributing to this collection, Rachel Kramer Bussel, Amie M. Evans, and myself, wrote memoirs from the perspective of being bottoms, of being sexually submissive females. This was something I hadn't expected. It took me by complete surprise since all the memoirs, in a sense, landed on my desk on the same day. It was too late to run out and round up a last-minute contribution from a domme, or from a woman who was neither a top nor a bottom. I wondered if this sudden situation would perhaps throw the overall tone of the collection off-balance. But I don't think it does. Fortuitously, each of the three pieces underscore the most salient issues of being a bottom—the hypnotic allure of pain and the depth of arousal a woman's body reaches when it is natural for her to submit sexually to the will of another.

In the case of Amie Evans, there doesn't seem to be a moment of doubt that bottoming is an exquisite sensation to be explored as fully as possible. That giving in to the unconquerable dual wills of her clit and her vagina is a type of surrender that makes her feel not just sexually but also spiritually whole. Indeed, her submission to her body's voluptuous demands is the underlying constant in a healthy relationship and professional collaboration with her life partner.

My twenty-five years of experience of being a sexual submissive has certain similarities to Amie's regarding how my body responds to it, but psychologically, we approach it from near opposite perspectives. I have rarely felt completely comfortable embracing my sexual masochism, in part because of the era I came of age in, where women were socially discouraged from any supposed antifeminist modes of sexual behavior. For instance, my unflagging desire to be bound and disciplined by older women meant I might be single-handedly undermining the liberation of women everywhere. It took years for me to learn how to boot the world out of my bedroom and simply let my sexuality be what it needed to be.

Rachel Kramer Bussel's significant body of nonfiction work—her magazine articles, her interviews, her essays, and her past *Village Voice* columns—perhaps misled us into thinking that we already know what goes on in her private life. She is the first to admit that much of her fiction already relies heavily on fact. If you are familiar with Rachel's work, however, what you will find written here will surprise and probably delight you. As I did, you might recognize some telltale experiences that wound their ways into Rachel's most popular stories. Yet here, in these pages, we get the other half of the equation: what really happened, how she came to be in the company of these people we've read about, be they casual strangers at play parties or intimate lovers. More important, we learn what she was thinking and feeling, and sometimes struggling with, as she spread her sexual wings and became the writer, the sex chronicler, that she is today.

So there's nothing new under the sun. There's nothing we do with our bodies or with one another that hasn't been done by countless others—with widely varying degrees of legality or social acceptance—for thousands of years. On one level, it's a comforting thought: It's a relief to simply be human when the smoke and mirrors are put away. On another level, it's humbling: What was the big brouhaha all about if, in the end, it was only lust? But on still a third level, new or not, sex is about life, and life is what we all share. Lust is a sacred tool that teaches us how to rejoice as much as it teaches us about the perils of excess or the emptiness of fear. We experience our sex lives as individuals, certainly, but there is an area of human sexuality where all our secrets remain the same, and in that secret exchange we validate ourselves and the ultimate joy of our existence.

Share with me now the smart, adventuresome, and, above all, entertaining memoirs; the one-hundred-percent-true erotica that has resulted in this, our entangled lives.

Threeway

2 + 1 = 3

IAN PHILIPS, GREG WHARTON, AND "ADAM GREENWAY"

Or Before Anybody Fucked Adam

IAN: His name, for now, for here, is Adam. A perfect name for the adventurous doppelgänger of a writer who would like to leave behind his workaday world and lose himself in the strictures and structures of his poems as much and as often as he would like to be bound and broken open by the possibilities within his porn. Perfect because Adam is the first man. All is truly novel to Adam. And he is the ultimate writer, for he gets to name creation, and all who follow must use or rebel against his words, his stories. And our Adam is also perfect because he too is a first man. My first man, our first man, to give a hard jutting angle to the rounded curves of Greg's and my perpetual 69, this marriage of two perverts, pornographers, and publishers. And our Adam will, I hope (I write this opening paragraph without anything having happened yet between all three of us), allow each of us to come together and make a new shape: a longstanding tripod between Greg and his husband (me) and Greg's best friend, Adam. Or, more fitting since all three of us have written and published porn, a squirming triangle: my mouth to Greg's dick, his mouth to Adam's, Adam's to mine.

Of course, this threeway isn't all my doing, obviously, any more than this essay is written all by me. But I was the one who volunteered Greg and Adam into writing this piece (all the better to find out what had been going through their heads when their mouths were too full to talk). And my crush on Adam was the spark that finally helped ignite the smoldering kindling between him and Greg. For Greg had been writing flirting e-mails to Adam at the same time he'd been courting with me. Court and spark—that is Greg in e-mail. He can be a very sexy and shameless flirt.

This was back in 2001. Yes, that's a lot of smoldering. But Adam was in a then monogamous and then five-year relationship with his photographer husband, Christopher, and Greg was in a monogamous twenty-year relationship with his social worker husband, Scott. Both relationships had had their bumps, and more were to come, eventually bumping open a window of possibility for Greg to move from Chicago to live with me in San Francisco in March 2002, and for all three of us to come together in San Francisco in February 2006. As for me, before my first book, *See Dick Deconstruct,* was published in June 2001, I'd been alone in the City for ten years and mostly celibate (due to lack of luck and, in time, lack of interest in retesting said lacking luck). That all changed when, after visiting Greg's website for years, I finally discovered his picture. I dedicated a story in *See Dick* to Greg, and he wrote back about that and my author photo, and, well, the games began.

But that's a different story of how a flaming online affair fleshed itself out into a partnership at all levels. This story is about what happened when we let one more in.

I call this threeway with Adam our experiment in pet-door nonmonogamy. We're opening our relationship wide enough to let in just one pet. We're happy to feed him all that he wants when he's hungry. And he doesn't have to be an indoor pet. He can come and go as he pleases—just as long as he puts on a great show when he comes. And from everything Greg has told me so far about their weekend together in New York, our pet does. Greg's nickname for him is Shooter. But I'm getting ahead of myself.

Let's get back to Adam. The first man, our first man. The chosen, shooting one.

Why him?

As I said earlier, Greg had been flirting online with Adam at the same time he was flirting with me. At first, both with Adam and with me, Greg's flirtation had begun as one writer contacting another, complimenting another: encouraging Adam after his first publication online, and praising a story I had published in *Best Gay Erotica 1999*. Asking both of us to submit to Greg's new Web journal, *suspect thoughts: a journal of subversive writing*. Sweet words and shop talk. And then, with successive e-mails, a bit more spark. A bit more court.

There was even a moment when Greg could have had the mad affair that started our marriage with either Adam or me. He felt that strongly about both of us. Greg told me this, later. Long after we'd moved in together in San Francisco. (As a well-burned former-celibate faggot, I was a bit hyperpossessive—read: insanely jealous—back in those first days. Especially if I'd known my fey-bear self was in the running with some slender doe-eyed boy.) I don't know if Adam ever knew this before now. I don't know if he could have been the future Mrs. Wharton. Or how serious Greg was with Adam to begin with. Did he want him for a collegial fuckbuddy, or perhaps more? It doesn't matter now, since they're each other's best friends—with heavy petting privileges.

And Greg knew I had a crush on Adam, eventually. Even though we'd been open about everything in our very happily closed relationship, I still was pretty closed-lipped when a man (or a succession of men) caught my eye as Greg and I strolled from our apartment in the Mission to our press's mailbox in the Castro and home again. Or about my various schoolgirl crushes on cute boys in bookstores and coffee-houses, two places where Greg and I spend a lot of our non-bookmaking time. Or, in Adam's case, when a man sparked my desires to touch his skin, kiss his lips, suck his dick, finger and fuck his hole. (In other words, a hard crush, or, as it's known by its less sexy nomenclature: an obsession.) But part of the reason it took me a while to tell Greg about Adam was that I hadn't felt all these desires for him instantly—because when Greg and I first met Adam in person, I was so madly in love with Greg that all I noticed about Adam was that he had a very cute face and beautiful wide, soulful blue eyes.

Okay, that's actually not true. It's a heavily gauzy look backward to make a better story. The pitfall of memoirists. More a sand trap. As easy to whack your way into as a virgin asshole in poorly written porn. To be nearly truthful, the im-age of Adam's face and his eyes stayed with me after that first meeting. There is something of the haunted poet in the ex-pression that his face and eyes create when they are at rest, when no one is watching, or when Adam's had enough wine to forget this world. *In vino veritas,* as the Romans liked to say. But *haunted,* perhaps, is not the best word. It does convey the otherworldly feeling I see in his expression, but I don't believe Adam is haunted by remorse over things he's done. I think it is more that he is haunted by unspoken, unacted desires. Behind his eyes, I sense a very turbulent, passionate, even terrifyingly beautiful world. Some of this creeps into his poetry and into his porn. But even there, I think he pulls his punches, much like I would eventually discover he does in his kisses. In kissing, there is even more truth than in wine. Adam's kisses are wet, full, and yet even as his lips part and his tongue pulls mine in, something is held back. There is a hint of tension in his lips. In his squirming tongue even. Quite a feat. But then, so is containing all that writhes within him. And someday, I hope to watch it all come out. Either in Adam's writing or in my mouth or in Greg's ass.

But again I'm getting ahead of myself. Jumbling up time too much. But time, here in this threeway of words about an ongoing threeway that is, at its best, wordless but not soundless, is as jumbled as our limbs are in our most frenzied daisy chain. And this is true for each of us, no matter how very different our styles of writing are—and it will show. If for no other reason than the writerly reality that we've written these segments before, during, and after the cum has been spilled and dried. And writing in cum is so tricky—it's much easier to write to make another come.

Fantasy will bump up against reality until the writers bump up against each other. The first paragraphs of this section that I wrote in February 2006 grind a bit too awkwardly against these paragraphs I'm writing now in August. As for reality, it will bump up against reality, because we writers have bumped up against each other. Each of us experienced a reality when we were together. Alone and not. The same is true as we recollect it here. We are alone and not. Our memories of the other are there, but so are you, the reader, and you bring another reality altogether. As we write, Adam and Greg and I are each trying to arouse the ghost of hot fucks past, inspire more to come, and make you squirm a bit wherever you may be sitting or lying now. So we tell the truth as much as we can remember of what we wish to remember and yet each of us knows, from not only writing porn but from being published for the pleasure (and pain) of doing so, that too much reality makes the erotic juices run dry. (Who knew the supposed high ground of realistic, or is that real, writing, aka literature, could be such a high, dry ground. Shriveled and cracked. Brittle earth. But supposedly the mountaintop all readers long to climb to.) Instead, there must be a bit of green. Which means a bit of water and a trace of shit. And there must be enough shadowy space for you, the reader, to slide in your images, your fantasies, your self. But all three writers will create that space differently here. I overwrite and so I come first. On the full-figured frame of my neurotic abundance of words, you can hang the plot of our story. More or less. I leave it to my boys to give you some hot holes, often gaping with silences or stuffed with contradictions and insights.

But let us go back to when I saw Adam's face only as the face of an acquaintance. A fellow traveler through semicolon-strewn thickets of words. Before I'd ever thought of coming on Adam's face, and Adam's face—the clear skin, the arousing marriage of sharp angles and soft curves, the prominent, expressive eyes, overall that of a slightly older and less innocent Elijah Wood—is a *bukkake* wonderland. It's a face that should be encircled by coming dicks. The more there are, the merrier I am. Till his skin is as beguilingly liquid as his eyes.

Can you tell I've yet to come on his face? It's obvious when I'm writing about something I've never done, isn't it? Whenever I wax poetic, flying high like Icarus on his waxen wings, flush with pornographic detail, that's fantasy. No harsh sunlight of reality to melt me down to earth. Now I'm more earthed when I'm earthy. But it wasn't the lack of great sex in my everyday reality that spoiled my most exuberant porn writing, it was the excess of it. (Thanks, Greg.) Why write when you can do. And now I've modified that, since Adam, to why write when you can do writers.

Okay. Once more into Adam's breach. Back to why Adam. Back to the writer I fucked after Greg, my first writer, first hole, first love. Well, back to Adam's face. (Then his back and finally his backside.)

When I first met Adam, I never thought to look any farther down. To look at the rest of his body. To search out his telltale swell. For this top, that's the swell of fabric and muscle when a man bends over or lunges forward to take the next step. Of course, at the right angle or in the right clothes (or lack thereof), no bending or lunging is necessary—on their part. The curve of the ass reads like a treasure map. But instead of an X, there is, with a little spit and a lot of fingering and tonguing, a welcoming O. Well, at least in a story or two of mine. In reality, I never caught a glimpse of Adam's ass till Greg undressed him in front of me, at my request. Instead, the second time I saw Adam, when he visited us not long after Greg had moved in, I managed to peep my head around the corner at just the right moment and catch only a glimpse of his back as he dressed in our living room, where the sleeper sofa was. And as an aroused newlywed afraid of seeming ungrateful or greedy or, more truthfully, afraid of losing the love of his life if he admitted to a newfound lust in his life, that glimpse forced me to fall back on old habits.

Here's where fantasy and reality bump hard.

As I said earlier, I'd been a mostly celibate and a mostly frustrated faggot for ten long years before I met Greg. My porn stories had become a place where I could do what I could not do in my daily life: control all the dicks in the room. They came for me, and they came on command. Granted, a lot of surreal goings-on occurred between that first flush and the final salvo, but I was as happy as the first Adam naming names. The expulsion from my garden of earthly delights happened anytime I stumbled my way through San Francisco's wasteland of real boys in real time. And so, seeing that bit of Adam's back and knowing that more than a few feet of rent-controlled apartment stood between it and the tips of my fingers, the edges of my lips, I retreated inward and reached for a scenario that is a tried-and-true old reliable in the pornoverse: Adam would just know how much I wanted him, he would know how much I suspected Greg wanted him—or maybe Adam wouldn't know or care about our desires. Regardless, he would want us so much that he would push past the hanging barrier of sunworn fabric that served as a makeshift door between our bedroom and the rest of the apartment; he would enter our bedroom, and Greg and I would put down our his-and-his nighttime reading, and Adam would strip before us and climb into our bed; fade to a very dynamic black.

Of course, that didn't happen. Reality—our realities—kept my unspoken fantasy just that. But four years later, after more fantasy and much speaking, Adam would be naked in that same bedroom and I would no longer have to conjure a single skin cell of him from my shopworn imagination. And we wouldn't turn the lights off once.

o o o

GREG: The wonderful truth is that Ian and I have an open pet door to our relationship and to sex. We're free to have sex with others as long as (a) we're doing it together when we're in the same city, (b) we share all of the juicy details of anything done without the other, (c) we always play safe, and (d) hell, there's no need for a "d." How amazing is that? Neither of us experience jealousy, because we both know how much we love the other and that sex with other men won't change that love or our relationship. And it doesn't.

We don't fuck around with others that often, but there's no reason why we shouldn't explore when the opportunities come up. They have, and they will again. Almost all queer men will think of other men and sex, and I'd probably be safe in assuming that most of the men who think about it go and do something about it—regardless of their relationships. We do it openly and with gusto. I love watching Ian enjoying other men, and it turns me way, way, way on to do it with more than one person at a time. I love putting on a show, and I love doing it in front of my honey. And he enjoys watching me enjoy myself with other men.

It's funny that one of the questions asked quite often of erotic authors (most authors actually) is "Have you done what you write about?" or "How much of this is true?" or "Do you really do that?" And I've often heard authors answer, "No, I'm an author." Or "It's fiction." But guess what? I *do* do that stuff. I have done most of what I write about. (Except for sleeping with my sister's husband, since I don't have a sister, or killing someone, for those of you who know some of my stories. . . . Some of it *is* fiction.) Much of what I've written *is* true, though real folks and memories fold together or warp into another body at another time or place and become new characters. But the sex . . . I've done as much of it as I could. Of

21

course, a lot of it happened at a later time than when written. Does that still count? What can I say? I've always been very sexual. I've had mucho sex. But I blossomed late. I didn't realize my full appetite (see the paragraph above for what turns me way, way, way on) or my full potential until I met Ian.

And with Ian, we made Adam our first pet through the door. He was perfect, is perfect for us. We both love him, respect him, and lust for him. He's comfortable because of our friendship with him. He's got an easy personality that's nonthreatening. He's also willing. Willing to kink it up with us. A bottom. Sure. Good for Ian. But a bottom that knows how to make another bottom happy. Very good for me. Yum. I'm hard as I write this just thinking about him stuffing his fingers up my ass and his mouth around my cock. Or remembering Ian fucking Adam while Adam's fucking me. Our own personal porn movie—only we're the stars. Can't get that without three people. Or four, but that's another story for another time.

o   o   o

ADAM: Our relationship started with words. Since the late nineties we have commingled on the page—online, and in print—but were separated by three states: me in New York, Ian in San Francisco, and Greg sandwiched between us in Chicago. This cross-country grouping would be re-created in bed years later, a transcontinental romp. Until then, we fed one another's sexual appetites with our written fantasies, living out our smutty daydreams in steamy stories and steamier e-mails, tightening slowly together into a mutually gratifying knot.

Greg Fucks Adam in New York

IAN: Somehow I went from being insecure about my body and my sexual abilities and simmeringly jealous, imagining everyone wanting a piece of Greg and him happy to rock the world of all comers, to being a little less insecure about my body, thanks to the good loving of my man, and wanting to get off seeing him rock the world of all comers. I wanted to see him make others' eyes roll up into their heads like he does mine. I wanted to see his incredibly welcoming asshole swallow dick after dick. I wanted to see him leaving others gasping and amazed at how much he could give while taking. And I wanted to see them take the big dick I so often couldn't. (I may be a blabbermouth, but I'm not, alas, a very big mouth. And my asshole. Well, too many not-so-repressed memories block that entrance.) I knew his dick would coax more than a few tears and a lot of dick-hardening (my dick hardening) groans from some well-deserving boy.

But when did I get so comfortable with the idea of making my husband the pass-around-party bottom of queer publishing? I don't know. There was always that nagging voice that said I should get comfortable with nonmonogamy because gay men and sex and monogamy may travel a bit of the road together, but not the whole highway to the death-do-us-part offramp. (Of course, that voice is the same voice that chides me while I write. I try to ignore it as much as possible.) And sure, some of it was toppish pride: You can fuck him now, but he's happiest underneath me. But mostly, I think it was because I found and continue to find Greg obscenely hot and an incredible lay (his porn-writing skills come from his well-lived and well-fucked experiences, fueled by a libido that can melt the walls of an igloo, the complete opposite of mine: nearly all fantasy and research and a bit of remaking horrible first dates less horrible). And, finally, I was slowly coming out of the voyeur closet. A few years into living together with Greg and I'd started to fantasize about how hot it would be to see him having with other people the very same sex we were having at that moment. Usually with the crush-of-the-day or some cute author we'd met. In time, that author became Adam. He was my obsession.

And Greg, as he has always done, gently coaxed both fantasy and the object of my obsession out of me and never laughed at me or belittled me for either of them. Instead, he was willing to play along. He was coming out of the exhibitionist closet himself. And, after all, he'd always wanted to have sex with Adam. Just not as much as I wanted to have sex with Adam. For as much as Greg loves Adam and loves to get it up for Adam, his "Adam" is another author, a writer who has no idea Greg's named a ginormous dildo after him and rides it like he's outrunning the Four Horsemen. (Yes, we have an author fetish. It's out in the open. So much of our libido is channeled into our writing and publishing that it, well, only makes sense that fucking with the people who wrote the words we loved so would be the ultimate culmination of the act of reading and writing and publishing them. The omega orgasm.)

Anyway, I digress, as always. My way of edging closer to the more emotionally embarrassing revelations that I feel lurk just beyond the edges of my peripheral vision as I sit and type. The revelations that make me naked to myself and all readers. Right now, it's telling of where my fantasies and realities collide throughout this threeway. But I can't not reveal them. Then I would be holding back. And as you know from my description of Adam's kisses, holding back drives me wild.

When I fuck, this can be a fun thing. When I write, it makes me miserable.

So what I shudder to reveal is what you, the careful reader, have already deduced. I'm off to the side while all the hot sex is happening in this threeway. So far, at least. In fact, if you skip to one of the "Adam" or "Greg" sections, you'll see how fast they get down to business. Clothes off and they're a human pretzel. Me, I'm always the last one naked.

Until I'm certain my actual body won't be rejected, I like to be on the sides, directing. Running the fuck. Just as I did in my porn. Except there it wasn't about avoidance, just the opposite. I'd write out extremely sexually detailed stories about things I was too scared to do in real life (have sex with any of the hot tranny boys I've had crushes on) or things that I'd done and failed at (have a successful first date) or done and made big mistakes because I was new to it, like any beginner (like bondage, domination, sucking a dick, fucking an asshole).

What can I say, it's taken a lot of therapy and pills and porn writing and sex with Greg to begin to make a real peace with my body, or, more accurately, my body image. An image congealed out of years of shame for being seen by others—and in time by myself—as short and fat and fey while a kid and short and fat and fey and hairy and little-dicked while a young and then middle-aged gay man in San Francisco. In other words, a bit of a misfit. (And this is probably a major reason why in my porn stories the misfits—and all my protagonists who I root for to come and to come big are misfits—always have the best sex. And love their bodies because they know their bodies and know how to have incredible sex with their realistically or fabulisticly imperfect bodies.)

And yet, for all my forward movement, I would still panic over how anyone I was attracted to would perceive me. With

Greg, before we met, it was months of: "What will he say when he hears my voice?" ". . . sees my body?" ". . . sees my naked body?" (Perhaps the most courageous thing I've ever done was buy a cheap camera that looked like an old-time diving bell to take naked pictures of myself to e-mail to Greg.) Once we were together and fucking like newlyweds, it was: "He's so hot. How did he end up with me? What happens if he bumps his head and recovers his real tastes?" Yes, that was how my mind often worked then—and how it still does. It's just that once our affair with Adam built up a good head of pre-cum, I was asking myself the same questions about Adam.

But how did we get that particular dick hard? It's odd; I can remember so much of our affair, except how it began. I know that a year ago, we were all sharing a room at Saints & Sinners, an incredible and incredibly fun conference for LGBT writers and readers in New Orleans. The hell that Katrina would un-leash was still months away. Instead, it was Adam's personal world that had been turned upside down. He and Christopher had just opened their relationship, and Adam was ready to let his well-cloistered inner slut out. Alas, Adam was, well, less ballsy then. Even now, he's more the one you throw against a wall while ripping off his clothes than the one who pushes you up against his hard and insistent desires. But last spring he was looking for sluts, and they were there at Saints & Sin-ners—hell, throughout all of New Orleans—and yes, I was still mooning over him and hoping he'd sneak into our bed, but he chased after the cute boys who wanted to take him home to Mom. I guess it only makes sense with those topsy-turvy laws of physical attraction. All the while I was looking for a boyfriend I found only dicks, so it makes sense that when you look for dick, you find a boyfriend. Well, sometimes, and not just in porn.

Adam went home to New York discouraged but also emboldened. He found a few playmates, had a few crushes that ended in tender kisses, but he wanted something a little rougher and nastier to round out his sluthood. He'd never done bondage but had a desire to experience it. We all knew a mutual foxy friend who was as skilled with tying up boys as he was with writing about it. Actually, we know several. But Adam and his Wilderness Daddy, as Christopher would come to call him, hooked up in the hills of Virginia and had a porn-story-inspiring time. In fact, Daddy Aragorn, my preferred name for Wilderness Daddy, and his partner had quite a threeway with Adam, and he wrote beautifully about it. Three, it seems, has always been a lucky number for Adam. And all the while this was going on, Greg and I were cheering Adam on. And waiting to hear the juicy bits from our good friend in Virginia. Somewhere in the midst of all these e-mails, Greg wrote Adam that we'd also be happy to tie him up when he came to visit us in February next year. And then I mentioned in an e-mail to Adam how Daddy Aragorn and I had swapped e-mails confessing our mutual crush on him. My crush was out of the bag, at last. Very easily slipped free. Just a brief aside, and then Adam wrote back of his blush. A casual, offhand remark. And somehow the landscape of our friendship grew a bit hillier with the occasional eruption of something more jagged, more angular, more erect in our passing commentary. And I began to call Adam "Crushling," partly in honor of my own crush and partly in honor of Daddy Aragorn's *Lord of the Rings* lust for Adam, his very own hobbit or halfling in the body of an Elijah Wood/Frodo Baggins look-alike.

Adam would write back a chaste bit about his sexploits. I then mentioned I wanted to see photos from his time in bondage. And before long, to get closer, even by proxy, to Adam's naked body, I was pimping Greg's ride. Or, as I billed it, his porn-star dick.

Greg, of course, was enjoying all this attention my bragging brought him, and he was adding his own flirty e-mails to the round-robin e-conversation, but he wasn't quite sure how much of his dick anyone would actually be enjoying when he would be staying at Adam's apartment in New York for an independent booksellers' convention that December. That's when I let Greg know, by way of e-mail to Adam (I was nearly always BCCing Greg in e-mails to Adam then), that Adam should feel free to make the most of Greg's porn-star dick while he was there. With my blessings.

This was all in early November 2005. Suddenly, by Thanksgiving, it would be I who was being blessed. The fantasy of their fucking in New York in December and again during Adam's visit in February was helping me to escape the reality that we'd just been informed by our landlord's lawyer that our apartment, the whole building actually, was going up for sale. Either we could buy our one-bedroom apartment (for $650,000) or we could settle (sell off our many rights as tenants under San Francisco's laws) or we would be evicted (under a California state law that allows landlords to remove a property from the rental market; no more rental property, no more renters; guess which one our landlord would eventually choose after a few go-rounds with all the tenants' lawyers?). One way or another, we were going to have to move from our rent-controlled apartment. Greg's home of more than four years. My home of nearly eleven. Where I'd written all my books. Where Greg and I had published all the Suspect Thoughts Press titles except his first one. And somehow in the new year, possibly before or even as Adam was visiting us, we would have to manage to find an apartment that could house us and the press and all our books in San Francisco's land of ever-shrinking rentals with ever-rising rents. By the weekend that Greg was actually in New York, I was throwing all my hysteria and anger over being uprooted, along with my homesickness for Greg, with whom I hadn't slept a single night apart since he'd moved in four years earlier, into dozens of phone calls and e-mails for a play-by-play (one of my three conditions for their playing together) or for pictures (another one of my conditions) of Greg rooting deeply in Adam's ass.

What I learned that weekend was: Thank the Goddess for my pornographer's imagination. It fueled me through various jack-off sessions as I waited to hear if anything had happened—and with the time difference between the coasts and the fact that Greg was working a trade show all day long, it took a while. Greg finally called me the first night after they'd had sex and were getting ready to go to sleep. I was all giddy with questions ("So what happened? Details!") and as soon as I heard there were photos, I wanted Greg to e-mail them right then and there. I had to see Adam's nice big red dick, as Greg had described it. Maybe there'd be a shot of Adam's ass. Maybe of Greg's dick in Adam's ass. *Please, oh, please.* All more fodder for my fantasies while I waited for Greg to come and act out just what had happened, while I waited for February and Adam to come so I could, hopefully, join in, while I nearly forgot that Greg's and my life had been completely upended by a simple letter (*Where are we going to live? How are we going to pack all these books?*). But the reality was that it was nearly three in the morning and they had to get up in little more than four hours.

And though I got a bit more information before Greg returned to San Francisco, I was left to wait and make up my own scenarios until Greg, jet-lagged and nearly drained of cum, returned home and improvised the highlights of their several nights of fucking. It was an amazing fuck as I got to do both Greg and Adam, whose positions Greg was reenacting with much gusto.

Much better than the photos. All four of them. Yes, that weekend I also learned another bit of realism to add to a future story: It's nearly impossible to take a good digital photo while you and another are having sex.

For that, you really need a third.

o o o

GREG: While the memories are foggy and differ on how exactly we flirted and what happened between us all before we actually started doing something about the flirting—as memories usually are—the end result is the same. We're peers in our love of words, best of friends, and compatible fuckbuddies. Nice combination. The only thing to improve it would be if Adam (and his husband, who does not share our bed) would actually follow through with their on-again, off-again plans to relocate to Los Angeles. That would certainly make for much easier travel to and from our new home in Oakland.

I really didn't know what might happen with Adam when I visited New York last December. I was traveling to do a booth for our press at a weekend-long book festival, and I was going to stay with Adam. He was going to help man the booth so we could have some rare time together. While Adam would have offered me a place to sleep anyway, despite the size of his and his husband, Christopher's apartment, it would be perfect that weekend, because his husband would be away with family. Ian had been very open in his not-too-subtle e-mails to Adam

THREEWAY

that Adam and I should fuck—with his blessing. But Adam isn't the world's best communicator. On paper, yes. E-mail, rarely. In person, nada. He never mentioned in any e-mail or phone call—to either Ian or me—that anything sexual would happen. And even though I've come to be the great communicator with Ian—discussing *ehhhvvverything* in depth (we're such old-school lesbians)—I don't remember coming out and saying anything daring to Adam, either. Maybe I thought he didn't actually want me that way? (That is, up to that night in December. I've since written very explicit e-mails to Adam. More for my benefit than his, since there is still never anything exciting coming back . . . yet. You'd think two pornographers could communicate feelings in dirty e-mails.) I didn't say anything until that first night after my arrival, after dinner, after watching some reruns on TV, when he was sitting there in just a T-shirt and flimsy shorts looking quite fetching—and I was so very hard and horny, wondering if it really might happen— that I finally just leaned over and said, "I want to kiss you." He took off his glasses and said something like, "I was waiting for you to . . ." or "Go ahead . . ." or . . . Well, that was easy. I kissed him—soft and sweet, at first, to match his lips, then harder, with more hunger. And not being a "beat around the bush" kind of guy, I immediately had my hand up his shorts leg to find no underwear and what felt to be a sweet, long, tasty hard-on waiting for some attention.

Feel free to insert here a montage of somewhat tentative groping. Tentative at first, anyway. We mashed lips, licked, bit, groped, fondled, and stroked our way out of our clothes and into quite a few truly fabulous and satisfying positions of raw sex. Both being bottoms, I didn't really know how it would go, but it turns out that we're very sexually compatible and can give each other great pleasure. We soon lost the tentative and

31

awkward gropings for a more sure-of-what-we-want 69 position of sucking each other off while stuffing as many fingers
up each other's assholes as we could. It was a wonderful start,
but the couch wasn't the most welcoming place for such positions, so we moved to his bed.

Later on in our threeway affair, when Adam came to San
Francisco, I took a much more forceful stance on getting the
anal attention I really wanted (read: getting fucked). But that
first night I thoroughly enjoyed fucking Adam's brains out—
for a surprisingly long time—in as many positions as we
could think of and one condom could take: Adam on all fours,
head down, ass high and spread wide, with one of my hands
pushing down on his shoulder and the other stroking his
cock; Adam on his back, legs pushed toward his shoulders, me
pounding and pounding; Adam on his side with one leg lifted,
me fucking him nice and slow . . . you get the picture . . .
hopefully more than one. And though it was a work weekend,
and though we did dine and hang out with many other
friends each night, we also managed to have lots of sex the
next two nights.

Oh, wait . . . the first night! That's right. I remember his
saying at some point before my trip that his husband doesn't
like to eat ass. Ah, poor baby. What a loser . . . I mean, loss.
Luckily, my husband loves to eat ass! And so do I. So after the
initial stroking of his boner through the shorts, and a taste or
two, I had him strip and I ate his ass out. I was still in my pants
at this point, and it seemed extra-naughty to have him spread
out on his couch in his living room—fully clothed—with my
tongue up his asshole. Then we proceeded. (How could I forget the rimming?)

My only failure was my attempt to take pictures for my
husband of the weekend, my first time away and with another

man. While I did take a few nice shots of Adam in various positions—and one of me that Adam took while I was sucking
him off—I didn't do a very good job of documentation. When
I was deep in passion (deep in Adam, actually), I didn't think
of the camera! But I did give Ian as much of the juicy details as
I could when I returned home, disappointed by the business
part of the weekend but totally satisfied by my sexual adventures away from home and the first time out of our relationship.

o   o   o

ADAM: My relationship with Greg started when he saw my
work online in *Outsider Ink* and asked if he could include my
work in his new e-zine, *suspect thoughts.* It was the first time
my work had ever been solicited, so I was naturally flattered.
We struck up a regular e-mail conversation, comparing notes
on books, writing, and our relationships. Greg felt that his
partnership had run its course, and I felt like my boyfriend
and I had become roommates, living platonically overlapping
lives. Greg and I were free to flirt and spark up the Internet
with increasing tension. Our e-ffair culminated in a swap of
half-naked photos and a short story I'd written about my proposed trip to Chicago and how we'd get together, but I didn't
have the balls to act on it.

Technically, it was one of the first porn stories I'd ever written, and I sent only the first half of it to him that concluded
with my naked arrival at our hotel room. I couldn't bring myself to share the second half of what might actually happen in
the fictional hotel room, but the idea of flying out to Chicago
to act it out instead flew through my mind. However, our brief
online fling would end shortly after I sent the story; both our

lives got complicated after that, and we had to focus our attentions elsewhere.

Ultimately, my words are my sex, and that was all I was prepared to share. Even though the sex in my relationship had been muted, I was afraid of cheating on Christopher and destroying our relationship. Instead, I funneled my rediscovered sexual energy into my work and started writing erotica, where I was free to explore without the threat of hurting anyone.

o o o

IT WAS WITH a new breed of jealousy that I learned Greg had ended his failing relationship and had moved to San Francisco to join his new love, Ian. Although our affair had taken place only in words, I felt as though I'd been cheated on and had lost the opportunity for it to be more.

Greg changed overnight; he was happier and making long-range plans for the two of them. I was amazed and jealous that he could make such a drastic change in his life. I figured Ian must be some incredible guy to inspire such a transformation. When I finally met them both, I understood: Greg and Ian are an ideal couple; they complement and complete each other while maintaining their own quirky personalities.

I stayed with them over a long weekend in 2002, and four years later I can finally admit that I would step out of their shower naked and dress in the living room, in a half-assed attempt to lure Greg into some kind of tryst. It had nothing to do with stealing him from Ian, or even snagging a little bit of Greg for my greedy self, but only to stroke my own wounded ego of having been the one not chosen. In my head I constructed this great wooing scene straight out of the tritest Harlequin paperback: Greg makes a move and I back away, claiming the trump card of my boyfriend back home. At least I'd know he wanted to fuck me. Instead, he scurried out of the room and jumped on Ian, who got a lot of lovin' that weekend.

After that, we saw each other once or twice a year, in San Francisco, New York, and then annually at Saints & Sinners in New Orleans. Rather than a third wheel to their relationship, I felt like a piece of their puzzle, since I'd been woven into their origins.

o   o   o

EVERYTHING CHANGED when my boyfriend and I opened the borders of our relationship. Christopher challenged me to break down the self-imposed boundaries I'd erected within myself and became my biggest supporter for living out the sexual adventures I'd only visited on the page and in my imagination. Perhaps my own fears of rejection had kept me inside the safe boundaries of my own work, where I could explore scenes I'd never consider seeking out in real life. I'd grown into a comfortable but insulated sexual existence and found it difficult to break out of my own internalized fantasy.

I started slowly, hooking up with my polyamorous friend, Steve, who'd had a crush on me for almost a decade without my being fully aware of it. He gave me the ins and outs of open relationships, and was responsible for saving mine from destruction as I faced this new frontier. Once Steve showed me how to open the door, I realized how much I'd lost by having it closed all those years.

When Greg announced he was coming to New York for a book fair and needed a place to crash, I invited him without hesitation. Christopher was going to be out of town, so Greg was free to share my bed. It was Ian, whom I'd befriended outside of my relationship with Greg, who saw this as a perfect opportunity for his husband and I to consummate our years-long attraction. Ian gave me carte blanche to entertain his hubbie, and for this to be the one permitted "vacation" in their four years of monogamous bliss. He set the rules: We had to be safe and enjoy one another, and Greg was to bring back tales of everything that happened—and pictures, if possible—to share the experience.

Despite the offer, I wasn't sure anything would happen or should. I was afraid of ruining the healthy relationship I had with Greg, and potentially upsetting his relationship with Ian, and for what? One weekend of sex? I sent Christopher off on his trip with the vague reassurance that nothing was going to happen; my cock had other plans.

Who was I kidding? Greg, if you've never met him, has a sexy charisma and rebellious charm. We'd grown a unique intimacy over the years of correspondence, and I trusted him implicitly, which has always been an issue with me. When he arrived, we had a quick dinner and watched some television, talking without saying anything while that awkward and thrilling tension built around us, like teenagers after the prom wondering who should go first. Then we were both silent and looked at each other, knowing the line had been crossed. "I really want to kiss you," he said. I asked him what he'd been waiting for.

After years of buildup, it was oddly familiar to have something happen. Avid kissers, we necked like horny kids, stripping off the few bits of clothing we'd bothered to wear. It was electrifying to stand up and remove that last barrier and stand fully naked before someone who appreciated what he was seeing. Our bodies blended into senses and touch, mouths on cocks and asses, fingers exploring skin and crevices, lips tasting sweat and flesh. Through all the years of abstract fantasy, I'd never considered the possibility of the actual live person, his tattooed body, shaved head, and porn-star cock lying on top of me.

While our first encounter was awkward at the outset, it felt natural to finally extend our relationship to include sex, with the full knowledge of both of our partners. I said quiet thank-yous to my friend Steve, who'd opened my eyes to the potential of polyamory, and an even bigger one to Christopher, who'd jump-started my libido.

Greg knew one thing I was after was a rim job, so after we'd had a chance to fill our mouths with each other, he flipped me over on the sofa and buried his stubbly face in my ass. It had been years since I'd received this type of attention, and he quickly had me groaning for more, and deeper, penetration. We adjourned to the bedroom, where we would be free to make more of a mess. We abandoned ourselves to primal urges, and worked through increasingly vigorous rounds of kissing, oral sex, and jacking off, until we were wrenching cum from each other. I collapsed next to him in sweaty camaraderie, and then we lay there and talked for an hour, our sweat and cum drying.

o   o   o

SINCE GREG AND I were both inclined toward monogamy, we fell into a weekend marriage: having quickie lunches, longer dinners with New York friends, and fucking like dogs in heat at home.

The second night we skipped over the preliminary awkwardness and got right down to it. Having had his tongue inside me, I knew I wouldn't be satisfied with less than his cock. It took little to entice Greg to fuck me, and we burned across the bed in a variety of positions, stopping occasionally to prolong the moment. I asked him to finish by coming on me, another internalized fetish of mine, and he jerked off on me, covering me in his spunk.

It was the first time that Ian and Greg had been separated since they got together, so we both made sure to keep him in the loop, phoning Ian almost directly afterward with the dirty details. We made a half-assed attempt to take digital photos for his viewing pleasure, but there were only three, and none of them really captured the moment. Ian nicknamed me Big Red after seeing them, but revised it to the sweeter Crushling in our following correspondence after confessing his own crush on me. It was one of the few moments I'd blushed as an adult.

Adam Fucks Greg While Ian Fucks Adam in San Francisco

IAN: The chasm between fantasy and reality: It separates the porn writer from the pornoverse as much as it does the porn reader. And it's nearly as impossible to leap for either writer or reader. But mid-jump, what a rush. Then, of course, comes the crash.

Or, in our case, the landing of Adam's plane.

But the crash is not always a bad thing. I love landing on or even in Adam. It's just that this weekend couldn't and wouldn't go as seamlessly as I'd fantasized—and all I'd done since Greg's return from New York was go to and from work, prepare for the holidays, brace for the landlord's decision on what to do with his tenants come January 1, and fantasize, fantasize, fantasize.

In the early mornings before Greg awoke (and when I was supposed to be writing), I'd sit in front of my antique iMac, dick in hand, replaying Greg's words in my mind, accompanied by body memories of his wonderful role play, while I stared at the blurry, too-close close-up of Adam's swollen dick. It looked frighteningly red, with a distended blue vein zigzagging across it. Almost like the skin of a burn victim. But I looked past this. I'd later see with my own eyes and taste with my own mouth that it had all been a trick of the flash. Then I'd look at an almost-as-blurry photo of Greg, eyes half-mast, face half in shadow, half in the light, swallowing Adam's dick. These were the two of the four "naughty" photos they'd managed to take that let me catch even a glimpse of what had happened those nights in New York. But that was enough.

The skills I've learned writing pornography gave me on those mornings what they've always given me: the ability to spin sexual gold from sexual straw. And because the operating system on my computer is too ancient to allow me to watch even snippets of porn, I've also learned to concoct quite the stories from still photos. To take the openmouthed face and supply the cry. Then again, one of my favorite turn-ons is seeing the face of someone I think is hot at the exact moments of their orgasm. I wrote a whole story that combined that fetish with my ability to make a porn video from a mere still and even dedicated it to Adam and his photographer husband, Christopher. It was all about a guy in New York who walked around the city with a blank Polaroid photo in his pocket that he would rub when he saw someone he lusted after, and when he got home and took the photo out of his pocket, voila, there was their face right as they came. That was an expression of Adam's I was living to see. Unfortunately, I had only a blurry photo of his dick alone and in Greg's mouth. No shot of his body beyond an even blurrier stomach. No pictures of his ass.

But then my Christmas came early as Adam took a self-portrait for Christopher's gift. It was of him naked in a bath-tub. In the first version, he was looking directly into the camera. Later, he reshot it and looked away. I got to see them both because Adam wanted Greg's and my opinion on which was the best photo. The earlier one allowed me to see a curve of Adam's ass, the later one a bit of his dick. But in the first one he was staring straight into the camera with those eyes I'd never been able to forget. And with a look that I wanted to see directed at me. (I later learned he was well lubed and well stuffed with a buttplug in that picture. That only added to my jerk-off fantasies.) Even if Adam didn't visit us in February, and there were times when it looked like his schedule wouldn't permit it, that photo was almost as good.

Almost. Then again, almost looked like it was going to have to suffice.

Since Greg's return, it had been nearly impossible to gauge whether anything sexual was going to happen among the three of us in February. Years before, when Adam had first vis-ited, Greg and he had gone sightseeing, and when it came time to eat, it took them an awfully long time to decide on the place. Two budding powerbottoms trying to be polite. Neither quite yet ready to top from below. After hearing about this, I joked that I should have bought them a double-headed dildo and put an end in each ass and waited to see how long it would take for one of them to start fucking the other. Obvi-ously, that was a cheap shot by a very nervous top who has to process his way to orgasm. Still, I got a good laugh. (Greg, too.

I still don't know if Adam laughed when Greg told him the joke.) And obviously by the time Greg got to New York, that indecisiveness was no longer a problem. Nonetheless, I knew them both well enough to worry that both could easily let their weekend in New York become a onetime happy memory. And when Adam came to visit, they would just fall back on that shoptalk that they do so well, of fellow publishers who happen to be best friends. Leaving me to seek out a dark, hidden corner in which to beat off. Endlessly. Besides, Greg's dad had just died in January, and now an eviction was looming. I had real major life drama to avoid.

So this Rumpelstiltskin spun more straw into gold. This time, it was through a series of e-mails to Adam blind-copied to Greg, filled with potty talk and porn scenarios. Questions about what got him off and what didn't. What Greg and I like. What Greg and I would like to do to him. What was going to happen, minute by minute, position by position, once he arrived. Along with lots of shoptalk about publishing and grief when a parent dies and apartment/lawyer drama. For Adam had become my friend over the years, too. And as obsessed with him as I'd become, I really did and do want to know him, inside and out. Part of seduction, mine and the other's, is the emotional undressing that occurs. The revelation of fears and hopes that is as tantalizing as when they are standing in front of me in tenting underwear with an ever-widening wet spot.

Occasionally, Adam would play along. Most times not. He would just reply to the everyday concerns and questions. Even when I gave a choice of subject header replies to let me know whether to back off about Greg and I bedding him in February (Red), or to keep going full throttle (Green), or to just let everything stay a nice, platonic friendship (Mrs. Wharton), he chose all three. Somehow, through a series of further e-mail round-robins, it became clear that Adam was looking forward to visiting us and seeing what might happen. It's just that I never knew fully, till I saw his hard dick in front of my eyes, how excited he was for something to happen. That he actually had been aroused by some of the scenarios I'd spun out for his trip from the airport to the bedroom that first night: starting with a blowjob from Greg in the car in the airport parking lot as I watched from the front seat and ending with the double penetration of Adam's hole. Not bad for one night's work.

No matter, I was more than excited and aroused for all three of us. And insecure, surprised, and giddy, and every other feeling that overflows when one's crush is coming to have sex with their husband in front of their eyes and maybe invite them along for the fuck. And to be fair to Adam, I knew then and I know now that I was trying, through my e-mails to Adam, to re-create some of that incredible clandestine flurry that had been the kindling of my original affair with Greg. Our endless e-mails and stolen phone conversations while Greg's husband had been at work were a modern-day *Dangerous Liaisons*. Seduction by words and words alone—until our first meeting in the flesh just days before September 11, 2001. That was a year of worlds ending and beginning.

And here I was, with more worlds beginning and ending, hoping that Adam in courtship would be just like Greg had been. (Greg has thoroughly ruined me, for the better. And I missed that early wildfire passion that has now, through years of living together as lovers and business partners, flamed into a deeper but different passion.) But Adam is Adam, and as I like to deal with my emotional issues by directing all the dicks in the room, Adam likes to deal with his issues by keeping all the elements of his life, and their attendant emotions, as separate as possible, because many of them are highly flammable and he just doesn't want to deal with the possible combustion. I can understand. I try to do all my combusting in print, too.

By the time Adam's long-delayed flight landed, I was so keyed up that I knew all my e-mail swagger had been fantasy. I was too afraid to do anything but fidget next to Greg as we waited, and I could only smile goofily once Adam got to baggage claim. Seeing him in the flesh, I wanted him more than I had before, in my fantasies. But I had no idea how I would be able to leap the chasm from my desires to his body.

Fortunately, reality after reality forced my overly scripted porno-tastic seduction-abduction-of-Adam plan to fall apart. There were lights and cameras everywhere on the rooftop parking lot, where, prior to 9-11, Greg and I had once made out. Greg had decided it would be too distracting to me as a driver if he blew Adam on the ride home. Adam was understandably exhausted from his very long flight and really not ready to become the world's most uninhibited exhibitionist. And I was tongue-tied and fumbling over my words. By the time I climbed the stairs of our apartment, my face as close to Adam's jeans-hidden ass as possible, my insecurity was straining to get my attention as much as my stiff dick. So, once upstairs, I played hostess. I had Greg get us some wine and snacks, and we sat on the couch and talked. It was already after one a.m. Somehow we got from the couch to the bed.

Once in the bedroom, I was hopping around the room like the overanxious teenager at his first sleepover that I felt I was. I turned on our "fuck lights," two vintage lamps that cast a wonderful amber glow, like hundreds of candles around the room. (All flesh, including my own, looks best by candle- or fuck light.) And next, still fully clothed, I was at the head of the bed with both of them standing at the foot, and I started to remember a bit of my script.

I asked Greg to kiss Adam. At that moment, I knew reality could be better than fantasy. Then I asked Greg to take off Adam's shirt—but with that, they were off to the races. Stripping down. Taking their own clothes off, and suddenly there was Adam standing naked in our bedroom with his dick jutting out ahead of him, nearly ramrod straight. His dick is long like Greg's, but thinner than Greg's thick slug of a cock. But Adam's head is larger, a beautiful, bright red bulb. Almost like a tulip about to blossom. Quickly, all of that was inhaled by Greg. But finally, after some serious deep-throating, Greg realized he hadn't shown me Adam's ass yet. He turned him around and I saw it at last. Unlike Greg's very curvaceous ass, Adam's is small, each cheek almost box-shaped from all the walking he does in New York. Like two of those biscuits they use to make White Castle burgers, those mini-hamburgers from the Midwest. Of course, not as small as those. But that fascinating hard-fluffy, square-round combination. Delicious.

As for what happened next, the three times we fucked that weekend blur together. It's odd. I remember so distinctly the next two days waiting and waiting to have sex. We'd go to breakfast, they'd check and answer their e-mail, and all day Sunday we watched lots of "Family Guy," "Little Britain," and Almodóvar's *Bad Education.* Much laughter and lots of Gael García Bernal. My two workaholic boys got an actual Sunday where they didn't work. Which I was very glad about. But all I wanted was to spend each day and night in bed. But we had three real people with three different cycles and desires, and that wasn't going to happen. Reality bested fantasy there. So why can't I remember the sequence of what really happened when we had sex? Maybe it's like the incident with the digital camera in New York. It's too hard to record an event when you're actually experiencing it. Perhaps that is the greatest difference between writing about fucking and fucking. It's very hard to keep hold of the authorial urge to record every detail like a camcorder. Too many other things make the mind as slippery as hands and mouths and holes.

Instead, I have only more, many more, blurry images: Adam waving me over the first time to join them on the bed as he kneels there with Greg sucking between his legs; kissing Adam the first time, actually all the times I kissed him—and it felt like I could never kiss him enough; Adam's half-lidded stare and almost-drunken lopsided smile he gets in the throes of sex; Greg's look that he flashes you as he locks eyes with you while your dick is in his mouth—like he's never tasted anything more exquisite, like he's never been so aroused in his whole life, like this is what he was born to do and he is thanking you with his lips and throat for giving him his calling; the little grunt that lodges in Adam's throat when he comes, the only way that first night I knew my blowjob had been a success till my mouth filled with his cum; the delight in Greg's face as he finally got fucked by Adam, sitting astride his dick and bouncing for all he was worth; Adam, with his telltale blissed-out sex face, staring down at me while he ground his ass onto my dick, now shy and retreating into its latex cocoon, while Adam coaxed it back out to play; my face, my mouth, inches from Adam's ass as he lay prone, waiting for me to spank him, and then watching his small, white buttcheeks flush and grow redder still as I slapped them until I could hear him cry out (which never came as my hand gave out long before his ass did, but we both had lovely souvenir bruises the next day); me inside Adam, who was inside Greg, my gut sweatily slapping his back and trying not to be embarrassed by the sound of it, by the reality of it, that I am not just a disembodied brain and I have a body and it's a fat body with a big belly, and hoping my dick was staying hard enough inside him as I battled both the shrinkage that always happens when I put on a condom and now the waves of body shame and monkey-mind chatter; looking across Adam's hip, while eating out his ass, and watching Greg suck on his dick from the other side until our eyes locked and, through our eyes only, since our mouths were too happily filled, smiling—all three of us ecstatically doing what we love with people we love—the perfect erotic moment of that whole weekend.

Of course, all good things . . . yadda, yadda, yadda.

So there we were Sunday night, after all were spent and done, lying side by side, three boys on a bed, naked and sticky with one another's spit and sweat and sperm, smiling, talking about books we have read and might write, gossiping about friends not strewn across the covers with us, almost dozing in the amber light. The end of that long weekend's last jump between fantasy and reality. What some might imagine is the busman's holiday for pornographers. But for each of us, a moment almost outside of time, three days where we didn't have to remember or respond to all that awaited us tomorrow. Monday. Our return to work. Adam's return flight to New York.

Monday. Reality's last laugh, its final crash. But from Friday to Sunday, what a soul-satisfying jump.

o o o

GREG: Adam's flight was seriously later than its scheduled already-late arrival. Adam had to catch a plane after work on a Friday night, so he wasn't going to get in until almost midnight, but it ended up being even later. Our best planned scenario of sex in the airport didn't happen for various reasons.

One being the hour and how tired Adam looked. Another reason being how bright the parking lot lights were and how menacing the cameras seemed to be. Goddess knows, having perverted homosexual acts in an airport might be considered anti-American and possibly even terrorist.

While I'm not opposed to—and in fact am excited by—the thought of sometimes being seen having sex or possibly being caught in compromising sexual positions, getting arrested by airport security/Homeland Security for anything is not high on my to-do list.

I'm not sure why, but I was also once again very tentative about ravishing Adam—at first, that is. Something made me feel hesitant to blow him while Ian was driving us home. (Is there a pattern here? I've wondered why I've been so tentative about him. All I can figure out is that it might be our long-term friendship and work relationship. But it still puzzles me. I'm way into sex and have never been shy in most circumstances. I've blown him before and will again. Ah, whatever. The good thing is that once we start, the hesitance in any form goes away.) The blowjob had sounded like a blast—even though the final blast of it was not to happen. I was not to make him come. Adam's cum was to be saved for Ian. (The things I'm willing to do—or in this case, sacrifice and not do—for my husband!) It was a brilliant idea Ian came up with, a little public sex for me and a little torture for Adam: having to sit still while getting blown by me as cars were buzzing by and then not even being allowed to come. But poor baby was so tired and I was unsure and we just did some teenage groping of crotches. Until we got home anyway.

Ian was great the entire weekend, making sure that, when we weren't eating or out and about, which wasn't too much during the weekend, since Adam had made it clear what he came for (and tourism wasn't it), we were fucking. And Ian orchestrated it all wonderfully, many times even micromanaging it. This was really cool and very sexy: to be told exactly what to do next. Oh, the first night? You know, I don't remember what all we did. I just remember Adam surprising my honey with a throatful of cum. Certainly Ian had planned for that, hadn't he? "Surprise," you say? Well, Adam didn't let on in any way that he was about to let it blow. Not that Ian would have stopped him, since he wanted to swallow as much of Adam that weekend as possible. But it was a surprise. You see, Adam, while hot and very willing in the bed, couch, kitchen, wherever, he has one fuckbuddy flaw—one big fuckbuddy flaw—for both of us. He doesn't make much noise. Almost none at all.

And Ian and I both love the noises of sex. Sweet talk. Nasty talk. Encouragement. Laughing. Moaning, groaning, and growling. And screaming out when the pleasure calls for it. Loudly and with gusto when appropriate. I wake the neighbors with almost every orgasm—no, back up, with every good pound, or grind, or pinch or slap or poke; anything with an intense sensation will bring a noise from my mouth. Ah, but Adam, no noise . . .

But despite that, he was—is—a good fit for us. (We all fit on our bed, which is a good start. In another recent tryst, we didn't all really fit too well on the bed, and I kept thinking we'd break the frame—or that I'd fall off of the edge of the bed as I was riding atop a fat dick with a bit too much enthusiasm.) We three get along great sexually—even with the lack of vocalization. All three of us like to suck. And all three of us like to fuck. We all like to give attention to asses. All three of us are kinky and enjoy a bit of pain. Ian as a serious sadist, me as a serious masochist—when encouraged!—and Adam somewhere in between. I say in between because he can chew mighty hard on my nipple, but says, "Yellow! Yellow! Yellow!" before I'm even warmed up on his. I say in between—except for spanking.

While I can take many forms of pain, especially tit play or a really hard fuck—*Mmm, Daddy*—I pull away from spanking unless I'm tied up. I need to be secured. Not that I don't enjoy it, because I do, but I can't take it without flailing around or reaching back to cover my ass. I don't ever scream out our safeword—I'm not sure I ever have—but Ian usually stops spanking me once I do my fish-out-of-water act. "Oh, Ian's not a real sadist then," you might say. But he is. He is just what you might call a kinder, gentler sadist. But he loves to dish it out, and he gets off on it big-time.

We probably should have seen it coming. Ian wanted to spank Adam. Adam wanted to be spanked by Ian. So they did it. And did it. And kept doing it. I was off to the side—mostly watching and encouraging. I wanted Adam to suck my big, hard dick while it happened, but I thought, and rightly so, that even though Adam wasn't thrashing or screaming out like I do, he might bite down a bit too hard. So I just watched and jerked myself off. Ian wanted to do it until he got Adam to scream out, to tell him to stop. That would have made my baby come right then and there, instantly. But that didn't happen. I wanted Ian to bring out the paddle (which I'm awfully fond of, with its furry side and hard wood side) or the crop (which I love very, very, very much, especially when used to lightly spank the underside of my cock and directly on my spread asshole). But both Adam and Ian were enjoying the moment too much for suggestions. So I watched. And watched. And watched. And I jerked off while I watched, and the spanking got harder and harder and harder.

Adam went home with bruises. No, serious bruises. A completely bruised ass. Black and blue. What's black and blue and red all over? Adam's ass after a weekend with us! Ian felt bad (I think, though I'm sure he liked it, too), but Adam's ass healed just fine. As did Ian's palms, which were covered in what could be best described as a callused blister. (We never did hear what Adam's husband said of the bruised ass. Did he notice?)

Adam also went home without the double-fucked asshole he requested ahead of time—though I've heard he since was rewarded with one by another couple. Attaboy! Not that we wouldn't have done it. Hell, I would have loved to do him together, then have them give me a ride. Next time, okay? But we didn't remember, didn't think about it. At least I didn't think of it. But we did nearly wear him out doing just about every other thing we could think of doing. And I never tired of a single moment of mouth, cock, hand, foot, nipple, or ass.

o o o

ADAM: I'd already planned to visit them in San Francisco before anything happened, to talk about projects and Suspect Thoughts Press, and to just visit with my favorite Left Coast couple. Ian saw this as a new opportunity for Greg and I to explore, with him orchestrating the whole event. As one who needs to have the full approval of the other party, as I do myself, Ian sent a lengthy missive asking how I felt about his being included in the sandwich. He set a color code for my responses: "Mrs. Wharton" meant I didn't want Ian to be active but would allow him to play director, "Red" meant that he could be involved but not a full-out participant, and "Green" meant that all bets were off and anything went. I replied with all three code words, unsure of what I wanted myself.

I lost my virginity in a threesome, and developed a taste for them; there are infinitely more physical combinations between three people than two alone. However, they can get emotionally complicated, especially when you step into someone else's relationship. The moment one person is favored over the other, egos can flare and feelings get hurt. The fantasy collapses or explodes. To have a pleasurable threeway, all participants must be engaged and the energy must complete a full circle.

I had no fears with Ian and Greg, and found it incredibly flattering to be the first exception in their relationship. And I'm an attention pig, so to find myself at the center of my friends' fantasies, the target for their love and ravaging, it was more than I could resist. The week before I flew out, I'd wake up in the middle of the night with my head full of fantasies and have to jerk off, planning what would happen.

To prepare for our weekend, Ian purchased three jockstraps in varying colors, blue for me, red for Greg, and black for himself. He mailed mine to me and insisted that I wear it on the plane. We planned a mutual suckfest in the airport parking lot, to be followed by a weekend of sex rivaled only by porn movies. The penultimate goal to be reached? Double penetration.

Unfortunately, life does not always work out the way you planned. My flight was delayed and by the time I reached San Francisco, it was nearly one a.m. (EST); I was half asleep. The parking lot was overly bright and monitored, so we skipped the preliminaries and drove the short distance to the apartment in the Mission, Greg and I quietly feeling each other up in the darkened backseat.

Ian laid out a light dinner and wine for us, a special occasion, as Greg and Ian rarely drink. Once we were done, Ian hastened us into the bedroom, rather than let the evening fade into morning without at least an appetizer of what was to come.

Initially, Ian played director, having Greg and I strip each other and kiss, moving us onto the bed, where he suggested which acts of stimulation we should perform for his voyeuristic pleasure. Being something of an über-bottom, it was incredibly erotic to be orchestrated into a live sex show, watching Ian watch us as we sucked each other off.

We gleefully romped through lots of kissing and touching, both being big on our oral skills, and finally enticed Ian to join us. He already knew one of my favorite things in the world was being rimmed, and was happy to gorge himself on my butt, while I had my mouth filled with Greg's cock. We moved through a variety of positions, merging our body parts and lips, asses, and cocks, reconnecting in different arrangements until we each shot off in sequence, covering Ian in a lake of release.

The days fell into a rhythm, with sex taking center stage in the middle of the day, something to be built up to over breakfast and to enjoy the afterglow of during dinner. We tried a variety of positions, and though double penetration did not occur, we did form a linked chain with me in the center. We ended in a heaving, sticky mess, legs, arms, and cocks comfortably entwined.

Afterward we lay naked and talked about books and writing. It's rare for me to be able to kick back and talk about the things that matter most, as daily life barely gives me enough time to work. In many ways, this was as stimulating as the sex, a postcoital denouement, and one of the reasons I'd wanted to slip into their literary relationship for the weekend.

Ian Fucks Adam in New Orleans

IAN: I have put off writing this section until the last possible moment. I've wandered out into the front yard and backyard of our rental home in Oakland to "garden." Puttering among the plants. Watering and watering, waiting for the words to flow from me. I've wandered the halls filled with my un-packed books I've yet to shelve, three months since we've moved in (I used the writing of this piece as an excuse not to do that). Hoping that chaos would drive me either to shelve or to write. Always evading the writing because what happened in New Orleans was, for me, the ultimate collision of fantasy and reality. And, since I aspire to write a novel some-day, which, most likely, if my shelving abilities are any indica-tor, will be published posthumously, I see portents in the fact that my fantasy of barebacking with Adam would collide with the reality of barebacking with Adam in post-Katrina New Orleans.

But that framing belittles the tragedy of the colossal batter-ing New Orleans took before and after the levees burst. This was no tragedy. We were in New Orleans because we had re-turned to Saints & Sinners, the conference where Slut Adam would be born, the conference where Saint Ian would finally get down off his pedestal. And even though it took me two days to muster up the courage to confess to Greg what I'd done, we're still together and closer than ever (oh, the ties that are bound in the hell that is moving, which happened only two weeks after I returned from New Orleans). In fact, the writing of this whole essay, and the e-mail processing that has gone on among the three of us about that "one night in New Orleans," has deepened our threeway relationship. We are all now pining to get together again, even if it means waiting till the next Saints & Sinners conference in May 2007.

The only real shock is probably to those who wonder how three writers could be so poor at communicating with words, their chosen medium, whenever they are in person.

And the only real shame is mine, which has blocked my writing till now.

Yes, *shame* can be a pretty melodramatic word, especially to someone who is prone to melodramatic moods, like myself. But *shame,* more than *embarrassment,* is the right word. Shame means knowing you shouldn't have done something that you did, full well knowing that you shouldn't be doing it. And that's just what I thought while coming in Adam's ass: *I shouldn't be doing this.* Yes, Greg and I had fantasized with each other, and with Adam, how hot it would be to fuck Adam's hole after the other had come in it. But that was fantasy. The reality was that, even though all three of us were negative, even though Adam was using condoms with his other men, even though Greg and I had had sex only with each other for four years, Greg did not want any of us to fuck without a condom. To be safe. And Adam and I agreed. It was the breaking of that promise that shamed me most.

But it was also on that night that this "good little boy" finally learned what "the heat of the moment" really means. Shoulds and promises melt like butter at that temperature.

That night started with me wanting to strip Adam's clothes the minute I was alone with him in our hotel room. Greg had stayed behind to pack the house for the upcoming move. This was going to be my New York—even though I'd busied myself for weeks with worry that without the spark of Greg, Adam wouldn't want to do anything with me, and even though I knew I'd be time-sharing Adam's asshole with Daddy Aragorn and his partner. But it wasn't until many hours later that we were alone again and I had to add to the wait because it took me forever to ask Adam if, well, maybe, you might possibly want to have sex with, maybe, me. He smiled and said yes and then, like in any good porn story, I processed that yes for thirty more minutes. Some of that was the emotional-revelation foreplay I need to be safe enough to begin, but a lot of that was just sheer nervousness—that stalling to reboot your brain after the total crash that occurs when all your blood has rushed to your dick and left your brain high and dry as you sit on a couch next to the object of your obsessions, and you have too many desires to act on and too little testosterone, chutzpah, brain cells, something, to pick one and run with it. Of course, Adam likes to be prey. He wants to be pounced on. In myriad ways. And hard. So he waited me out, patiently, but wouldn't initiate beyond that yes. Somehow, I remembered to lean in, and we began to kiss. Soon we were standing and I was stripping him in front of a wall-length mirror. He had his back to it, which meant I got to stare at his backside when I'd break away from kissing him.

Honestly, I had no idea what I wanted to have happen. Well, certainly at some point in the weekend, I wanted to fuck him. But how that would come about, I had no idea. Really, my biggest goal that weekend with Adam, besides spending as much time naked and kissing him as possible, was to get him to make some noise. A lot of noise. In fact, Daddy Aragorn and I had talked about a spank-off over Adam's butt. Whoever got him to make the most noise won. Of course, we never got as far as deciding how the winner would take his victory lap— and a full day and night of conference events kept all four of us from getting together. So that night, I figured I'd do what always got Greg's mouth running—I'd rim Adam. We made our way to the bed and, after more kissing, Adam lay spread-eagle before me, a butt buffet. I spread his small, muscled ass cheeks wide and tongued him for fifteen or more very happy minutes. You might think fifteen minutes of your tongue in an asshole would be tiring on your tongue, perhaps even boring for your ever-impatient dick. Wrong. I could lift my eyes and see myself surrounded by Adam's ass. I could look up his back to his head, gently moving back and forth on his pillow. I could hear soft little moans when his face wasn't in the pillow. It drove me on. Then I remembered how Adam had said he felt the crush of another's body on his to be very erotic, and as a fat man who's always afraid of crushing another under his weight, I realized I could give him one hell of a crushing as I rubbed my hard dick between his ass cheeks.

And now I was on top of him, and he turned his head to one side, looking blissed-out, drunk on the pleasure of my rimming, of my weight, of me, and he said, "I know something else that would be good inside me," and he slipped my dick into his asshole. It was hot talk, and Adam looked so incredibly sexy, and then he did what drives me wild in that position and leaned up and we started kissing. My fantasy was becoming real. But I couldn't revel in the moment. I couldn't let loose and enjoy. I was in shock, a very pleasant physical shock, that this was happening. And yet my brain was sounding a distant alarm. *Are you inside Adam's asshole? Are you really fucking him without a condom? No, no. You're just rubbing against his asshole. That's all. No, he's not. Yes, he is.* And on the fight went as I lay on top of Adam, fucking and kissing him. And, believe it or not, I kick myself for not making the piggy-most of those moments as much as for the actual breaking of my promise to Greg not to bareback.

But finally, I knew I was going to come. And I told Adam, thinking if I was really inside him and that this wasn't right for him, he'd push me out. Make him keep my promise to Greg for me. And he said, "That's okay." And I came—now convinced I was only rubbing his asshole. Distancing myself from my broken promise to Greg and my passion with Adam and losing out on the moment. Yes, even a pornographer can fail to make the most of what should have been a very Grade A, porn-hot moment. And so I continued to be both in the bed with Adam and wherever the place is that you go to when you are in denial. Adam rolled over and began stroking his dick, and I continued to kiss him while I fingered his cum-filled hole (yes, I too wondered how the cum got in his hole and wasted another hot moment) until he gave a very deep-throated grunt and shot a beautiful load that, if I were there now, I would eat up to bring the moment full circle and close it.

But I can do this only in memory. And I do it quite often now that it is safe. Now that Greg has forgiven me, I can return to that bed and grind away at Adam's ass with gusto. I'm returning the reality back to fantasy. The terrible guilt and fear that ate at me until I told Greg everything on the phone two days later is gone. Now, I just have the shame that I once wrote such an antibarebacking porn story with no idea of just how easy it is to slip. That I could be so one-note in my fake piety. And shame that this night happened at a conference for an AIDS organization. Actually, that's more embarrassment at the idiotic irony of it all. And finally shame that I never told Adam, till he read this essay, that I'd broken my promise to him to keep that night "our little secret." I think Adam finds secrets, like his somewhat secretive identity here in this piece, hot. I can see why. He's written about "men of mystery" and is truly one himself. But then again, he's a poet. It comes with the territory. As for me and secrets, their heat burns right through me and I bleat them out. Instead of a confessional poet, I'm a confessional pornographer.

And with that said, it's time to leave the booth. Hail, Mary.

o   o   o

ADAM: The one thing we all looked forward to was escaping to Saints & Sinners in New Orleans, and to vacationing in that sexual blend of queer artists and writers that we counted ourselves among. There was only one problem. . . . Before they could make their reservations, Ian and Greg found out their apartment in San Francisco was being sold and they were being evicted. Between the tight deadline to pack and move, and the expense, only one of them was going to be able to attend.

Ian was elected to go, but we worried, without Greg, would anything happen between us? We are both nonaggressive and often spend more time processing and ensuring that the other person is interested than actually fucking. The night Ian got in, we had a long conversation, and I realized that we had a lot of the same sexual insecurities, not necessarily a fear of rejection but a reluctance to project our fantasies onto someone else; we both preferred to live in someone else's fantasy and get them off rather than force our own agenda.

Sweetly enough, the one specific moment that paralleled my time with Greg was Ian asking if I'd like to fool around. As mentioned here by both Ian and Greg, I can be something of an enigma when it comes to sexual signals. I spent so much of my rural queer youth pining over straight boys that I could not have, *should not* lust after, that I had been forced to internalize my own fantasies and live them out only in the safety of my imagination. A true sexual introvert who is only now beginning to break out of the prison he'd created for himself, I'm still learning how to express my desires outside of fiction and fantasy.

Additionally, the majority of my sexual experience has been with older men, and I love playing the corruptible boy to their daddy, a relationship that I've happily achieved with Daddy Aragorn and his partner. Perhaps it is the subjugation of my desire that forces me to make the other person responsible for the fantasy, or maybe I'm just an egomaniac who wants to be wanted; either possibility would be a great topic for my shrink.

We undressed in front of a wall-sized mirror so we could watch our naked bodies merging, kissing, touching. With my back to the mirror, I watched Ian watch me, and reveled in his appreciation. I'd been a shy and awkward boy with body issues similar to Ian's, only in reverse, but as I'd blossomed into my mid-thirties, I could finally stand in my naked skin and allow someone to look at me without the urge to depreciate myself by noting the too-skinny torso, flat ass, or bump of acne over my shoulders. This egotistical moment in front of the mirror was a huge step in overcoming the innate shyness that had kept sexual exploration outside my reach.

Ian led me to the bed, and we found our pace and rhythm, building into a nice friendly friction. After our last time together, Ian knew what to do to get my attention, and flipped me over and went to work on my ass with his mouth. He served me up like pudding with his expert tongue, working with the skill and determination of a true deviant to melt my inhibitions away. Inspired by his ministrations, I knew I had to have more.

It was three o'clock in the morning, and we were in that no-man's-land of the early morning when reality ceases to exist. We were the only two in the world at that moment, and I did some hasty rationalizations. I knew for one hundred percent certain that Ian was HIV negative. Ian and Greg no longer used condoms, nor did I with my own partner, because we play safe outside of our relationship. From our tryst in San Francisco, I knew that Ian, like many men, has trouble performing with a condom. As quickly as my brain fired up these facts, I'd gotten Ian on top of and inside me, au naturel.

Just before he came, Ian let me know. It was a second rash decision: Instead of asking him to pull out, which I didn't want, I encouraged him to finish what he'd started. We crossed a bridge together, connected by our own flesh and flaws, and in my own way, I felt as though I was helping us both find a way to expand beyond our self-imposed boundaries. He shuddered into me, and I jerked off afterward, sated but feeling a little bit guilty for my selfish act.

As we went to sleep, spent and exhausted, I realized what I'd done: I'd broken my own pact with Christopher and myself. Worse, Ian told me later about his own promise to Greg, which I'd broken, too. Living in the moment, we often forget the repercussions of our rash actions, and I shamefully asked Ian to keep it our little secret; in hindsight, I felt like the old man who'd molested me when I was eleven.

It wasn't until writing this essay that I found out Ian had disclosed what had happened to Greg and had wrestled heavily with his own conscience. It pained me to hear it, for there are few people in the world that I would hurt, but never my friends; sometimes you can do more damage through silence than with harsh words. This is my apology to Ian for asking him to lie about something that I'd encouraged, and to Greg for breaking the confidence of our friendship.

The rest of the weekend, we had little time together, but what we did have we made the most of. We talked late into the night, about writing, relationships, and our own self-inflicted wounds, and joined together, as if we were healing each other's insecurities, bolstering our confidence out in the world. Ian and I learned how hot it is to ask for something from your lover: a kiss, a blowjob, a touch—and to link your fantasies together.

○ ○ ○

GREG: I missed Ian something fierce when he was in New Orleans. I missed his company, his warmth and his compassion for everything, his sense of humor, his smile, his place in the bed, his hands, his cock, his mouth.

But I was happy that he went on the trip. He needed to be there for the press. He wanted to be there for himself. He deserved to get away and to see friends. And that included Adam. And while I felt like I was missing something—both from not being at the conference for conference things and from not being able to play with Adam—I was really excited that the two of them would have time alone.

Yes, like my amazing husband who encouraged me to fuck another man while I was away in New York, I wanted them both to enjoy each other in every way possible while he was away in Louisiana. And I didn't feel a drop of jealousy.

Ian didn't tell me about fucking Adam without a condom for at least a day. I think he even avoided talking to me on the phone the whole next day. Yes, I think he called late the next night. He told me later that he was afraid to tell me, that I would . . . I would what? There's nothing for me to say. We're all negative. What's done is done. When we play next, we'll once again play safe—or at least we'll wear condoms when we fuck.

I wasn't mad. I wasn't even that shocked. I love them both, and the fact that they fucked without protection doesn't change anything. It just makes it that much easier to see why barebacking happens so often.

Lust is a power unlike any other.

Until Adam Is Fucked by Greg and Ian in Oakland

IAN: I've said enough. I'm tired of writing. I want to step away from the computer and find my husband and my lover waiting for me in the bedroom just beyond the far wall of this office, waiting to perform for me, waiting for my husband to sit on my dick while my lover slides his dick into my husband's cock-stuffed hole, waiting for my husband and then my lover and then me to come, and then we will wipe each other off with our mouths, our kisses resuscitating all our dicks until my lover can straddle my cock while my husband and I fuck him together.

It's pure porn, pure fantasy, but we have years to make it real.

o o o

GREG: Not that I haven't mentioned to Adam how much I wanted him to come visit—soon!—many times since his trip to San Francisco, because I have, but while writing sections of this essay, I realized just how much I want to see him again. I've found myself rock-hard, dripping wet with pre-cum, and ready to jerk off while typing. And I have. At one point I knew I'd never get the paragraph to read right until I had some focus back, so I took the situation in hand (ha, ha!), stuffed a buttplug up my asshole, and gave myself a fierce wank.

That hasn't happened many times when I'm writing. I can read another's porn and get turned on—though not usually enough that I feel the need to stop and play with my dick—but most of my stories have been written without the need to come mid-story.

Speaking of cum, here are some things (okay, a lot of things) I'd like to do to or with Adam when we next play: I'd like to shoot my cum all over his mouth and face—again. I'd actually really like to do that right now. Maybe I'll take a break from writing and jerk off while I imagine it in better detail. I'd like to fuck him in our dining room with him lying on his back on our antique barn table, his legs spread as wide as they can go. And I'd like to fuck him really, really hard, pound him without mercy until he screams out—which, in my fantasy, he does—or at least until I can't control my orgasm anymore, then I'd like to pull out, roll off the condom, walk around to the side of the table, and stuff my cock in his mouth, where Ian's conveniently already is, and make him eat our cum as we ejaculate at the same time. I'd like to have Adam slide his cock up my ass while I'm already sitting on Ian's cock and have them both fuck me at once. I think the shapes of their cocks would work well in that position. Yes, I'd like that. I'd like to play with Adam's asshole for a while, then slide in a big buttplug. Then I'd like to make him kneel in the shower, and I'd like for Ian and me to pee all over him. Then I'd like to call him silly sex names such as "slut," "cumbag," and "buttboy" while he jerks Ian and me off at the same time. That's hot—on his knees with a hard cock in each hand. After we come all over him, we'll let him jerk himself off. But I want to see him eat his own cum, so he has to jerk off into his palm so he can swallow it. I'd like to get on all fours and while I suck on Ian's cock have Adam fuck me with my favorite fat dildo. Then after I've made Ian come, I'd like to have them switch positions so that Ian fucks me with my dildo while I suck Adam off. I'd like to watch Ian fuck Adam's brains out and take pictures of the entire fuck so we have them to look at later in between fuck visits, when Adam's back in New York. Then Ian can jerk off watching me jerk off looking at photos of him fucking Adam. Perfect. Yes, I'd like to do all of the above. Sounds like a great weekend! Adam, when are you coming to visit again?

o   o   o

ADAM: I've often imagined myself in a threeway relationship, not just in the bedroom but in a living situation. I've always felt more comfortable being with another couple, rather than being the sole focus of another person. Perhaps this is because as a writer, I need time alone and am forced to choose between my work and my boyfriend. In a tripod relationship, especially with two other writers who understand that need for space, there is always another person to spend time with, and there's usually at least someone who is in the mood the same time you want to fuck. Although my relationship with Greg and Ian will not fully develop into that ideal, the times we have had, and the future times to come, will give me a taste of that dream. In the meantime, I will continue to flesh out my fantasies on the page, and to know that out there, someone is getting turned on and we're having one big orgy.

o o o

WORDS CONTINUE to earn my respect. This essay has been a journey for all three of us, and has helped foster understanding of the thoughts, insecurities, and fantasies running through our minds over the course of our threeway. It has opened doors to discuss and disclose some of our more private thoughts and flaws. For myself, it has been a healing opportunity to be described with love and objectivity, and has helped me reveal my motivations and the reasons for what I withhold. I promised the boys that I'd give them ample chance to get me to respond vocally, and loudly, at our next tryst, whether it be in New York, Oakland, or New Orleans. Until then, we'll have to console ourselves with our memories and our plans for the future.

A Picture in a Frame

For E

MARILYN JAYE LEWIS

I.

What's in a name? An identity, for one thing. A name can serve as a spotlight—an unwelcome one, at that—exposing the identity of a real person with a real life somewhere. A life thick with its own intimate relationships—relationships that might not appreciate the kind of salacious secrets that get revealed in an erotic memoir. Mine, specifically.

What do I call her, then, if not by her actual name? How do I conjure a suitable other name for the woman whose twenty years of illicit trysts with me have been at the root of much of my most popular erotic fiction—even when the stories were sometimes about men? A woman who better understood me sexually long before I understood myself. A woman whose fertile imagination in the bedroom deserves some sort of lifetime achievement award. How do I choose a suitable other name for a woman like her? And yet have it be a name brimming with the same type of rejoicing sound as the name her father gave her when he brought her home from the hospital nearly fifty years ago?

Think about it: What is in a name? Then consider your most precious lover and call her by a bunch of sounds you've never called her by before. Never mind that for some unknown reason, she stopped speaking to you a year ago and so won't hear you calling her now. Let that confounding part go and focus, instead, on how it might feel to once again lie naked with her in a bed somewhere, laugh together, share a bottle of red wine, perhaps, while passing a cigarette leisurely between you. Become aroused over her mouth's uncanny ability to make you come and then call her suddenly by this other name, blurt out the foreign syllables that have no memories attached to them, no visceral meaning.

It seems to me there is so much in a name. Love itself can be buried within a name, clinging tenaciously to it. And yet in order to protect her identity, I must choose a new one, pick a name, any name, slap a moniker down on the paper and get on with it already, begin the telling of the lurid tales. Any name will do for now. I could call her E and no one would know the difference. What matters most is to keep the rest of it as accurate as possible. For instance, how it felt the first time, hearing her sexy voice in my ear when we were at a dinner party and still practically strangers to each other. I'll tell you how it felt: I got wet between my legs. She leaned close and told me that she knew I was a dirty girl. She whispered it tenderly, ensuring that her meaning was felt acutely in my clit. She wanted me as aroused as possible, if only because we were in a room full of oblivious people, including her significant other. We were fully dressed, and she wanted me to feel nonetheless exposed. I did feel exposed. I knew I was a dirty girl;

still, I tried hard to hide it, to resist her furtive seduction and behave myself, not publicly lust after a woman who belonged to someone else. I wanted to be good. Ironic, then, wasn't it? Her quiet suggestion that what a dirty girl like me needed was a good spanking, and that I should call her when I thought I was ready to be over her knee.

What is it about lust and its attraction to voices? Why is it that certain voices speaking low in our ears can somehow touch us between our legs? Further proof, in my opinion, that our senses are a gift from God. Not a distant paternal sky-god; I'm a believer in the personal immediacy of an all-pervasive inner God, and the eroticism of certain voices is something I exult in. I don't credit it to a meaningless, chaotic universe but to a universe of creative purpose instead. That lust can be so joyful is proof enough for me of divine intent in the cosmos. The sound of E's voice was part of her sexual instrument, and her voice turned my sense of hearing into something sexual as well. An aural exchange of lust. What else but a divine being could have guessed beforehand that ears might prove useful in a universe of love? That the allure of a single voice could get the dirty wheels whirring and slick that place between a girl's legs, ready it for probing fingers or something even more extreme? Hallelujah for the sound of voices, then, in the world of love.

E was by nature a top, although she wasn't committed to it as a rigid lifestyle or in her sense of fashion. Over the years, she owned various leather jackets, leather belts, and black leather motorcycle boots, but not because she had a particular fetish for leather. She simply liked wearing it sometimes, plus, for a while, she owned a motorcycle. Yet she also wore plenty of T-shirts, sweatshirts, blue jeans, and sneakers. She was tall—six feet two inches—and nearly one hundred ninety pounds. She towered over all of us in our crowd, which aided that impression she gave of being sexually dominant. There were a couple women that E had been an all-out bottom for, but mostly she liked to be on top, at the helm of a sex scene, directing the action, meting out either mild torture or delicious punishment as a given scene required. She was excellent at one-on-one sex but just as imaginative in threeways and orgies, as long as they were women-only scenes. (There was an incident in the early 1980s involving E and a queer man in Los Angeles, but that was so out of the ordinary for her as to qualify it as a shameful secret, divulged to only her closest New York City confidants years later when she'd had too much to drink. Still, to her credit, she may have fucked the guy in L.A., but she had topped him, too, making him come all over his own shoes.)

The details of E's life before we met are sketchy to me. I recall snippets of stories she told about first loves and first lusts: a forced enema here, some cunnilingus on top of a washing machine there, but nothing more sticks with me. Sad that I could have been lovers with a woman (albeit clandestinely) for nearly twenty years and have such insufficient knowledge of who she'd been apart from me, of who she was as an individual or what those needs were that extended beyond her desire to punish me and make me come.

I don't know if all bottoms are self-centered and narcissistic. After all, bottoms have a reputation for serving, for desiring to please the top. But for me, being a bottom has always been about receiving pleasure, even about taking more than my fair share of it, about reveling in erotic indulgences and metaphorically gorging at a banquet of all-out lust. In short: *Gimme, gimme, gimme; fill up my aching void.*

For the uninitiated, bondage can seem freakish, even scary-looking, and the equipment for administering discipline might send a chill up one's spine. To the nonfetishist, it might seem incongruous that someone who exposes herself willingly to painful and degrading punishment could be in fact a self-centered narcissist, gorging at a banquet of lust. Yet that's how it has always felt to me, difficult as it's been to explain why I have the particular needs I have, why it's erotic for me to feel psychologically bared and physically vulnerable. For me, a top with a lot of rope, a leather strap, a good imagination, and real stamina is nothing less than a blessing from heaven. It means I will be exposed emotionally as well as between my legs, and it also means that a veritable smorgasbord of new and unusual ways of making me come is near at hand. Being bound through most of it means I won't have to lift a finger, either. All I'll have to do is receive, as in: receive my punishment from a well-aimed leather strap; receive the thick dildos up my holes when I least expect them, or the clamps with heavy dangling weights on my clit and nipples, her mouth on my swollen labia, or maybe the high-powered Hitachi Magic Wand.

Okay, I'm simplifying it. Indulgent as it can be, trust is the underlying current of Eros in that whole scenario. Without it, one is doomed at the outset. Without implicit trust, undertaking a bondage and discipline scene, regardless of how imaginative the top might be, is like embarking on a psychological suicide mission. There's nothing erotic about it. E, however, was like the proverbial Earth Mother. She could always be trusted to nurture me along with administering my punishment.

II.

There is a black-and-white photo of me as a little girl in Cleveland, in 1963. The style of house we lived in back then was called a California A-frame. It was brand-new at the time, furnished top to bottom in the then obligatory Danish Modern. It was a beautiful, if compact, mid-century house; I had an idyllic childhood there. The photo of me sitting demurely in a living-room chair was taken by my loving grandmother and captures me in my shy, well-behaved, perfect little white girl world. Like every other child on Earth, though, I wasn't always an angel. I frequently found myself on the receiving end of a blistering bare-assed spanking, a punishment I dreaded as if the sky itself were falling. Pain and humiliation so acutely disturbed my otherwise ideal world that something as simple as an ordinary spanking filled me with irrational terror. Not so strange, then, is it, that at the center of my sexual persona, I have always been that shy and trusting little girl, trying my best to behave? After all, it was my first spiritual starting point for exploring a very scary world.

In the sense that sexual opposites can be powerful aphrodisiacs, it's no wonder that even by the age of five, I was erotically attracted to older girls who tried to persuade me to misbehave. Even though I was too young to understand yet what I was feeling, I have a crystal clear memory of that first time, at age five, when I responded sexually to another person.

It was while playing in the basement of our second house in Cleveland with a slightly older girl from next door. She proposed that we play house. Her idea of playing house, however, was unlike any game of house proposed to me before. She told me to lie down on the couch, which I did, and then suggested that she would be the mommy and I the baby. Then she moved to pull down my pants, explaining that I had been bad, that I'd wet myself and was going to be spanked.

In real life, a threat like that would have caused me to burst into tears. Yet for some mysterious reason, the idea of getting spanked by her didn't feel threatening at all, it excited me. I was completely entranced by what she was preparing to do to me, and I couldn't have been more crestfallen when my real-life mommy appeared at the top of the basement stairs and informed my little girlfriend that it was time for her to go home now.

The enchanting experience had lasted just long enough, though, to cause me to seek out slightly older girls who might be willing to spank me. Surprisingly enough, I did find one very agreeable older girl when I was seven or eight, who carried out the actual spankings on my bare ass quite a few times before I wasn't allowed to play with her anymore. But mostly my erotic life was lived in my head. I had sexually charged crushes on most of my babysitters and on a few teenaged TV actresses from that era. My secret inner world brimmed with lurid fantasies of spankings and other humiliations suffered at the hands of these seemingly ordinary girls. I had a full and wonderful childhood in all the usual senses of the word. But the childhood I experienced in my head was nothing less than X-rated.

When I learned to masturbate at around the same age, that inner world grew even more lurid, fueled as it was by brewing hormones and by the family dog accidentally licking me between my legs one afternoon when I was innocently changing out of my bathing suit. It felt shocking and incredible, what the dog did, and it gave me an idea of something else I might want to do with girls. At that time, I had no idea that oral sex existed or was in any way common. For me, the naughtiness of licking a girl between her legs, or being licked by one, was the dirtiest thing I could imagine. Then, at age nine, when I had my first orgasm from masturbation, the world in my head became positively addicting. Nothing in the outside world could compare to the erotic one unfolding at a wicked pace inside my head, as I brought on orgasm after orgasm, day or night, every chance I could be alone. It caused me to become even more shy as I grew older, though, perhaps even pathologically withdrawn, making me incapable of dealing nonsexually with real people in the real world.

Luckily for me, I suppose, the erotic scenarios of discipline and sexual humiliation that played out in my head were often more satisfying than the physical encounters I had with actual people. For one thing, my vivid imagination helped me become a popular erotic fiction author later in life. But when I met E, when I was all of twenty-two and had already had unsatisfying sex with more men and women than I could count, I was not prepared for how explosive it would feel to finally encounter a flesh-and-blood woman, a "slightly older girl," in fact, who could take the sex in my head and make it just as satisfying in the physical realm. I guess that's why we stayed lovers for almost twenty years.

Not that it ever felt like twenty years while it was happening; it felt like a mere heartbeat. And I'm not sure why we never hooked up as aboveboard, out-in-the-open, committed lovers, why we were always fucking each other in secret, with our respective committed relationships taking place on the side. I suppose I have the rest of my life to try to analyze that misguided idea, but for now what intrigues me more is that E and I met at all, and that our sexual rapport with each other was so inspirational and satisfying.

III.

How do I describe the hypnotic allure of pain, or at least certain types of pain? When I was thirteen, I secretly read the infamous French novel *Story of O,* and I was thoroughly aroused reading about the pain O experienced in her many degrading sexual encounters. How could I have had a predisposition, by age thirteen, for enjoying something like that? I've often wondered about it—what makes me a sexual masochist—but I've as yet to reach any reasonable conclusion, even thirty-three years later. The chapter where O is sent to live with Anne-Marie in the house by the Fontainebleau Forest was a chapter I read over and over again. Even though I enjoyed the entire book, the scenes where O endures her whippings at the hands of women rather than men kept me riveted. Specifically, the scene where O, who's been stripped naked, is tied on a platform, thighs forced apart, and whipped between her legs by another woman never failed to make me come. I wanted to be O, never the woman administering the punishment.

The first time I visited E at the apartment she shared with her girlfriend in Queens, I was nervous. This was well past the dinner-party episode where she'd told me to call her when I was ready to be over her knee. We hadn't had sex yet, but at least I'd made the phone call. It had taken me nearly a month to get up the nerve to go that far. I wasn't sure I really was ready for her. I knew sex with her would involve a lot more than just spankings. It would run the whole gamut of sexual discipline. By age twenty-two, I had willingly engaged in rough sex and endured a couple of uninspired spankings at the hands of men, but that was it. Actual bondage and discipline, and the accompanying pain, was still unexplored terrain but a world I was longing to experience, especially with a woman.

E took me on the grand tour of their modest railroad flat, the type of apartment where one room follows another, where there are no doors except between the kitchen and bathroom. We walked through the bedroom to get to the kitchen. The large bed was unmade, and leather restraints were permanently attached to the bed's legs. I could see them plain as day. She noticed me eyeing them but didn't say anything. Naturally, I wondered who tied up whom; E's lover was just as formidable a dyke, in stature and temperament, as E was. I couldn't picture either of them being the bottom. Still, I kept my curiosity to myself. I had already reverted to that shy little girl who was trying her best to behave.

E didn't have sex with me that day, even though she knew I was quietly dying to be touched by her. She waited another *month*. I guess she wanted to be sure I was jumping out of my skin with my desire for her by the time she laid a hand on me. When it finally happened, when we went to bed together, the release was sheer ecstasy.

It's hard to believe it now, when I look at the years that followed our first sexual encounter, the familiarity, the occasional spats, and, overall, the love that eventually flowed between us; how could it have been possible that I was ever as wide-eyed and nervous as I was that first time? Yes, E towered over me physically, she had a few years' worth of experience in B&D already, and she was technically older than I was, yet she was still only *twenty-three*. It seems ludicrous now, in hindsight, when we are both pushing fifty, that she could have felt so much older, so much more mature than me. But she did.

She was masterful at seduction, even back then, that first time we were in bed together when, to my great disappointment, she didn't spank me—making me wait, instead, an additional two weeks for it. She knew how to prolong desire, to draw out the anticipation and make the thrill last. Just being with her that first time overwhelmed me, even though she didn't spank me and we (mostly) kept our clothes on. There was a moment when she had me on my knees on the floor, bending over the edge of the bed. Two of her fingers were working my soaking pussy, two fingers were wedged uncomfortably up my ass. She had warned me to keep my mouth shut, not to make a sound while she drove me into utter ecstasy with those fingers. I'd obeyed her to the best of my ability, delighting in the twin feelings of pleasure in my pussy and pain in my asshole with only a frantic whimper. For that, my panties had come down around my thighs. Other than that, though, and a breathtaking round of cunnilingus to finish me off for the evening, we'd both kept our clothes on.

For me, a promise is a promise; I take it seriously. If a person promises that I'm going to be spanked the next time we meet, it will behoove that person to keep that promise or the quality of our relationship is going to suffer. E was always true to her promises. During our next sexual encounter, two weeks later, she got right down to business.

My first erotic spanking with E was not the traditional over-the-knee kind, as I had been anticipating. For one thing, for the first time in my life, my pussy was shaved painstakingly clean. Back then, only girls in the sex industry or in the BDSM scene had shaved pussies. Porn videos hadn't saturated our lives yet, bringing kink into our everyday world. It felt freakish to have a shaved pussy back then, but E relished that kind of detail in a B&D scene, so I willingly accommodated her.

On the bed, she tied my wrists together in front of me and spread my legs, tying each of my ankles somewhere up over my shoulders. It was the first time in my life I had been tied up. It felt frightening, in the way that a thrill ride feels frightening: Your belly flutters; you question the soundness of your own judgment at the final precipice before the drop into oblivion. But it was also unspeakably arousing for me, to at last feel so forcibly exposed.

E knelt between my legs, my hairless pussy soaking, swollen, and spread wide for whatever whim struck her fancy. She leaned over me then, close to my face, her voice assuming that tender, sexy tone I had first heard in my ear that night of the dinner party. "Mommy's going to spank you now. You're sure you want it?"

In the tiniest voice I'd ever heard come out of my mouth, I peeped, "Yes."

"Yes, what? Tell me what it is my baby wants."

"I want Mommy to spank me."

It had never occurred to me that she would take on the role of mommy and call me her baby. The safety imbued in those words, the sudden feeling of blind trust, overwhelmed me, rushing into my heart as the stinging slaps began landing on my ass. It was a painful spanking, and it went on for one hundred blows, all of which I had to count, audibly. If she couldn't hear or clearly understand me, she'd start all over at "one."

IV.

It's fourteen years later. We're fourteen years older, each in our hormonal peaks, sequestered together in a cheap, rent-by-the-hour motel room out by JFK. By now, we are used to being absolute sluts with each other. I'm wearing nothing but a pair of black four-inch spiked high heels, silky black stay-put stockings, and a blue plaid schoolgirl skirt. A clear acrylic buttplug is stuck up my ass and has been for at least an hour already, keeping me feeling stuffed full and stretched open, the inside of my rectum viewable and somewhat magnified through the clear acrylic. E loves this, the fact that she can see inside me through the buttplug. Four small lead weights are clamped tight to my hairless labia, gravity causing the swollen lips to pull painfully downward, but to me it feels delicious. I get aroused by this kind of steady pain so near my clitoris. We're allowed to smoke in the room, thank God, and we're also sharing an expensive bottle of Bordeaux. Those really lousy, locally made porn loops are on the closed-circuit TV. We've rented the room for a four-hour stretch. We'll know when it's time to leave because the porn loop on the TV goes off when the allotted time is up.

E removes my schoolgirl skirt—my wrists are bound tightly together with rope so that I can't remove the skirt myself. She wants to take a picture of the progress the clamps are making at extending my labia. My face is not visible in the photo. She captures me strictly from the waist down. I'm kneeling on the motel-room bed, wrists bound in front of me, the black stockings on my thighs making my shaved cunt and the area surrounding it seem impossibly white, highlighting the four lead weights hanging down from my labia, looking very nasty indeed. It's a Polaroid snapshot; digital cameras haven't been invented yet. E winds up selling the Polaroid photo later that evening for two nickels (a nickel for me, one for her) to a very horny married man that I never meet but who lives on E's block in Brooklyn. He treasures the photo, but he thinks we're a couple of freaks.

At the motel, we've been having a full afternoon. Prior to our tryst, I had been told by E to fill an entire student's theme notebook with the words, "I'm a bad girl and I need to be spanked." It had taken every moment of my spare time for several days to accomplish it, but I did. The theme notebook is filled with page after page after page of the same damning sentence. E peruses the finished result and chuckles merrily, picturing me finding enough time in my overloaded schedule to scribble the same ten words over and over again until the notebook's many pages were finally filled.

Because of what's written in that notebook, I know I'm going to be seriously spanked and made to kneel in the corner with my skirt raised in back, exposing my red and burning rear end in the infamous Catholic girls'-school tradition. It's one of the things I cherish about trysting with E: We'd usually talk on the phone days beforehand, plotting in detail the various things we would do when we got together, and then we'd do them, with very satisfying results.

However, one of the spur-of-the-moment decisions E had made that day in the motel was that for the duration of the scene, I was not allowed to be on my feet. Atttractive as my already long legs looked while I was wearing those four-inch spiked high heels, when I was not on the bed, I could only be on my knees. If I needed to use the toilet, I could at least lift myself up onto the porcelain bowl, but I had to crawl there and back—not as simple as it might seem when my bound wrists were factored into the equation. This was why, when E finally asked me to retrieve the theme notebook from my backpack, I had to clumsily crawl to her, carrying the notebook between my teeth.

In my adult life, I've done a number of B&D scenes with both men and women, but none of those stand out as particularly enjoyable. I'm not a "lifestyle submissive"; I've never been interested in seeking out a full-time mistress or master. I don't like the spectacle of dungeon scenes or public play parties. I don't even enjoy threeways. I'm only into one-on-one unobserved sex. It isn't that the typical ritualized B&D scene holds no appeal for me—it actually does. I find it very erotic—when *others* are doing it. I'm especially appreciative when other submissive women are exhibitionists who want their ritualized sexual humiliation observed by someone who isn't participating in it. I'm a first-class watcher. And I'm decadent enough to be even happier if cocktails are involved. So it isn't that the scene itself turns me off. It's more that I've had little luck enjoying scenes with partners I wasn't infatuated with in some way, and I've had disastrous results doing a scene simply for the sake of doing a scene. A couple of my experiences felt like wide-awake nightmares—for instance, scenes I did with men whose motivations for wanting to hit a girl I'd grossly misinterpreted. I did one eight-hour stretch with a man in a hotel room that felt about as erotic as eight hours of rape, battery, and psychological trauma. The other scenes that didn't go well weren't because of my scene-mates being psychopaths, though. It was simply that, for me, other playmates have always paled when compared with the instant sexual rapport I had with E, and her disarming humor and imagination.

There were times when even E took me too far, when the pain inflicted on me was excruciating and short-circuited any feelings of sexual gratification. I recall vividly a time when she attempted to fist me when my body wasn't ready to accommodate that type of an intrusion, and the acute pain of it had me on the verge of blacking out. But with E, those rare moments ended with her grabbing me in her arms and saying, "I'm so sorry, baby. I'm so sorry." It was never her intention to hurt me in a bad way. For people who don't enjoy pain at all, that's probably a tricky differentiation to comprehend. But for people who are sexual submissives or masochists, it marks the difference between a good top and a heartless one. And it's part of why I feel that effective tops, both males and females, regardless of whether or not they've topped me, are among the most giving, innately gentle, selfless, and emotionally intuitive people I've known.

Obviously, I can't speak for all submissives, I can speak only for myself. For me, being erotically attracted to, perhaps even fixated on, sexual discipline and humiliation has never been a completely comfortable fit, as far as my intellect goes. I was raised in an era when, if a woman had any brains or social awareness at all, she considered herself a feminist. During the women's movement and directly after it, there didn't seem to be any sexual gray areas for women; either you were intelligent and stood up for yourself or you were stupid and didn't. In my public persona, I've always been comfortable taking charge, taking on added responsibilities, even being a leader. In the bedroom, I'm the complete opposite. In my business life, I don't react well to people making decisions for me or expecting any type of subservience from me at all. During sex, I can get aroused only if someone else is taking the lead and telling me what to do.

In the early years of my adult life, this was a dichotomy that confounded me. In certain business or social situations, it would have been mortifying to me to have it be readily known that I was a sexual submissive, because in my mind, simply being one didn't make logical sense. It was like sleeping with the enemy or surrendering to the oppressor. Why would any woman in her right mind willingly do that? To be honest? Intellectually, I still don't know. Emotionally, though, I gave up trying to be logical and decided instead to allow myself to be whoever I needed to be in this world. Somehow, I found my own spiritual balance.

I suppose to most people, sexual dominance is what makes logical sense. Especially since in our society, success means being on top. But for someone like me, being on top during sex is nearly impossible. I'm okay with a strap-on, especially for anal sex. I can fuck a man or a woman up the ass and approach sexual euphoria while doing it. I think it's because I can so easily tune in to how much I enjoy receiving anal sex. I've somehow managed to become an okay spanker for the same reasons. But I can't seem to go beyond that. I recoil at the thought of causing anybody actual pain, or degrading them, or causing them to feel humiliated. It doesn't arouse me sexually at all.

When I was twelve, I had a boyfriend a year younger than I was. We were both virgins, all we did was kiss. It was really only puppy love; still, it was an intense case of it. His mom had died of cancer, and he and his brothers were being raised by an overly protective, strict disciplinarian father, and I used to feel very sorry for my boyfriend. One afternoon, we were hanging out together in my basement, where there were both a pool table and a Ping-Pong table. Unexpectedly, my boyfriend, the object of my extreme adolescent affection, bent over the Ping-Pong table, handed me a Ping-Pong paddle, and asked me to spank him with it.

"I can't do that to you," I blurted. "I don't want to hurt you."

Still, he practically begged me. "But I want you to. It's okay to hurt me."

The sight of him bent over the pool table, even while fully dressed, was too provocative for words. I understood what he wanted from me. By age twelve, my private erotic world was already steeped in fantasies of spankings and corporal punishment of all kinds. I wanted to hand him back the Ping-Pong paddle and beg him to spank me with it instead, but I was too shy. In fact, I admired his candor, that he trusted me enough to ask something like that of me, to admit that he wanted to be spanked. I would have given anything in my twelve-year-old world to have been able to admit that to him. And yet, even while understanding viscerally how much he wanted to be spanked, the truth was that I couldn't hurt him. I was physically incapable of causing him any pain, even though I knew he was very disappointed in me for not even trying.

It's that visceral understanding of a complicated sexual need that has led me to at least try, as an adult, to accommodate certain submissive needs in my various lovers. Based solely on my body of published works, it's been no surprise that a number of younger men have found their way into my private world, usually uninvited, wanting to be topped by me. As politely as possible, my huge ego not wanting to adversely affect my book sales, I sent them all on their way. They had no inkling of who I was as a real person, what my needs might be, they saw me only through the guise of their own fantasies. But one young man was different. He wasn't into humiliation or pain; he didn't want to be topped by me. What he wanted instead was the safe place of mommy; pain- and punishment-free. He wasn't into infantilism or the whole "adults in diapers" scene. It wasn't about being a baby, it was about wanting to get lost in the erotic world of the maternal.

The man was a stranger to me. And as so many others before him had, he came into my life uninvited. Still, it touched me that he saw me as a woman who could fulfill that primal a need. He was so insistent, so eager, that I agreed to do a scene with him. I agreed to at least try. It helped that I was a lot older than him; it gave me a good starting point. Other than that, all I had to offer was a vagina and a pair of tits with extremely sensitive nipples. It turned out that was all I needed. The rest of being "mommy" came from the heart's imagination. I discovered that I could get completely aroused by having a grown man, a perfect stranger no less, suckle at my tits, pretending to be my son—one of the most intimate of bonds, faked to precision. I took the responsibility seriously, knowing that the success of the scene hinged on my maintaining a dominant maternal stance and not shifting into my usual shy little girl persona.

Miraculously, having never been a mother in real life or so much as a positive influence on anyone younger than me, I summoned it from somewhere, the maternal instinct. And the pièce de résistance of the whole evening? With his fingers working deep in my vagina, I unexpectedly ejaculated for the first time in my life. Now, how primal was that? The fluids gushed out of me in a flood; they flowed and flowed, like the waters of life; I left the couch cushions soaking. We were both mesmerized by what had happened to my body. After nearly forty years of believing that only certain girls could ejaculate, I was suddenly one of those girls and, judging by the sopping condition of my couch, I seemed to be making up for lost time.

Sadly, though, in hindsight I know that the encounter was one of the rare instances where I went out of my way to put another's sexual needs before mine in a scene. I was usually too self-absorbed, even hypnotized by receiving my own pleasure/pain, that I never stopped to so much as wonder what might be in it for the top. I got only as far as determining if a top was effective or not for my own needs.

In these last few years since I've stopped doing scenes, having settled, back at age forty-three, into the first truly monogamous relationship of my adult life, I've had a lot of time to think about my past behavior as a bottom and, subsequently, the behavior of the dominant men and women I got involved with. At last it occurred to me to at least *wonder* about what they might have wanted from a scene. How did they derive sexual fulfillment from being on top? And, ideally, what could the bottom offer that helped the top feel sexually fulfilled? I realized that I didn't have a clue. The needs and motivations of a sexual dominant, to me, were a huge blank canvas. Tops were my sexual opposite, and yet I knew nothing about what might make them feel whole. It was then that I realized the depth of my own need to feel overpowered and sexually exposed seems to have been bottomless. Trying to fill that void in me had been all I'd focused on, either reveling in my satiation or blaming a given top for not being able to fill the bottomless pit of my needs. Maybe I'm oversimplifying it, but it seems that my willingness to be present at a scene was about all I actively contributed, leaving the rest strictly to the top to provide.

It was all that self-damning contemplation that brought me to the conclusion that the most effective tops truly were among the most giving, selfless, and emotionally intuitive people. Not to downplay the sexual gratification tops get, not to make it sound like sexual domination is a mission of mercy for the self-absorbed submissive. I know that there's a complementary thrill in both giving and receiving punishment, even though I experience only one half of that equation and don't relate sexually to the other half of it. I at least understand that there's a unique fulfillment derived from causing a willing bottom to suffer, and that to make that suffering sublime takes patience and compassion. To be willing to cause pain to another human being in the first place, or at least this type of pain, takes courage. To fine-tune the pain or punishment so that the erotic power of it builds for the bottom and then crests over and through her like a wave of grace takes skill and care. It makes me feel all the more grateful for the experiences

I shared with E. I was grateful to her while it was happening, I wasn't completely selfish. I just wish I'd shown her my gratitude a little more consistently.

V.

I prefer rope that's made of a natural fiber, such as sisal or manila. And rope that's twisted, not braided. Being confined in chains or by leather restraints doesn't arouse me; being tied with rope does. The simple act of having my wrists tied together gets me wet between my legs.

I learned through trial and error that I don't like whips or martinets, birch rods, or leather-covered paddles. But I can get sexually aroused from just watching a top remove his or her leather belt. If my legs are forced apart, the anticipation feels even more exciting. But to feel a leather strap snapping against my aching clit, my swollen labia, or my soaking hole, I'm willing to hold my own legs open. Before the strap so much as touches me, I'm already in an erotic swoon.

If my hands are tied and I'm blindfolded, I instantly become a most compliant submissive. I love a world of darkness and restraint—to be bared from the waist down, to wait in that darkness for my punishment, whatever it winds up being. I love the peculiar fear that fills me then, the acute sense of unnerving expectancy. I'll take a cock or dildo up my ass without a struggle. I'll feel profoundly grateful for the penetration, in fact. I'll perform oral sex with abandon, too, preferably on my knees.

I don't know what it is about the state of bondage that both soothes and excites me. I'm capable of having sex like a "normal" person does, and I can have orgasms from traditional intercourse. Yet bondage heightens the pleasure for me. Punishment makes me feel special, singled out for a secret kind of attention.

I know it's rooted in my childhood. Not in how I was treated as a child but in how I experienced the world in private. I know that doesn't come close to explaining it—why, through most of my waking days, I did whatever it took to avoid any type of punishment, physical or not. I didn't want to misbehave, never willfully intended to be bad. Like most children, I walked blindly into trouble and then was horrified to discover that whatever it was I'd done without really thinking was now going to cause me to suffer. Yet, alone in my bed at night, with my fingers between my legs, I couldn't get enough punishment and humiliation.

In my early teens, corporal punishment was still legal in my junior-high school. I was an intelligent student, I usually got A's, but there was a period during the fall of my eighth-grade year when my parents were divorcing and my mind was always wandering. I couldn't seem to make myself pay attention. School, and everything about it, suddenly bored me.

My history teacher that year, Mr. Cook, held me back after the class period one morning. When we were alone in the classroom, he handed me back a recent test I had taken and there was a big red D at the top of the paper. I was shocked. I never received D's, but I didn't try to defend or explain it. I just stared blankly at it.

He said, "I know there's some trouble at home right now, but in my class, I expect you to leave your trouble at home. If you don't start paying attention, I'll take my paddle out and use it on you."

I was appalled. I knew he was serious. A lot of the teachers kept paddles in their desks, and we all knew that he was one of them.

He said, "You have until Friday to get it together. You're going to retake the test on Friday, and if you get an A, we'll forget about this D. Anything less than an A and I'll keep you after class again and paddle you. I'm not afraid to do it, either. I'll call your parents and get their permission if I have to."

I felt stung and humiliated, just from his words. I was terrified of getting paddled. Nothing as severe as that had ever happened to me, least of all at school. I wasn't afraid of his calling my parents. It was the threat of pain and humiliation that motivated me. I wanted to avoid it at all costs. I studied like a crazy person, then, and started paying attention in class. When the next test rolled around, I got an A. Mr. Cook placed the graded test on my desk in front of me. He didn't say anything like "good job" or "that's better," he just looked at me. It was a look that seemed to say *I know how to make you behave.* I'd avoided the paddling, but I felt humiliated anyway.

I never understood this dual response in me. One teacher threatens me with a paddle and I felt appalled. But once, while staying at my best friend's house, after sneaking out in the middle of the night with her and smoking cigarettes, her father caught us and threatened to beat me with his leather belt for misbehaving under his roof, and I was instantly smitten. I fell in love with him. And it wasn't a mild crush, either. I was sexually obsessed with him until I was twenty-five years old. I had orgasm after orgasm, imagining that leather belt of his landing on my naked ass and on other more sensitive naked areas.

It's a fetish, I know, but I don't know the "why" of it. It has something to do with a nuance of intimacy, I think. A paddle is a hard, cold object, after all. Whereas a leather belt or strap might retain some of the human warmth of the person wielding it. At least I perceive that a person holding a leather strap is more connected to it. Which I guess is why a spanking is, for me, the most intimate punishment of all. I wonder, if Mr. Cook had taken me aside and threatened to take off his belt and beat me with that instead, or threatened to take me over his knee and spank me, inappropriate as that would have been in junior high or at any other time, would I have become sexually obsessed with him, too? My instinct is to sigh and think, *Probably.*

I know it's part of why I don't like to participate in dungeon scenes or public play parties. I need a certain nuance of intimacy with my partner, and I also need to feel that what we do is secret. It's one characteristic all my childhood sexual fantasies shared: Regardless of who I imagined was punishing me, they always punished me in secret, and it was that secrecy, that one-on-one attention to my humiliation, that made me come.

Contrary to what people have believed about me as an adult, that because I write erotica, I must be an exhibitionist who wants to get fucked by everybody, that's far from true. I need my sex life to take place in private, with someone I have an emotional attraction to. I write erotica because I feel compelled to do it, perhaps even neurotically compelled. I do purposely try to create a sexual experience for the reader when I write. Reading is a quiet, internal process, a process that I'm, in a sense, abetting. And reading about sex, in particular, is often a very private, if not secret, affair.

My compulsion to write erotic stories began in my teens, although it wasn't something I felt comfortable about back then. I wrote the stories because I was so overly preoccupied with erotic thoughts that I needed some kind of escape valve for them. It felt as if the stories demanded to be written. But once they were down on paper, I destroyed them. I was afraid of their ever being found and read by someone, *anyone,* least of all my parents.

It wasn't until I was well into my escapades with E, in my twenties, that I was finally able to show someone the stories I'd been compulsively writing (and destroying). The first story that I showed E was more like a forty-page love letter to her, since it had been spawned, full-blown, after one of our secret B&D lovemaking marathons.

She was moved by the story, in the best possible way. I think she understood for the first time, really, the depths of my desire for her and how much I was getting off on the things she was doing to me in bed. I felt relieved that the story seemed to bring us closer together and she hadn't regarded me as some kind of freak for writing it. Still, it was a private gift, one meant for her eyes only. She read it, in its entirety, after work one afternoon while we were in the women's locker room. In those days, we both worked deep in the bowels of a large museum in New York.

After she read it, she folded it and stuffed it in the pocket of her leather motorcycle jacket. Then we went outside, hopped the train, and headed to her apartment in Queens. By the time we got to her apartment, we'd forgotten about the filthy story, stuffed in the pocket of her jacket. She took off the coat and tossed it onto the couch. Within moments, her lover was wearing the coat, getting ready to head out the door in it—out into the big, wild world of New York City, with forty pages of damning, pornographic evidence of our affair tagging along with her.

It was comical, really, the degree of acute fear it instantly filled us with. How E and I both stood there, motionless, staring at her lover in that coat, at the fat wad of papers wedged inside one of the coat's pockets. *How on Earth are we going to get that out of there before she leaves the apartment?* I wondered. And I was quietly despairing for another reason. Unbeknownst to E, her lover had already confronted me once, taking me aside in the lobby of their building one night, telling me in no uncertain terms, all two hundred towering pounds of her, that if she ever found out that I was fucking around with E, I was going to be in serious trouble. And I believed her. I didn't stop fucking around with E, but nevertheless, I believed her. I was going to be in some kind of ugly trouble if we got caught, and I didn't think it would involve being put over the woman's sizable knee.

It wasn't that the story was documented proof of an affair between E and me. But it was handwritten by me, dedicated to her, and filthy as hell. It was another one of my humble masterpieces that wound up destroyed. This time, torn to shreds and set on fire in the fireplace. At the last minute, before leaving the apartment, E's lover had felt the bulge of papers in the coat pocket, yanked it out, and tossed it blindly onto the coffee table.

After that episode, although E continued to inspire my erotica for years to come (she still does, in fact), it was never again openly dedicated to her. Though she did read all the books and stories I wrote, and was always proud that her life served as an inspiration for them.

She was creative, as well. A wonderful painter, she painted huge close-ups of cats and dogs in vibrant, shocking colors. And sometimes she painted people.

I have a Polaroid picture in a frame. It's a picture of a painting she once painted. The painting sits on an easel in her kitchen, almost completed. It's a painting of a naked woman, from her neck to her thighs, against the background of a closed venetian blind. The same blinds that hung on my bedroom window. I own only a Polaroid of the painting, because E sold it for a lot of money several years ago at a gallery showing. Still, it was a painting of me, with hints of another woman E loved who lived in Bavaria. Both of us were tall brunettes with big bones. I never saw the other woman naked, and she never saw me. But when I look at the naked female form in the picture, I know intimately which parts of the female image painted there were inspired by an intimate knowledge of me. And I love the fact that it stays a secret, how intimately E knew me. How many times she had both caressed me and hurt me when I was naked.

Most of the things I've written here about the sex life I shared with E, my submissiveness, my sexual masochism, my proclivity to have an orgasm when in the throes of violation, humiliation, and pain, were difficult things for me to come to terms with in the beginning. Privately, I berated myself for having such "sick" needs, for being so willing to allow myself to endure a type of base humiliation that I could never deliver to someone else. It made me think I was self-destructive. It made me think that underneath it all, I hated myself and wanted to see myself destroyed. However, the actual experiences I had with E, the sexual exchanges we had, filled me with such bliss, such a feeling of arousal and then erotic sublimation, that I couldn't resist seeking out those experiences with her over and over. With E, I never felt as though I wanted to be annihilated or destroyed. Life felt like a gift. I felt lucky to be alive, to have such a thing as an orgasm at all.

Eventually, I made complete peace with myself. I can accept myself for who I've been even while I don't often understand my behavior. Simply because I long for my punishment, for that secret, one-on-one attention to my humiliation, doesn't mean I don't like myself. I exult in the unpredictability of private life. In fact, I still treasure the eroticism of the whole scenario: the shy and trusting little girl, willingly taking her punishment. And I've somehow learned to treasure the other side of that coin: the top who willingly delivers, who cares enough to try to make me come. These things that I've learned, I know because I met E in the first place. She helped me open all those doors.

In our late thirties, her younger brother died from AIDS. He died in E's arms, in his old bed at home. E felt his spirit move through her when he died, "joyfully," she said. But it didn't keep her from grieving for him for a couple years. Or from turning to drugs, like mainlining Demerol or heroin, to deaden her broken heart. When we last made love, she wanted to be the bottom. I complied to the best of my ability, but it was difficult for my heart to be in it. How could I top the woman whose own dominant nature had been my sexual salvation for so many years? It didn't feel like real sex, somehow. She had an orgasm from it, from the specific thing that she had asked me to do; still, it felt like we were both drifting aimlessly in space. After that episode, we reverted to being just friends. Friends with a colorful history that we loved to reminisce about.

Eventually, we both found new lovers, people more suitable, I suppose, for our approaching march toward middle age. Menopause wound up coming early for me. And while it's been traumatic, it's also been a blessing. It's given me perspective, helped me see my sexuality from a quieter, less hormonal frame of reference. It's been educational to be able to stand back from who I've been as a lover and see myself calmly, instead of always being so hopelessly mired in the thick of my complicated desires.

In some ways, I find my sexuality reverting to the eroticism of my childhood. Meaning that the erotic world that unfolds in my head, blossoming daily in exquisite detail, doesn't come with the added compulsion to constantly act on those ideas. It's an empowering place to create from, actually. It doesn't mean I don't have regrets—I have so many of them. But I have joy, too.

A couple years ago, I wrote E a letter, finally taking responsibility for my self-centered, often annoying behavior over the long years. I told her how much I loved her and what it had meant to me to have her as a lover, what she'd taught me about myself, and what I wished for her future. She called me then and said she'd never received a more beautiful letter in her life.

Why she stopped speaking to me a year after that is a complete mystery. But I don't press the issue. It makes me sad, but I suppose that after twenty years of being there to cater to my every salacious need and whim, she's entitled now to a little privacy.

This Insane Allure

BILL BRENT

I. Wounded

All day long, they know. There is nowhere to escape their staring and pointing. The dirt and gravel are spit away, a bit of it swallowed. The bloody nose has been cleaned up; the fat lip has stopped its bleeding. But it's still grotesquely large, a wound that stares at me every time I catch my reflection in a window or a mirror. It's a deformity, a giant accusation of failure.

I am twelve. This is the sixth or seventh time so far this year. I've lost count. Whenever I get off the bus, I know there is a fifty percent chance someone will try to kick my ass before I leave. Someone will try to spit his evil into me like venom. *Fuck you, faggot, failure.*

o   o   o

I AM FORTY. Just now, on this sunny afternoon in July, my lover persuades me to go swimming in the creek where we are vacationing. I hear a serious, mysterious rustling in the brush on the northern shore. Two rattlesnakes dance together, heads bobbing to and fro several feet above the ground. I call my lover over as the dance continues for several minutes. We watch, enraptured. We can't tell whether they are fighting or fucking. Sometimes they are so close.

Throughout this week, I have been watching *Bareback, Bareback II,* and *Bareback III,* by Dick Wadd Productions. Hour after hour, I watched gangs of hot, masculine men with giant pricks and pulsating buttholes fuck, suck, rim, felch, fist, kiss, lick, spit, chew, and otherwise share every sort of carnal knowledge available between men short of licking blood, drinking piss, or eating shit. I felt like an intruder. I was envious. It seemed wrong that such intimate rituals should be so readily available to the paying public.

○ ○ ○

SUZANNE VEGA writes knowingly of "bad wisdom," worldly knowledge one acquires before one is old enough to assimilate it in a healthy way. Here is one of my narrow escapes.

When I was in college, sometimes I'd respond to personals in the "pink section" of *The Advocate.* One of the ads I responded to was Ron's. The ad was very basic; he wanted young guys for sensual massage.

What Ron really meant was internal massage. As in prostate. With his cock.

Ron had a nice cock. It had a pronounced upward curve, a tendency I've noticed is fairly common among the redheads I've bedded. Given his cock's extreme curvature, he really should have done a better job of introducing his lads to its pleasures. He had a lovely, black-tiled double shower, complete with douching hardware. Yet he never showed me how to properly use the thing or otherwise prepare for his fuckings. That's America for you: We expect everyone to arrive ready-to-serve. Gay men basically do a shitty job of mentoring their young. Neglect is a kind of wounding we don't often acknowledge.

Ron was a lawyer whose clients included San Francisco bathhouse owners. He was politically active at many levels. On his bedroom wall hung a framed document signed by John F. Kennedy, his hero. He lived way up in the hills, in a gorgeous house with a sunken living room and a sweeping view of the western half of the city, clear out to the ocean, several miles away. His lifestyle had a grandeur that I'd never imagined I'd get a glimpse of.

We saw each other off and on for two years. Occasionally, someone would back out of a social commitment, and Ron would call to see if I was available. It was a fair deal. He'd take me out to dinner, I'd get to see a musical or something, and eventually we'd end up back at his place to fuck. I think that he really liked to screw chicken, but he went with young college guys because he couldn't risk getting caught with a minor. Eventually, he stopped returning my calls. I supposed that I'd grown too old for him.

Once, on a Saturday night, we went to see *My Fair Lady*—oh, the irony—with his housemate, whose actual name I never learned. Everyone called him "Vera," which I guess made Ron "Mame," although no one ever called him that, at least to his face. Afterward, Ron drove us to Polk Street and went into a bar. He came out with two guys who accompanied us back to his place. One was a skinny, nelly young queen with glasses and dark, straight hair. The other was a model-gorgeous guy with a tan and dark, curly hair. The queen was really aggressive and started putting the moves on me in the car. He seemed quite immature.

Back at Ron's place, the four of us ended up in bed together while Vera headed downstairs to his own room. I wanted to suck Ron's cock, but it became clear that he had designs to fuck the gorgeous guy and had brought along the aggressive one to fob off on me. I couldn't really blame Ron; the gorgeous guy had one of the most spectacular asses I'd ever seen. But that still left me with the aggressive queen, who wanted to fuck me badly. I went along with him up to a point, but when it became clear that he was sadistic, and in particular enjoyed battering boys' holes with his cock, I fought my way out from under him rather than become the latest victim of his rape. I also sensed that if I let him penetrate me, I'd be damaged in some unspeakably profound way. I just knew I'd catch something. I was always getting syphilis or crabs back then, or my rear would just get intensely sore for a day or two when guys would fuck me badly. In retrospect, given the timing, this guy could have infected me with HIV. This was about a year before the first reported cases.

Some sort of drug was imbibed at that point, and I declined. I jumped out of Ron's big bed and went downstairs to see if I could play with Vera. I liked his sense of humor, and I'd wanted to have sex with him for months. Soft, his dick would put most men's hard-ons to shame. He was willing then, and we tried to get him hard, but he was way too drunk by that time of the evening, and perhaps I avoided AIDS then, too, as Vera's favorite pastime was to spend long evenings on his stomach at the bathhouses and take all comers, as it were. Oldest story in the world: The biggest dick belongs to the biggest bottom. Yet I knew that even with his monstrous cock, he wouldn't damage me like that other guy had intended to.

                                    ◦ ◦ ◦

ALMOST EVERY INNOCENT thing I did or said at that tender age of twelve could be perverted by my peers into some form of lewdness. It's ironic, then, how I ended up labeled the pervert. This engendered a paranoia and self-consciousness about my acts that haunts me to this day. Ultimately, though, we each choose our behavior, so it doesn't really matter. Others may plant the seeds of worthlessness, but we're the ones who till them. If charity begins at home, then so does cruelty.

This world wounds us all. The question is, What do you do with that? Certain trees have marvelous ways of incorporating their wounds into new patterns of growth. Thus, I aspire to have the intelligence of a tree.

I forgive myself for my innocence.

I forgive myself for my guilt.

I forgive myself for my shame.

I forgive myself for my blame.

I forgive myself for combining so many drugs at one point this week that my memory flickered out for roughly twelve hours. I blame the Vicodin. Meanwhile, my body continued, entwined with my lover's, through various acts of sex and sadomasochism sufficient to fill a feature-length porn video. I was lucid throughout, yet later I could recall only fragments. He says we did amazing things together, yet I have no memory of them. What rare part of me was erasing the experience as I was enacting it?

I've never had this experience before, and I wonder whether some part of me had to die to give it birth. Some parts of us are meant to die early. Thousands of your brain cells will die by the time you finish reading this.

o o o

I DRIVE TO L.A. on business. My good friend, with whom I usually stay, gets lucky and has a date staying over for the weekend. Thus, I end up at the notorious Coral Sands Motel instead. I am thirty-nine years old.

There is no love in this wounded place. I have tasted enough of its inhabitants to know. I walk past an open doorway and pause just as this young, black musclestud with nine-plus inches of fat, solid horsecock hammers it home to a squealy whiteboy bottom for the whole tweaking neighborhood to see. Not nine stroke-mag-story inches, not nine AOL inches, I'm talkin' 'bout nine-plus inches of the throbbing, meaty dingus itselfus. I have seen enough cocks to know. I, being the pushy bastard I can sometimes be, walk into the room and close the door. Private Party. Do Not Disturb.

I saw this dude earlier in the day, checking me out as I marveled at his trim physique and luscious, born-to-be-tortured pig nipples, but he looks even better up close. I mean, can we ever really get enough shave-headed young black gods with dicks the size of Casey's mighty bat? I would say no, sadly. We must await them like Napoleon awaited Waterloo, like Custer awaited his Last Stand, knowing that their sultry, studly ways will be our undoing.

So I watch him fuck this squealyboy bottompig's buttcrack (*sans preservatif, mon dieu!*), and I start yanking on those nips of his like they were my one and only ticket to ride. Meanwhile, squealyboy gets the squealyhole plugged full of yours truly. I just have to make him shut the fuck up. It's not a bad blowjob. Well, too bad for squealyboy that our young black god's mega-plunger uncorks a rivulet of mucky, brown, bung-holewater onto the sheet. This purge ends his urge. Studcock takes this as his cue to exit, with me aiding and abetting his escape.

Sometimes there is no love. In those viral, synthetic moments, sex is a competition sport, and I just grabbed myself first prize.

I have savored enough flesh to know.

We go to his room. I lock his door possessively, meaningfully. He asks me, "So you don't party, and you use condoms. What are you doing at the Coral Sands?"

"It was not my original plan," I replied. "A mixture of coincidence and circumstance."

Well, I wash him off good, and then we swap a bit of nipple lust while I give him a San Francisco deep throat, as he gasps, amazed that I can really choke his honker all the way down and keep it plugged in. But that's just the warm-up act. He does a hit of speed, and I ask how he can stay so hard. Viagra, of course. God bless the blue diamond. So I take full advantage of this glorious mess that the Dark Lord has laid before me. *On the floor, get to work, tweakerboy.* He chows down on nipples, cock, then balls, and finally the bunghole. His huge cock, which has been moderately hard all along, throbs sky-ward as soon as tongue touches hole. Oh, man, what a fuckin' rimjob. I don't think I've ever had my butt eaten this good. Reasons for living, gentle reader.

I abuse his torture-starved nipples for half an hour and get him to breathe through the whole ordeal with no objections. Verbal abuse. Foot worship. He asks Daddy if he can put on his piss-drenched clothes. Out comes a yellow sleeveless T-shirt that reads "Daddy's Little Boy" and a stinky jockstrap. He's so fucking cute in that gear that I just gotta haul off and slap him hard, harder, harder. Then me with the mindfuck, threatening to shit in his mouth while it's worshipping at my hole. Then he, begging me to call him "nigger boy," which I do frequently and with gusto. A lifetime of political correctness goes swooshing down the drain in one huge flush! At one point I call him a "shit-mouthed party-trash nigger-boy butt sucker." He shoots a huge load and falls over with my foot still crammed down his throat. "Thank you, Daddy Lord White Master, Sir."

o o o

SUMMER 1993. My mother is dead at forty-nine. My boyfriend and I are not communicating well. I have broken up with my girlfriend; she is now in an alcoholism recovery program. I am having trouble finding work, and I am broke. AIDS is killing people all across America, with San Francisco as Ground Zero. I have been HIV positive for three and a half years. Combination therapy is still several years away. I have no health insurance, and I am a patient at San Francisco General Hospital, using the name of a classmate I had a crush on in sixth grade. It's a low point. I am thirty-three years old.

I am bored and lonely. Where can a poor boy go to get laid on a weeknight in this ghost town? I end up in the alley at My Place. There's too much grabbing and grasping for me to relax. This punk boy and I pick each other out. I tell him that this scene is too crazy for me and invite him home. We drive up the hill to the apartment that I haven't paid my half of the rent on for this month.

We arrive. The anticipation is thick. I light a fire: very romantic. I indicate a basket of condoms. We strip and tear into each other: feral, savage, violent. For several hours we are a tangled mess of fury and urgent need. We bite, we claw, we slap, we dig under each other's skin. I grind my face against his armpits until I reek of him. His necklace cuts into my flesh like barbed wire. We fuck atop giant floor pillows, a makeshift bed next to the fire. Somehow the condoms, three feet away, never get used. This is never discussed. Angry punkboy dick thrashes into me over and over. I fuck his grungy, skinny punkboy ass.

Finally, he shoots. Ninety seconds later, he is out the door. I am furious with him, more furious with myself. My rage keeps me up all night. I pound this fury into an article on how to negotiate safer sex and boundaries with strangers. It's full of good advice I've just learned the hard way. Bad wisdom spun into gold.

o   o   o

SOMETIMES I THINK that I achieve through writing the kind of release that others achieve through crying. I started writing down my thoughts and feelings about the same time that I started getting assaulted at school. Somewhere along the wounded path of adolescence, I lost the ability to cry tears on all but the rarest of occasions.

Writing, then, is a sort of antivenin.

Every eight hours I poison my body so that a greater poison within does not kill me.

May those who pity me drop dead upon reading these words. They have no idea how grateful I am.

It is the first week of December 1996, my first week of HIV combination therapy. I have not made this decision lightly. I am at my lover's home, thirty-six miles south of my own. I am thirty-six years old. For a week there is a war raging within my body: the virus versus the meds. I am a dreadful mess. It is all I can do to drag myself from the bed to the toilet several times a day. In my delirium, I write a five-thousand-word murder mystery, the longest piece of fiction I have ever written to this point. It gets published. The virus disappears from my blood. The battle is won, if not the war. I am reborn, for a time.

II. Intermission

So I wrote that in 2001, but then I confronted a lot more darkness than I ever knew my soul could hold. I got hooked on crystal meth.

Fucking has brought me more darkness and more light than anything else. Fucking and fighting, love and hate, all so close.

I tried crystal meth three times, in the mid-nineties, with two different men I was fucking. The first two times were blissful, but the third time was disturbing. It jarred me, the degree of power that the thin white line held over my friend—this insane allure. The only way I would engage sexually with him while he was on meth was to "top" him with his own crystal—in other words, I was the sole governor over when and how much. I was a sadistic bastard—I granted him only two snorts all night long. (I did only half a line myself, and simply so that we could share the same relative headspace.)

It was the only time I ever topped him. I loved exacting my revenge—tying him up and executing all the cock-torture and hole-reaming acrobatics he'd performed on me hitherto. Yet I couldn't shake the feeling that it was the crystal he was bottoming to, and not the bottom-turned-top. So I walked away from that scene, muttering, "This stuff's *too good.*" And then I walked away from crystal for seven years. I told another man I was fucking in 1999 that I would never get addicted to that crap.

Then I did anyhow.

So, how?

Visually, Wayne was a fortysomething version of Willie Nelson. That's one of the funny things about fucking so many different men—eventually you get to fuck a reasonable facsimile of everybody famous.

We meet at Fort Troff, a wondrously sleazy, twin-towered adult playland-in-a-warehouse equipped to accommodate a dazzling array of sexual interests. I saw it featured in a bareback sex movie, *Pigs at the Troff,* and knew I had to visit Atlanta someday to check it out.

The club is everything I've hoped for, and more. It doesn't open until midnight. Dimly lit concrete surfaces and horizontal wooden plank walls.

All night long, Wayne and I keep showing up on the periphery of each other's scenes with other men. At last, we both come up for air at the same moment, with nary a dick or hole in either mouth, long enough to strike up a conversation. My ride (who has been riding me in more ways than one) has just informed me that he is leaving soon, so it's time to put up or shut up. Wayne is more than happy to put up.

We leave the club in his small pickup. About half a mile out, Wayne asks if it would be okay to pick up a buddy of his. What am I supposed to do, say no? It's his truck. We pull into the parking lot of another sex club, where his buddy is waiting in the parking lot. After brief introductions, the three of us head out to the interstate. Dirk is silent. Our thighs rub against each other's in the cramped, tiny cab.

I am confused when we pull into Wayne's driveway and his friend is still in the truck with us. Now I learn that they are exes who just live together now.

Or at least that's Wayne's version.

Wayne has charmed me into breaking two of my rules: (1) Don't go home with strangers who pull surprises, and (2) Always have a ride out of Dodge. I think I've done a good job of tracking our route back from Fort Troff, yet I'm not even sure which town I'm in now.

It is close to six a.m. We are sitting on chairs and a couch in the front room, and Wayne wants everyone to smoke a bowl of crystal out of Daddy's big pipe.

It sounds weird now, but for a couple of years, this was no big deal. When I traveled, sex on speed was pretty much part of the trip. I was off duty in every other sense during that vacation, so why not?

Mostly, though, sharing a pipe served as a way to connect. Communion. Group mind. All that be-here-now focus I would have to learn to achieve down the line without the need to tweak. Anything. Least of all, myself.

So we smoke together, and soon I am ecstatically shotgunning meth vapor in and out of Wayne's mouth. He keeps diverting my attention to Dirk, though. We pick at the donuts that Wayne bought on the way home.

Wayne and Dirk have a discussion offstage, then inform me that Dirk's sister is coming over to buy a puppy, maybe even two, from the squealing litter that Dirk has bred. We can play until she calls Dirk on his cell phone to give the ten-minute warning, but then they will have to sequester me in the "guest room," which is really just a sling and a bunch of boxes stacked against the walls. No bed.

The meth makes me have to piss. Dirk trails me to the

bathroom, so I piss on Dirk. Dirk directs me to his cock. Cocks go in and out of mouths. Wayne documents the whole initiatory scene. I still have the CD of photos: pictures of myself, bent over Wayne and Dirk's toilet, pissing on Dirk, then sucking Dirk's dark, bloated, uncut monster; a bit later, pictures of Dirk in the sling, head cocked in postcoital rapture, sphincter winking, my cum dribbling out of his anus. *Click. Click. Click.*

There is nothing special or magical about these photos. I look just like any anonymous tweaker with a mouthful of dick. My cock has three kinds of cockrings on it. I need a shave and a haircut. My irises are as big as buttons. We both look like emaciated wrecks.

Suddenly, Dirk's sister is around the corner. So now I lie alone in the playroom, covered with a blanket, rocking gently in Wayne's sling, doing my best to relax and possibly even snooze a bit (*On speed? Fat chance!*) while Dirk's family visits . . . for two hours!

Dirk's six-year-old niece wanders down the hall while the adults are distracted in conversation. I am trapped. If I call out, it will blow their cover. If I don't, she will see me, since the door does not hang right and it is impossible to close it completely. Later, I will learn that all the doors in the house are like this, and that this is one of Dirk's tricks to ensure that Wayne can never have complete privacy while Dirk is home.

I don't want this to be happening. I try to erase myself. I will myself to be invisible. I'm really glad I insisted on this blanket.

Finally, Dirk's sister calls out, and her little girl replies, "Mommy, come look! There's a man in this room!" The little girl is quickly scooped up and taken away.

Despite this glaring lapse between my hosts' onstage and

offstage lives, the brood will remain for nearly another hour. *Tick. Tick. Tick.*

At last they depart. Dirk is overjoyed because now he has two puppies' worth of money to take to the bank. Wayne at least has the decency to be contrite.

The rest of the day settles into a blur of douching and Web surfing. I learn from Wayne that Dirk's family was ready to place him in Georgia's mental institution until Wayne agreed to give him a place to live. Yet Wayne sleeps on the couch, while Dirk has the only available bedroom all to himself. I suppose they could make the sling-and-boxes room into a second bedroom, but that would require focus and commitment, which are two things in short supply among tweakers. When you're high on speed, the first things to go out the window are your senses of priority and proportion.

Dirk takes me aside later and claims that he owns the house and can prove it in court. I also hear from Wayne that Dirk has been up for at least several days prior to my arrival. Furthermore, Wayne has a behind-the-scenes agreement with the owners of Fort Troff never to grant Dirk a club membership. Apparently, it's the only place in town where Wayne can reliably escape Dirk's stalking. In a later chat, Dirk is sorely puzzled as to why he can never get a membership.

o o o

THE NIGHT PASSES, and I need to get to my plane in a few hours. Wayne picks up on my apprehension and offers to handball me. I am touched yet skeptical. He assures me of his prowess. We smoke one last bowl of meth, and suddenly I am a lot less skeptical.

All of the visit's past trials are forgotten as we ride together, one body of synergy rocking back and forth in the snug harbor of Wayne's sling. Fewer than a dozen men and women have fisted me to wrist depth, yet within fifteen minutes, this old pro with the red bandanna is in for the night. I am so transported that I don't even mind too much when Dirk walks into the room.

At least he isn't carrying a fucking camera.

As the fates are my witness, this is the most shattering yet therapeutic reaming I've ever received. All the hardness and tension of the past two days melt out of me as I contract, hard and full and at last connected to something greater than myself, with no chance of turning back. And finally, overjoyed, I erupt.

Fifteen minutes later, Wayne is in the kitchen, humming and confident. While he fixes food, I call the airline and change my reservation, since we have played too long to get me to the airport comfortably on time. Despite my precarious finances, I agree to pay the one-hundred-dollar ticket-change fee in order to stay another day and relax in Wayne's warm and agreeable grip.

By the time I finish my call, food is ready, so I postpone calling my friends Cal and Jim, who are picking me up in Sacramento. Wayne serves the best-tasting meal I have had in a very long time. In both the bedroom and the kitchen, his hands are gallant. Basking in our reflected aura, even Dirk seems more benign. Maybe I've met my Prince Charming on meth.

Wayne drives me to the CVS pharmacy so I can get some medicine for my new cough. He takes me to his worksite; he introduces me to his clients, and we walk through the woods and fields behind the lovely house he is designing. It's romantic. Who is to say whether this is better or worse than the grounded experience of sane, careful, and comfortable old lovers? The highs are higher, and the lows are lower, to be sure, and with Wayne, I feel like I am absorbing the arc of an entire relationship within the space of three days. Not to mention that amazing hand.

The meth space is like that sometimes. Often, while I was doing meth, I wondered how many hours I was burning off the end of my life by sacrificing them to the urgent and pendulous now. "Do you really think it is weakness that yields to temptation?" asked Oscar Wilde. "I tell you that there are terrible temptations which it requires strength, strength, and courage to yield to."

We return. Dirk picks up on that warm current still flowing between Wayne and me, and he is jealous. Maybe he is just angry that we were gone for so long. I remember that I need to call Cal and Jim, but for some reason I can't get a call out of Wayne and Dirk's phone. So I send them an e-mail, four hours before I'm scheduled to land, to let them know I'm staying an extra day. I promise myself to call them again later, just to be sure they know.

Wayne needs to do some work at his computer, and so I ask if it would be too distracting if I sat on the floor at his feet and worshipped his cock with my mouth. Wayne says sure, that would be wonderful.

But Dirk is in the room, and he can't leave us alone. I start to wonder whether Dirk has ever let go of anything in his entire life. I suspect that if he has, then he has calculated the exact cost and measure of the loss, and is no doubt still harboring grudges against those who made him pay. And I am sure now that though he was up for days before my arrival, competing with him to stay awake is fruitless. Clearly, he is much more experienced than I am at this game.

So I suck Wayne's beautiful cock, but I can't really lose myself in the hypnotic trance I seek because I am aware that Dirk is watching my every move. He's a ghoul, a black hole, a vacancy. The longer he remains, the more I am aware of how he puts exactly nothing of value into a space. Maybe I'm just paranoid from the meth, but I get the distinct impression that Dirk expects to be entertained. He seems to have absolutely nothing to contribute.

o   o   o

"DON'T YOU HAVE A LIFE?" I scream, at the end of my patience. "Can't you leave us alone for even a few minutes? How long have you been up? Don't you ever go to sleep? Why the fuck don't you get away from me?" And on and on, as my fury unravels.

Dirk storms out of the house and takes off in Wayne's pickup truck. At least I've gotten my wish, I think. Tomorrow I'll be gone, and Dirk can have Wayne all to himself again. Yet suddenly Wayne is all about pulling together any drug-related materials and leaving the property as quickly as possible. "He'll probably call the police now. We'll have to take the van. The brakes are shot to hell, so we'll have to drive really slowly."

We creak and crawl across Atlanta, slithering through the stop signs. "All I really want is to fall asleep next to you in a safe bed in some anonymous motel." I sigh.

"I know a place," Wayne assures me. "We'll need some money, though—I'm tapped out this week." Soon we are at an ATM and I am withdrawing a cash advance on my credit card.

It's okay, though; I figure it will be worth it to get a bit of peace until it's time for my plane to leave tomorrow.

Then, once I've paid for the room with my expensive cash, I realize that Wayne's not interested in settling down for the night. He has outmaneuvered me once again, this time into a notorious Atlanta sleaze pit, a sex motel where he can continue the party. I learn that the locals refer to the neighborhood we are in as Slut Valley. Wayne hides the hazardous van behind the rearmost building, since he fears that Dirk will come prowling around, tracking him down. I wonder how many times this has happened before.

Wayne skulks off in search of moist, tender flesh not mine. Frustrated, I set off by myself across Slut Valley, figuring I can burn off my anger with a long, healthy walk, and then perhaps crawl into bed while Wayne is still out tricking. It's a good idea. I end up conversing with the clerk at the all-night combination skateboard store and head shop a mile away. It feels good just to connect with another human being who isn't psychotic or running covert agendas on me. Just some guy behind a cash register.

Eventually, I return to the motel, relieved to see that there is no sign of Dirk, but Wayne is in our room with two other guys. They are smoking crystal. I ask if they can go to the other guys' rooms, but it turns out that they are just prowling and have no rooms of their own. I keep a very close eye on my belongings.

In the morning, Wayne treats me to a diner breakfast and escorts me on the shuttle train to the airport, where we say good-bye. Once we separate, I am shaky, crashing from the meth and cumulative stress, but I breathe a huge sigh of relief. As I walk up the corridor, I call Cal and Jim to let them know I am boarding the plane. But Cal is furious with me; he explains that Jim circled the Sacramento airport for close to an hour the previous night, searching for me in vain. Cal informs me coldly that I will have to find another way to get home from the airport. I call a good friend and give him the short version. He agrees to drive from the Bay Area to Sacramento and peel me off the runway.

In summer 1970, my family was sweltering, trapped in the Central Valley desert, where Dad was stationed with the Navy, of all things. For entertainment, sometimes we visited the drive-in movies in redneck Armona, where we kids hunkered down with our pillows and blankets atop the folded-down seats of our beat-up station wagon and tried not to get caught sneaking looks at the X-rated movie on the screen behind ours. I was the most successful at this.

On the way home, I made an innocuous remark, which incited Mom to snap, "Oh, Bill, you're so gullible!"

"What's that mean?"

"Look it up."

When I did, I was devastated.

And at that moment, I resolved, with all the certitude that only a ten-year-old can possess, that I would never be gullible again.

o   o   o

THIS MEMORY RUSHES back at me as I am pinned beneath the seat belt, crashing from my record-breaking three days awake, twitching as I try to read back the apology I have fitfully tapped out to my newly estranged friend Cal on my five-year-old iBook, the "toilet-seat model," far too big for my wobbly coach-class food tray. This heightens my already acute sense of claustrophobia.

Hi, Cal—

I am sorry that communication between us got so fucked up. I've tried to write this e-mail three different times, at least, because I got swept abruptly into the middle of a situation that could have had life—

I feel like I should have some closure to this pain soon, but I cannot even reliably keep from passing out at the moment. I think it would

I think I fucked up in one way by playing a crazy person's game back at him in order to

I want someone to show me myself somewhere in the near future that reassures me that I am going to recover from my sense of well-being. I want someone wonderful to leap forward and show me that I am going to get over my sense of profound loss—loss of my confidence, loss of my health, loss of my purpose.

I feel like I am owed more of an explanation, yet I know that it doesn't matter. Closure may be irrelevant. I am just grateful to be alive today. Even feeling miserable is better than not having the chance to ever experience feeling rapture. I want to know that I can find my way back to being fully engaged in my, fully capable of managing my life, and

I want someone wonderful to be me in such a surprising and massively acknowledged way that I can't possibly have been given the gift out of a sense of obligation. I want to see the results of my commitment to improving the world.

We are such a small, insignificant piece of a puzzle that I may never get to see completed.

I took too much crystal and I wasn't prepared for the loss of safe houses in hostile territory. Cal's sanctuary and especially any of my hope that Wayne and Dirk could provide one, after being invited,

I am in shock and grieving. I am the witness to and incidental victim of a trauma so recent that I cannot possibly analyze it yet.

Maybe not even tomorrow. I've been under a lot of duress, and what I really need is a large bowl of chicken soup, a lot of herbal tea, some hugs, and to sleep in my husband's arms, and I can't even drive because I'm so exhausted. I just realized that eventually I may be called in as a witness to a situation that may take months to be brought to trial.

My past twenty-four hours have been telescoped into a treadmill of disorientation and confusion. I can't even finish this email because we're already being told to close our computers so we can land in Dallas.

Please, when you have a moment, call Wayne Barry and he will give you a coherent explanation of why I didn't call you yesterday. I did the best I could under situations where I was being threatened physically and aggressively.

I am too fragile to explain the sequence of events of the past seventy-two hours. Maybe next week. In the meantime, I am asking Wayne to call you to provide corroboration at your work.

I am about to lose my ability to type. My star is so dim and afraid of burning down to a dead black cinder much sooner than I had originally thought.

I can't keep going with this entry. I keep spilling ginger ale on myself, I cannot fnish most sentences, everything in my world that matters seems hard to get and not worth maintaining.

I want a day so golden that it puts all of my endeavors back up for consideration and praise. Not because it's Bill Brent, but because it's a local force of nature that changes people's lives in the best, most enduring way possible for them. I want to do something wonderful. I want to help us all get what we need. I want to be indelible, and I want to give this life my best possible

*shot. I have no idea what that means, though, and I'm
frustrated with spilling so much ginger ale because I was too
distracted by trying to finish a complete thought. I am not
competent of that right now. I am sketchy, and I haven't learned
how to love my new hero status or reward myself for it. I want to
be satisfied with myself, and I want to hear wonderful stories
about how my art changed people's lives and always will. I am
so burnt out. I can't possibly ask for a less likely miracle.*

*I hope I get it anyway. I want my cough to go away. I feel
that the toxicity level of this weekend was so high that the
medicine I brought for it was expected*

I can't write. Not right now. I can't even think clearly.
Love,
Bill

III. Wounded, Again

My head pounds furiously. The flesh concealing my jawbone
begins to throb and swell as forbidden tears crash angrily
through the eyelid gates. An elbow bleeds freely after its sudden smash against the asphalt. The sharp-edged gravel pierces
and stings the flesh beneath my skin.

All this sensation rushes in on me at once, where moments
before I was numb, literally paralyzed with fear.

Two girls step forward to drag me away. It's always two
girls, never the same two. It's like I'm in this black comedy by
Beckett or Sartre, cast in the role of Suburban Adolescent Je-
sus, and they keep changing the actresses playing the Virgin
Mother and Mary Magdalene without consulting me first.

o o o

IT'S OKAY, THOUGH. Later today, I will be riding my bicycle in big, slow, lazy figure eights, staring at the earth while dreaming of flying and perpetrating long, painful, bone-crushing tortures against my attackers. Guns and ropes. Shattering limbs.

On my good days, I march home from the bus in a rage, up-ending the furniture and heaving aloft the piles of laundry my parents have left for me to fold. On bad days, I shut my door (if only it locked) and stare catatonically at some portion of my bedroom wall for hours, fantasizing my grand fuck-you to the world, in glistening, stop-frame detail, as I twist my body onto the orange girders of the Golden Gate Bridge and catapult into the sunset, kissing the clouds for one miraculous moment of fiery abandon before my body smacks against the turbulent, unforgiving waters, which surprises me because it doesn't hurt even a fraction as much as the asphalt of my junior-high play-ground, since by then, of course, I am already dead.

Pain and flight. I can't run, I can't stay.

Kids who are besieged by physical assault tend to regard themselves as unworthy of love. Any self-esteem I had seemed to be predicated on my ability either to pass tests or to win the approval of others (same difference, actually).

I'm the joker in the deck of love. I can show up in any player's hand, at any time, and my value varies according to the context. Nothing about me is fixed.

My place is no place. I am most at home when I am most nomadic.

I attribute this partially to years of being uprooted as a child. Thus, it is hard for me to believe in institutions or any form of structure predicated on long-term goals. Imperma-nence is my worldview. Gypsy feet clad in Reeboks, that's me.

o o o

NEW YEAR'S EVE, 1979. Every man wants to be eighteen forever. That moment is mine. My new friend Terry is fortysomething. I don't think he was ever eighteen. He takes me to see the Northpoint Theatre's midnight showing of *Tommy*. !! *Happy New Year* !! "Listening to you . . . I *hear the music*." I remember the overamped opening credits and the first five minutes of the movie clearly. Then a black abyss until the closing credits.

Terry and I return to the sleazy tenement he manages for a slumlord. We drink champagne, toasting to the new year, and then I pass out again. I awaken in the middle of the night, submerged beneath covers, surprised to find Terry's hard, snaky, slender dick down my throat. I finish him off in a daze, then quietly pick up my two pillows and a blanket, and move to the couch, where I will sleep for the remaining two weeks of winter break, before resuming dorm life. Neither of us ever utters a word about this violation.

Terry was my entrée to San Francisco gay life. I was his pimply Pygmalion project. He had the romantic mind of a frustrated courtroom interrogator (which he was, having been to law school but never having practiced). I thought I was in love with him. I listened to him and thought I heard the music. Sadly, I had a tin ear for romance. Our conversations were more like cross-examinations where I was always prosecuted. Like a good little victim, I always returned for more, hopeful that this time I could defend myself successfully. This was love. After years of being singled out as one of the school faggots in redneck Fremont, I thought it was what I deserved.

Terry's cock was the first to penetrate me. He never taught me to relax, or explained how to clean out. "You'll be sore for a day or two after the first time," he informed me as preparation for taking my cherry. He was right.

Two years later, Terry took me to a place in Westlake called Bruno's. "Order the Steak Bruno," he advised me. "It's not on the regular menu." So I did. While we were waiting for our meal, he coldly intoned, "I hope you brought enough to pay for us both." Another of Terry's sadistic surprises. Terry, more than twenty years my senior, owned a successful printing business at Serramonte Center, while I was typing my way through college, living on peanut butter and Campbell's soup, and renting a converted pantry closet for eighty dollars a month in the fog belt. "You need to learn not to invite men out to dinner and expect them to pay your way."

I dug around in my pockets. I had five dollars and eighty cents. "How much is Steak Bruno?" I gargled.

"About fifteen bucks each. Plus tip." Visions of a long night in front of a sinkful of restaurant dishes danced through my worried head.

Of course, I didn't enjoy a bite of my meal, and of course, Terry relented with his cat-and-mouse game and paid the bill. I think this was a pretty effective way to guilt-trip me and ensure that I'd acquiesce to sex with him. I'd have done that anyhow. But I can't remember a thing we did in bed together; the rest of the evening is an unhappy blur across my memory. The one moment I recall with startling clarity is after we'd finished having sex, when I went to the bathroom to wash up. I actually looked at myself in Terry's big mirror, gritted my teeth, and muttered that famous phrase, "Never again."

I ran into Terry once afterward. I was walking past Mitchell Brothers and saw Terry coming my way. We exchanged mutual, contemptuous tightenings of lip that were more grimaces than smiles. Neither of us spoke a word or slowed our gait. For once, I'd met him on equal ground. Pygmalion had finally dumped her chiseler and left the room.

o o o

OF COURSE, I'm not innocent. No one ever is. No one forces you to fuck that ass or to take that hit or to stay in that room. It's always a choice. Often I found myself in situations where I probably should have bolted, but once you're high, that's not always a smart thing to do.

We can always find a reason to hook up, or pick up, or stay up, or fuck up. But if we are unafraid, we can always find a reason not to. Fuck fear. Be here. Wake up.

We begin by running from hetero homes, but once we've started bolting from life's unpleasantness, it's hard to stop.

Some of us never do.

o o o

IT IS JANUARY 2, 1990. I am twenty-nine, in a small room at Test Center #1 in the Castro, and a counselor is telling me that I have tested positive for HIV. Happy fucking new year. Everything in the room intensifies at the shock. An ugly lime-green print on the facing wall suddenly brightens. The fluorescent lights buzz more loudly. As I leave, I say to the counselor, "Thanks for doing what you do," although, frankly, she has shown all the empathy of a dead clam.

When I walk through the front door, my partner, who lost his previous partner seventeen months before, asks me, "Any surprises?" All I can do is nod mutely and stifle my tears. I am no longer his only HIV negative boyfriend. He shows no emotion and continues visiting with a mutual friend for a leisurely two hours as I sit nearby in silent grief. I contemplate variously whether this is callous indifference or his version of shock, but he never bothers to explain, and never bothers to express any sorrow, even though he may have infected me.

Fast-forward to February 2005, about five months since I last used crystal, or any recreational drug, other than two cocktails and a glass of wine. I feel fantastic. This ex, however, has endured a seemingly endless series of severe health problems over the past couple of years. He is still using meth. It's hard to believe there's no correlation. In fifteen months he will be dead.

For Valentine's Day, I send him a copy of Richard Bach's transformative book, *Illusions*. Bach's meditation on impermanence was my high-school graduation gift from my very first boyfriend, who still writes me love letters from Mexico twenty-seven years later. On the flyleaf, I have inscribed to my ex, "Change your thinking, change your life."

One day in mid-1992, I wrote in my notebook:

Flow out of your life the things that no longer serve you.

o o o

ON INDEPENDENCE DAY, YET.
It will take me two more years to leave this ex.

o o o

I NEVER SHOT UP with Tina, though she let me stand next to her fire. That was the firmest boundary I set with myself regarding crystal use. Combined with my strong babysitting and self-preservation instincts, it was the easiest to adhere to. By the same reasoning, I have never owned a gun. I know I'd be all too capable of using it against someone I didn't like.

My friend Rex was a denizen of M4M's online sex board. I used to call his living room "the LAX of sex." The trick-tracks that have crisscrossed this sleazy geezer's swinging sling, from which he would hold court for four or more hours at a stint, would read like a Who's Who of Bay Area Tweakery. Rex was the Blanche DuBois of the meth set.

July 6, 2004, ten p.m. So here I am at Rex's, where we have been getting high and chatting, naked, for an hour or so, and I shyly ask our fuckbuddy Carey if I can suck his dick as he comes on. Carey is an injection user, so this will be a bit of a delicate balance, but I am the best boy in the world right now. I wait willingly, patiently, on the bathroom tile, submissive at his feet, head in his lap, while he shoots himself up.

Contact. Liftoff.

I figure that Carey will want to be plowed mercilessly once he comes on; instead, I find myself lifted off the ground and carried in his strong embrace. Actually, I think we walk downstairs together, and then he flips me, but things are moving very quickly. I do know that I get somewhat of a contact buzz from his shot as my ass slams against his charmed, Viagra-hardened cock. *White light, white heat.*

Carey tells me that shooting meth makes you feel nine feet tall. After he fucks me into the stratosphere, I believe.

The next morning, seven a.m. I've just had my briefcase stolen by a guy, appropriately named Rob, whom Rex discovered on Craigslist around midnight and invited over against my reluctance. Now Rex and I are wondering what to do next.

"Why is everyone so serious?" Carey bursts out. I am stunned by his absolute selfishness. Carey's high is fading and, man, is he getting bitchy.

My illusion of the intimacy between us shatters as it smashes against the edge of daylight. I loved watching Carey's smile dawn slowly across his face like the sun emerging from a dark raincloud, as our eyes locked and the world faded from sight. Then he flooded me with his essence, his blazing crystal piss, our baby, triumphant over his fear of failure. But was it worth this insult?

In my mind now, he shrivels to the size of my little finger, his once-turgid penis now a mere speck on my memory. His brain shrinks to the size of a rice grain, his soul no greater than his tiny, whiny voice, laying it all out for me like an annoying siren. *Bill,* warns the annoyance, *just keep doing crystal, and in a few years, Carey's life of dull duplicity can be yours: Your life-partner's abject rejection of you for the rest of all time. The flights from dealers whose ex-convict boyfriends chase you down in the dark to settle accounts. The relentless tension at the back of your brain as you strive to find the next safe place to get loaded and laid, more perfectly, more absolutely, more recklessly, as your options trickle away. The desolation as you run and hide fruitlessly from the tragedy of your own inner horror. Your love of the buzz, screaming at you, louder and harsher, until you lose forever the buzz of love.*

Mid-morning, I overhear Carey talking on Rex's cell phone. His tone is irritated and caustic—abusive, even. Later he tells me it was his dealer! I am amazed—if I were depending on my next fix from someone who was supposed to drive more than a hundred miles to deliver the goods, I'd at least act polite. Then I remember that Carey has owed my own dealer money for more than a year. The one with the ex-con boyfriend.

Soon Rex and Carey are back in the sling, hacking away at each other like seesaw marionettes. Part of me feels vacant, like a ghost, like I've already left the building. At more poignant moments, though, I feel a surge of compassion and forgiveness, tinged with just a touch of envy. It's so simple for them. All they want is to get high—higher than God—and to stay suspended in that walled-in sky for as long as their bodies will allow, to declare their defiance of nature and society, in a room free of judgment. And just for right now, they have what they desire, while I sit in the next room at Rex's telephone, in front of his ever-surfing computer, which brought me this predicament, dialing number after number and communicating with my lover more meaningfully than they can ever hope to in a million slamming, hammering, yammering hours of sling-fucking: I am pleading, explaining, describing, questioning, humbling myself, asking for help.

I've taken that first baby step toward home.

The test is over.

It feels good. It hurts.

It's real.

> Rue the day you threw your care away.
> –AUTHOR, FROM HIS POEM *BILLSLIST.NOW*

Amphetamine didn't even exist before 1887, nor meth before 1919. Every war since then has been fueled in part by meth aggression. We still don't fully understand the range of its effects, nor its potential for brain damage, either alone or combined with the residue of the hundreds of caustic chemicals used to process it, half of which are explosive. Its abuse potential is legendary. We don't know how to eliminate its unpredictable, negative impact on human behavior.

Or how to reverse the damage done.

Travelers on the PnP Highway sort readily into three discrete categories: the Dream Pilots ("dreamboat" is too antiquated), the Burnouts, and the Faceless Crowd.

Carey was clearly a Burnout. It was hard to believe he cleaned up enough to teach at UC during the school year. He changed his phone number right after my robbery.

Rex was a member of the Faceless Crowd. Very few tricks ever returned for a second visit. Later, they recalled him vaguely and with wan distaste, a bad trip they'd taken through the Blanche DuBois Funhouse of the Overpartied Mind. Rex moved to Pasadena within sixty days of my theft. Maybe, after surrendering my pipe and lighter to his custody that balmy day in early July, my one-thousand-five-hundred-dollar mishap accelerated his decision to leave. He sent me an e-mail: "Off to la-la land I go. . . ."

Late that summer, I reconnected online with Dean, a strapping Dream Pilot, and invited him to stay overnight while my partner was away. Despite my tepid request that he leave his party drugs at home, he indeed brought "a bit" of Tina (it's always "just a little") and some GHB, since he thought I might change my mind. Fortunately, my commitment to stay clean was strong enough to decline, though I did hesitate for a moment. I wouldn't dishonor my agreement with my partner. And my fuckbuddy was gracious enough to refrain as well.

The term "fuckbuddy" is odd. Men are buddies in sex and war but never in love. In PnP parlance, "buddy" inhabits a strange netherworld somewhere between friend and acquaintance. We respect our friends; with our buddies, though, we can be as fucked up and nasty as we please. Consciously or not, everyone who wants the Buddy-in-a-Genie-Bottle is seeking to deny accountability for his actions.

Yet Dean, who would rather be out finding a buddy who will party with him tonight, listens patiently as I outline my saga with Carey, Rex, and Bobby the Robber. "Can you imagine what will become of Rex in SoCal?" I muse. "Those boys will eat him alive."

"I don't know what Carey's Ph.D. is in, either," Dean tells me. "I doubt he even has one. He probably made that up."

"But why?" I ask.

"Who knows." Dean shrugs.

∘　∘　∘

IT IS 2001, the dawn of my three-year Space Odyssey with Timeless Tina. My partner and I meet Devin, a meth-slamming, muscle-god Dream Pilot whose ass just won't quit. Neither does my rocket. *Punk rock,* baby. I eat his galactic dream hole; I plow him into a meat-puppet stupor, shoot deep inside his five-star ass, and suck out the whipped cream for dessert till his rocket shoots stars. But later he stays in the shower for half an hour because he's scared that bugs are eating his skin from the inside out. Meanwhile, SFPD is towing away his fancy foreign two-seat vibrator for parking in front of a driveway by mistake. His business is inexplicably going down in flames. Maybe we blame the dot-com bust.

Three years later I meet him again, in another town, and our eyes lock across Rex's hellhole like we were cosmic, twin-towered, Kamikaze speed-freak pilot-punks mooning each other one last time over Pearl Harbor, Hiroshima, Hanoi, Baghdad, New York, New York.

I am already trying to kick, and I watch Dev shooting a cocktail that is *not* featured on the HIV formulary into his love-starved, bug-filled blood. He has just graduated from maybe his twenty-eighth twenty-eight-day stint at whitebread cliquey-boy rehab camp and clearly he *still* gets it not.

We're there to party, though, so of course I *still* suck his cock, I *still* fuck his ass, but it's not nearly as good as in years gone by. Is it just his ass, I am wondering, or have his war stories put me off? Doesn't matter. Three years ago, his was arguably the best fucking tail I ever ate and spunked. This time, I do not ask for his phone number. We never meet again.

o   o   o

CUZ PUNK ROCK, in my weary, wary opinion (consider the source) is really about accountability in the absence of a false god.

And crystal is anything but—just a stupid, mean fuckin' drug to do regularly, unless maybe your life has crashed and burned all on its own, and you just need to blot it all out for a while by fucking everything in sight. Which was me, back in '02, when a bad business deal stuck this broke badboy with a bankruptcy.

But I never . . . stuck it in my skin . . . I just sucked it . . . from the outside in.

Me, I'm just lucky I could crawl back out before it sucked me too far down. Or maybe I'm a bit too smart to deed my soul to a glass pipe and a traffic-jam generation of lost little boys.

But *don't follow me,* this bumper sticker across my ass warns, *I'm lost, too.*

Would I do it again? I hope not.

Was it worth it? Yeah.

Cuz I learned so much about my limitations. "You test boundaries," a therapist told me last year. "Mostly you have gotten through life unscathed by that." Yes. Resilience. Look how quickly I got my life back on track once I gave up on PnP. Not everyone wins his trial so adroitly. I forget that. And I had literal tons of support. But I asked for help, so I'll take some credit for that.

Today I'm not a Burnout, I'm not a Dream Pilot, and I'm certainly not of the Faceless Crowd. I'm something far more dangerous, a scrivener of queer truths. Your basic Burnout is someone who has become overloaded on something and has lost the capacity to experience it in a satisfying way. Often we become overloaded because we use it as a crutch to compensate for something found lacking in ourselves, or our lives. Sexual burnouts are usually unhappy in other aspects of their lives as well. Drug casualties are always that, most especially our lost buddies still speeding down the crystal autobahn.

Don't burn out, don't fade away.

Okay, I know I'm dancing around the question. Do I miss it?

Rarely, but this is when I miss crystal the most: When I'm fatigued and my spirits need a lift, at the end of a long, dusty day, and the sun is streaming through the slatted blinds of the picture window facing into our bucolic redwood grove, just off the front porch, I want to pick up a clean, elegant glass pipe, perched exultant amidst the beauty and majesty of nature . . . and then smoke something that completely violates its balanced and simple perfection.

That is when I miss crystal the most.

o   o   o

ONE OF MY FAVORITE ADS on M4M depicts a guy's head in multiple exposure. It's definitely a tweaker's project. It reminds me of that final moment in *All About Eve* when Eve's wannabe poses with Eve's acting award, reflecting herself endlessly in the mirrors of her own fantasy. I guess this collage-homage to egotism is meant to convey his ever-changing array of facial expressions, deep thoughts, pushy bottomhood? Whatever. His ad's headline reads, "HOW WILL U GET 2 HEAVN IF YOUR [sic] AFRAID TO GET HIGH?"

To which I reply, HOW WILL U LIVE THRU HELL IF YOUR [sic] AFRAID TO COME DOWN?

Sometimes I still think I'm missing out on that party. So what? I'm hosting my own party now, without all the messy complications of sex and drugs, and it feels fucking great. I have no one to impress, and I trust my friends—and they really are *friends,* not just acquaintances or "buddies" who might rip me off. I obey my new king, do the next right thing, humble yet strong, grateful yet free. I drive to the store, I water the garden, I say a little prayer for you, and you, and all of you, too. But then, buddy, you're on your own. No more caretaking eternal adolescents. I fix the dinner, and I kiss my man on the forehead as he types at the computer. He gets all my spare time nowadays. God knows he's waited long enough.

It's enough.

I went to maybe fifty twelve-step meetings the year I left the party. After the first couple months, though, I realized that I was already applying the twelve-step principles actively and continuously in my life, and that I didn't need that particular program to remain serene. However, I derived therefrom one basic guiding principle for conducting my affairs. I call it Bill's Fabulous Two-Step Dance:

Step 1. Just keep doing the next right thing.

Step 2. When you are not sure what that is, *ask someone you trust.*

. . . and if there's no one around whom you can trust, then ask yourself: *Why the fuck not?*

I'm holding out for more this time around.

o   o   o

IT IS LATE ONE EVENING during the week. I am forty-four, and my dick is hard. Mike drops his trousers and bends to his task, his desire, his joy. His partner grabs me from behind and locks his hands around my chest, against my nipples, grinding into me, humming breath into my ear. The bedsprings heave and release in time to our passion.

Mouth full of my cock, Mike trembles, ejaculates, then towels off. Soon his partner and I are pumping our pornstar-quality cocks down each other's wet, suctioning throats like a well-greased derrick. He tugs my tits; my dick jumps and I tug his back; his dick jumps, and we repeat this horizontal dance again and again. *Punk rock,* dude!

There's magic and power in three urgent men getting off together in the same room without the distraction of porn and pipes, the imposition of toys and props, or any unspoken agendas whatsoever. There's beauty and bliss in the act of three willing men, piloted by their pricks, letting their eyes, lips, tongues, nostrils, throats, and spirits follow.

Sounds vanilla? Maybe . . . maybe not. So what? It's real.

After an hour of submission to the horned gods, I am happy to arise, pull my clothes back onto my body, and depart in satiated grace. It's clean. It's simple. It's enough.

o   o   o

THESE DAYS, my goal is to experience my sex life as an extension of my art life, and my art as an extension of my sex. Love me, love my ass, love my art.

Punk fuckin' rock, dudes.

Oh, fuck metaphor. There's still nothing like a really perfect blowjob.

So, see, there *is* continuity to my life, after all. And my place is right here, right now. God knows I've waited long enough.

It is an inestimable relief.

° ° °

WE ZOOM ACROSS the desert, the ocean, and the sky. We think we know something. We barely have a clue. We cannot see how dark this Dark Age really is, so dark is it here that we can barely see one another.

Who am I?

I'm an infant. I'm an instant.

Just like you, dear friend.

Live and forgive, but never forget. Try not to spend all your time here learning the same foolish lessons over and over. What a wearisome, worrisome way to waste the day.

Despite AIDS, American gay men are among the most privileged and free people in today's world. Try to abuse neither the privilege of your freedom nor the freedom of your privilege. Be grateful. Respect.

We all know that life is not a dress rehearsal.

Does it ever occur to you that life is a musical fucking comedy sometimes?

A Greek tragedy of incomprehensible inner horror?

A blues song of nearly intolerable depth, grief, and beauty?

A comic laff-riot way wackier than anything that Mel Brooks, Charlie Chaplin, the Marx Brothers, the Three Stooges, the Warner Bros. cartoonists, or three generations of disaffected sketch show writers could ever, ever, conjure up in their wildest wet dreams?

That maybe a really good shit really *is* as good as it gets?

Who are you?

When you start using crystal, you have that weird sense of the improbably possible that you have only a few times in your life: when you start school; when you lose your virginity or fall in love for the first time; when you meet a mentor who really challenges you to make your life count; and when you look at loss and realize that there's a profoundly positive aspect to change.

And probably . . . according to my best sources . . . just before each of us dies.

You stop time. However briefly. And you are no longer just a bystander at the circus. You are thrust into the center ring. However illusorily. But you gotta remember this: It's only a pageant. Only a cabaret, old chum. And when the lights go down, you gotta pick yourself up, dust yourself off, and move on down the highway.

So, as you are changing, and whenever you can actually stand back for a moment and realize that you are changing, blow that mirror a kiss. Because who really wants to do one hundred thousand prostrations over a mirror with a straw up his nose?

That's painful.

And I'm already in enough pain.

So who am I?

I'm an infant.

I'm an instant.

I'm a graduate of the Tina Crystal School of Muddled Reality, Class of '04.

And I'm finally . . . here.

Coda

Now it is April 2005. Lately I am flowing things out of my life with a vengeance. The cell phones, sold 'em on eBay. The credit card, chopped it up. The excesses of sex and drugs, history. My ex crosses my mind only briefly now and then. I realize he has been too distracted to maintain our friendship, whereas I'm now too engaged to bother. Keep it simple. Elemental. Transcendental. Gypsy feet in Skechers, that's me—but no longer sketchy.

o　o　o

I AM AT THE triannual S/M Fleas, a kink community swap meet in San Francisco, with my friend Lola. We are selling off pieces of our past, relics no longer relevant. Right now I am post-leather, post-dildo, post-watersports, post-drugs, post-post. Is there anything left? Do I care?

I am left. And yes, I care a lot.

I survey the passing crowd. Each of us a hobo, trudging along the dusty trail, shouldering a stick tied to a bandanna holding hopes, fears, delusions, successes, disappointments. All dancing the dance of the wounded in our own singular way.

A nondescript, beady-eyed guy shows up on my radar scan. Not the least bit fetish-looking. He wears a dusty green corduroy suit jacket over a plain T-shirt and cheap chinos—the kind of clothes I am used to seeing on the closeout rack at thrift stores. At this point, I have gotten really good at spotting the likely sociopaths. I nudge Lola. "Check out this dude," I say. "Now, his fetish is *so* deep, *so* dark, and *so* disturbing that he *can't even talk about it* with anyone here. We can *hardly even imagine* what it might be." Nonetheless, I picture him vivisecting drugged and comatose twelve-year-old boys in a shack somewhere down a very long and twisted dirt road.

We both giggle. What else is there left to do?

Don't check out. Just keep showing up. *Don't* burn out, *don't* fade away. And once you're really here, dancing that dance that is righteously, rightfully yours, just keep on taking that next right step.

Leap now and then.

It's really the best possible revenge.

Public Sex

A Bottom's Confession

AMIE M. EVANS

MY PUSSY IS FAMISHED. It's forever hungry. A bottomless pit. No matter how much it gets, it always wants more. It is ungrateful. Demanding. Spoiled. Unappreciative. My pussy is starving; it tells me so all the time. First, in a gentle prodding way with a small tingle in the lips around its opening. It beckons, ever so slightly. *More, please.* Then, with more insistence, it calls out, sending forth moisture. *More, please, now.* Finally, it will not be ignored. It stirs up its neighbor, adding her voice to its call. My clit electrifies. Agitates. *More, we say now.* The please is gone, and with that, the want transforms into a need. My pussy is insatiable.

o   o   o

IT TOOK FOUR DATES over the course of four weeks before Adrian even kissed me. Our second date on an evening with a freak late-November snowstorm, however, had an incredible amount of potential for a first kiss. After dinner, as we stood on the center platform of the empty Back Bay T station in Boston, I thought to myself that this would be a very romantic spot for a first kiss. Both of us bundled in winter coats, scarves, and gloves—neither of us wearing hats—with a light dusting of fragile, half-melted snowflakes on our heads and shoulders, waiting for trains that would take us in opposite directions to our homes. The empty underground T station with its dirty concrete walls and floors, resident rats, and unidentifiable foul odor. A public spot, but empty of people.

We stood with only an inch between our noses as the two almost empty trains simultaneously pulled into the station surrounding us with a deafening rumble and a gust of cold air. Adrian grabbed me, pulled me into her arms, into a spontaneous, passionate first kiss. Her arms wrapped around me, our mouths half open, our lips touching, our tongues engaged. Then we separated, rushed to our trains—hers outbound, mine inbound—and from behind the windows watched each other as the trains pulled out, whisking us into the snowy night in opposite directions, the taste of each other still on our lips and a yearning for more deep inside each of us. I could hear the musical score building as the trains rushed in and climaxing as they pulled away. Each of us struggled to catch one last glimpse of the other.

But that isn't what happened. Adrian's train arrived first. She didn't kiss me. She didn't even watch from the window as her train pulled away. There was no music, and I was left alone on the platform, feeling butchier than I was.

As I said, it wasn't until our fourth date that Adrian kissed me. To be precise, it was the exact end of our fourth date. The part where after dinner I had invited her up to my apartment and we had talked for an hour before she said she had to go home. I walked her down the two flights of stairs to the common area. Her hand was on the doorknob; I was perched on the last step just to her right so as not to get hit with the door when she opened it into the small entryway. But instead of opening the door, she turned suddenly, placed a hand on each of my upper arms, and pulled me off the step into her. Adrian wrapped her arms around me, her tongue forced my mouth open, and she kissed me deeply. Over the course of the hour we'd spent talking, I'd given up the possibility of getting a first kiss from her, so I was completely caught off guard. I stumbled forward. I fought to find my footing and not to fall to the floor on my ass. I felt as if my tongue was engaged in a wrestling match with hers. But as soon as her lips touched mine, I immediately felt a tingle in my clit. After she kissed me, she bit my neck. Not too hard, but with enough pressure to leave a small mark on my pale, easily bruised flesh. Enough to cause me to catch my breath. Enough to stir a deep need in my cunt.

In hindsight, that first kiss was a microcosm of our future sex life. There was no buildup, no soft, closed-mouth pecks preceding the openmouthed, passionate kiss. No hug or cuddling when it was done. In fact, there was no warning at all that a kiss was going to happen. Adrian swooped in, took the kiss, bit my neck, and left me wanting more. The pattern is now clear, but at that time it was our first kiss and for me that meant soon, very soon, we'd finally start to fuck.

It had, after all, been four weeks—an entire month. And The Fuck was what I was after from her. From anyone, really. I wasn't looking for a relationship, just sex. Casual, easy sex. This first kiss, unlike any other first kiss I'd had, promised me, no, guaranteed me, sex—possibly rough sex. It clearly announced its intentions. It wasn't shy or questioning. It didn't express wonder about what possibilities the future might hold. It said, "I want sex, not love." And I was perfectly happy to oblige it and her.

o o o

I AM ADDICTED to sex in public. It isn't the idea of being watched. It would be an easier addiction to manage if that were the case. There are legal, safe places to go and lots of willing volunteers—a few who will even pay—if I simply wanted someone to watch me get fucked. I'd actually rather that no one saw me. Instead, my addiction is about the thrill of the possibility of being caught engaging in a sex act in a public space. I don't want to be caught; it is the potential of being discovered that heightens the pleasure of The Fuck. It increases the stimulation to all of my senses. Electrifies my nerve endings. The very idea of fucking in a public place turns me on instantly. The fact that it is socially unacceptable and against the law just makes it that much more exciting.

I have to admit that I keep a list of public places I want to have sex in and another list of public places where I have already had sex. It's juvenile, I know, but nonetheless, I update the lists with the same joy I felt as a child, when adding a much-wanted gift to my running gift list or removing a present from the list once it had been received. The most elusive place I want to have sex in that is currently on the list was the first place I added to the list when I started it: a confessional in a Roman Catholic church. I'd settle for any confessional, but ideally in my fantasy, it is an old Gothic church still equipped with the ornately craved wooden confessionals, complete with the sliding black screens, low lighting, and real velvet kneelers. The church itself is dripping with baroque details, crammed with stained glass and large statues of saints with gold leafing—a perfect example of religious excess.

My favorite public place to have sex in is a parking garage. By far, I prefer the multilevel aboveground garages that reach into the sky, but belowground garages and flat open parking lots, like those at malls, will do just fine in a pinch. My favorite spot is always the roof of the aboveground garage, with a clear night sky over head. One time, my lover and I were so bold as to have strap-on sex on the hood of our car on the roof level of a public parking garage in Central Square, Cambridge. Just thinking about that night makes me wet.

∘ ∘ ∘

THE FIRST JANUARY after Adrian and I started to date was bitter cold. Despite the early-November storm, hardly any snow fell that winter. Instead, the temperatures plunged into the single digits. In the Back Bay section of Boston, behind each row of brick town houses, instead of yards there are service alleys. Businesses and home owners park their cars there, store their trash in Dumpsters, and get deliveries through back entrances. At one time, I am sure these alleys were gentile and pleasant, and occupied by servants and nannies, but now rats as large as small lapdogs and the homeless forage and fornicate here. It is impossible to park on the upper end of Newbury Street, but Adrian had a free parking spot between two Dumpsters in one of these alleys behind the pet store where she worked.

It was into this spot she pulled her car at twelve midnight on a Tuesday night that January, after having had dinner and drinks in Cambridge. The alley was empty except for a few rats that scurried from under the Dumpster as we parked. She turned off the lights and cut the engine. The cold immediately started to sink into our warm enclave. As I undid the three buttons on my jacket and pulled it open to reveal the taffeta dress with the plunging neckline she had been eyeing all night, Adrian slid her seat back.

I smiled and smoothed out the skirt of my dress as she removed both of her gloves. She reached across the seat with one hand and I leaned toward her. She kissed me hard; I could feel the yearning in her. I'd been toying with her ruthlessly all evening. Her mouth was soft, wet, and warm, and she tasted like gin and cigarettes. Adrian pulled away, and I leaned against the back of the seat. She lifted up my skirt, revealing a white lace petticoat. She growled low and deep, then quickly pulled up the lacy layers to uncover a black satin garter belt and my shaved pussy framed between the straps attached on either leg to the tops of the stockings.

"I want your blood and your soul," she whispered as she slid two fingers into my wet cunt. I moaned and carefully rocked my hips toward her hand. "You're wet," she said, as she pumped her fingers deep inside me. "I want more of me deeper inside you."

Adrian continued to stroke her fingers in and out of my cunt as she worked my clit with her free hand. "I want to fuck you with my fist," she whispered in an even voice. I groaned as the idea of her fisting me, something we had yet to do, filled my mind with possibilities. "I'll tie you up on my bed and fuck you whenever I want," she continued as she thrust her fingers deeper inside my cunt. "I'll fuck you until you're raw, and still you'll beg me for more." Her fingers, slippery with my juices, worked my clit as she spoke. I came as the last word left her mouth.

Adrian licked her fingers as I pulled my skirt back in place.

We were both breathing hard. The scent of sweat and sex permeated the air. The inside of the windows were covered with steam, so we used a few napkins to wipe it off. We giggled and kissed deeply. We'd revisit this spot frequently over the next few months.

∘ ∘ ∘

VAGINAL FISTING is the ultimate fuck-you to straight men with bad attitudes who think that all dykes really need is a good dick. It cannot, like a dildo, be interpreted as a replacement penis; it cannot be seen as an imitation of heterosexuality. Two dykes fisting is as lesbian as it gets. And yet, part of the turn-on of fisting for me is actually having my lover invade my body with her flesh. To have her flesh inside my cunt.

∘ ∘ ∘

ADRIAN SLIPPED ONE FINGER into me. My pussy was so hungry it felt as if it had stripped the muscle and flesh from her finger, leaving it a small, bony stick barely felt. She added another finger on her next thrust and my pussy called out to me, *More, please.* I felt the cry traveling up from my cunt along my bloodstream, forcing its way to my mouth. With each thrust of her two fingers into my pussy, it called out, *More.* My pussy beckoned, and I clenched my teeth to prevent the words from escaping. Adrian added a third finger and worked my clit with her free hand. For a moment, I thought my pussy was satisfied, then the call came, more insistent, *More, please.* I swallowed hard, forcing down the words and the need.

Adrian pulled her fingers out of me. Now the distance

from her to me seems wide. *More.* I felt the demand inside me, then the head of her cock down there against my lips, the push as it forced itself up my cunt. But with each long, firm thrust, the want increased. *More. Give me more.* The call traveled directly out of my cunt through her cock to her clit. It made its way up her bloodstream to her mind, where it exploded as if the idea was hers. She withdrew her cock with a sucking sound and left behind an emptiness. I heard the sound of the lube pouring out of the bottle, felt the silkiness of her four fingers as they entered me all at once. "More": the word that issued from my pussy, exited my mouth, and filled the room. She pushed forth with all five fingers. My cunt resisted. It behaved badly, as if it were a spoiled child. It pushed back against her hand as if it had not invited—no, demanded—that her hand come in. As if it had not welcomed, encouraged it to enter. It refused to open. Refused to grant her access. "More," I screamed, and my pussy opened just long enough to consume her fist before closing tightly around her wrist. My cunt was full. Calmness spread over us while neither of us moved, her hand captured in my cunt.

o o o

WHEN YOU OFFER yourself up to someone as a human sacrifice, to be entered, consumed, desecrated, your body submits. At the moment of penetration, when your lips spread and the muscle at the opening of your cunt widens to allow her hand to enter you, your body relinquishes control. Your muscles shift to allow for the fullness, the length, the width. They stretch to accommodate the flesh, bone, and muscle of her hand, wrist, and arm. Your legs open wider, your hips thrust forward to meet her, to pull her into you. Your body, your cunt opens greedy for the fullness of having her fist inside it. A cavernous emptiness is awakened, and your body wants, aches to have it filled.

Desire, the kind of desire that comes from somewhere primordial, deep inside your blood, to be taken, to be used, to be filled, to be spiritually cannibalized. There is an all-consuming want, like the craving of an addict; it grows into an obsession when you don't get it. Your mind allows the thought of having it to consume you in a poor imitation of the real thing. While your pussy may throb to be touched, it is your mind that is addicted to fisting, your mind that craves consumption. For your mind must release control over itself for your lover's fist to enter you. Your mind has to bend to its knees, submit itself willingly to be lead through the gate. Your body would never accommodate the invasion, intrusion, possession, the desecration of your cunt if your mind didn't shift, bend, and melt. The moment of consumption—the exact point at which the broadest portion of her hand, the knuckles, pokes, prods, slides, or is sucked into your body, you become receptor—a controlled being. The fucker sucks power from you, forces pleasure from you, pulls moans and sighs from you, and you put out because . . .

o o o

IT IS THE BIGGEST DILDO I have ever seen. I assume it is a novelty item for displaying on one's mantelpiece or coffee table, but I don't ask. It is four feet long and easily two feet wide. A thick vein runs up its circumcised shaft, ending in a crown with a pee hole. The detail is incredible. A real piece of cock art. Large, oversized balls support it at the base and prevent it from tipping over due to the weight of the large crown at the top. It is a flat shade of industrial black, made of firm jelly rubber. One hundred fifty dollars. We giggle at it and point like amateurs or virgins as the leather-clad clerk with a shaved head and spiked collar stands, waiting to unlock the case and pull out our selection.

The giant cock sits in a large floor-to-ceiling display case behind chicken wire instead of glass, on a shelf surrounded by other jelly-rubber sex toys and novelty items. A lifelike cast of a fist and arm comes in two sizes—but we already have our own fist. An assortment of drastically different styles of buttplugs, from pencil-thin to liter-bottle-big, grace the shelves. The options seem endless. But a cock is what we are here to acquire. A big, fat cock. It is our first cock together. We want it to be exactly right.

We've already been to the women's sex shop, but none of their offerings were right. Too long, not fat enough, too small—I left there feeling like Goldilocks. So we are here, at Marquis de Sade, the gay male leather shop in the South End, to find our cock.

"If you want a good cock, go to the cock worshippers," Adrian had proposed as we walked out of the women's store.

And she had been correct. Long, fat cocks. Short, fat cocks. Long, thin cocks. Short, thin cocks. Cocks with veins and without. Cocks with balls and without. Cocks of all kinds line the walls. It is cock heaven. An odd place for two dykes?

Adrian stands next to me, her hands in her coat pockets, waiting expectantly to see which cock I'll pick. After all, it will be *her* cock. She'll wear it. "Black," she'd said at the women's sex store. "No pastels or animals." At Marquis de Sade, cocks come in only one color—flat, industrial black. Not a Buddha or dolphin to be found on these shelves. Nothing looks like anything except a real cock here.

"That one," I say to the clerk, pointing, "and that one." He unlocks the case and hands me the two dildos I have selected. I wonder if they had to lock the cocks up because people tried to steal them. But I don't ask. I hand one cock to Adrian. I hold the other in my hand. My fingers aren't able to make their way around it; an inch separates my fingertips. I hold it by the base and give it a shake. It wiggles a lot. I hand it to her and take the other one. It is heavier. Firmer and slightly wider without being longer, and it has a raised vein running down its shaft. Adrian and the clerk watch as I put it through the same test. I contemplate if it is too big. Too fat. I wonder if the balls will get in the way of the harness. I put it up against Adrian's crotch to see what it looks like. The clerk laughs with us.

"This one," I say, handing it to the clerk.

"A fine choice, if I do say so myself. And *I* know cock," he says flatly as he returns the rejected dildo to the case. At the counter, he rings us up and puts the dick in a paper bag. As we leave, he yells, "Have fun, girls. Don't do anything I wouldn't do." The two other male patrons look at us and then laugh knowingly. We giggle. Our fifty-dollar jelly-rubber cock in the paper bag is clutched to my chest as we walk out to the street.

o o o

BECAUSE THE SUCKING, forcing, pulling—the giving up of—is as consuming to you as the taking is to her. The giving up is what turns you on.

o o o

JUNE OF THAT YEAR was rain-soaked. Adrian and I drove an hour and a half north to Ashland to spend four days with her parents at their golf time-share in the White Mountains of New Hampshire. Everything I packed to wear for the trip was wrong for the weather and the location. When it wasn't raining, heavy fog hung low, obscuring the spectacular views of the mountaintops, and moisture seemed to have permeated everything inside and out. The air was unseasonably cool, and my sundresses and skirts did a poor job of keeping me warm. The one pair of jeans I had brought immediately got muddy and wet on our first walk in the woods. I was not prepared for New Hampshire, having expected it to be more like Atlantic City in the woods than actual wilderness. Nor was I ready for the implications of what the invitation to spend time with her parents on the family vacation meant for us as "a couple."

After all, we weren't a couple, nor were either of us looking for coupledom. But by now, eight months after our first date, I felt more inclined to keep her around than to discard her for someone else. This trip felt like a couple's activity, and everything, including my ill-selected wardrobe and her mother calling me by the first name of Adrian's last girlfriend, took on more weight than it would have just a few months earlier. I, despite my continued insistence to myself and my friends, wanted a relationship with Adrian.

On Monday night after the sun set and the never-ending rain stopped briefly, Adrian and I set out for a walk after dinner. I wore a blue-and-white flowered sundress, flat sandals, and a sweater, and she wore jeans, boots, and a long-sleeved T-shirt. We walked down the poorly lit dirt and gravel road, past rows of condos that looked as if they belonged in a more urban environment than this wooded recreational area in New Hampshire provided. Past a playground set off from the side of the road near the lip of the woods, two poorly maintained and seldom used clay tennis courts, and the pool house with its inside pool in a glass structure reminiscent of a greenhouse, and its outside pool surrounded by a six-foot wooden fence, onto the main paved road that led to the golf course.

The golf course, with its open unlit grass and patches of trees, promised us the seclusion needed to have sex. A small river marked the edge of the time-share complex's property and ran the full length of the far end of the green. Next to the river was a small grouping of trees in various sizes on a slightly sloping hill. This was our destination. We had seen it earlier in the day and agreed that it offered a secluded area for our walk's destination and a good cover for sex.

The green was pitch-black when we started across its lush, thick grass toward the cropping of trees. Despite the fact that the rain had stopped, the sky was still full of large clouds, so no light from the moon or stars could make its way to us. Everything seemed to be working in our favor that night. Halfway across the green, however, it became clear that the closer we got to the river, the thicker the bugs were, and we reluctantly decided to head back to the time-share unit before we were completely covered with bumps from mosquito bites. Disappointed that our venture had not panned out as we had hoped and both wanting very much to have sex, we headed back to the dirt road.

"Perhaps tomorrow," I said as we walked past the tennis courts.

"We leave tomorrow," Adrian said, then grabbed my hand. "I wanted to fuck you in New Hampshire."

We laughed and she pulled me into a kiss in the middle of the dark road. Over her shoulder I could see the outline of the swing set, the sliding board, the teeter-totter, and the jungle gym tucked into the edge of the woods.

"What about that?" I said, pointing over her shoulder to the outline of the massive wooden jungle gym.

She turned and looked where I was indicating, then back at the road. No one was outside on this dreary night. It was too wet and cold for families or seniors to walk around. Everyone was inside, playing board games and cards or watching TV. The few sparse streetlights were situated so that the playground area was almost as dark as the golf green. Adrian shrugged and smiled. Then we ran holding hands across the playground's patchy grass to the jungle gym next to the wood's edge, giggling like kids.

The jungle gym was made of wood and heavy plastic. It was standard fare, with a variety of rungs and notches for climbing, two slides, monkey bars, and platforms making tunnels between the sections. I climbed up a series of rungs and sat with my legs dangling on the platform. I was surrounded by brightly colored plastic panels with circles and stars cut out of them. These formed the walls of the fort section of the jungle gym. One of the sliding boards was up three rungs to my left, and the monkey bars were over two panels and up two stairs to my right. It was dark enough and protected enough that I was sure no one would see us from the road.

"Perfect," Adrian said, spreading my legs and hiking up my dress.

"Stop," I said, swatting at her hand.

"Make me," she said, grabbing both of my wrists and moving forward between my legs. I was up high enough that I could wrap my legs around her midriff, so I did and locked my ankles behind her back.

"Now what are you going to do?" I teased her.

She simply let go of my wrists and pulled my legs apart. I playfully kicked at either side of her as she pushed my dress the rest of the way up, revealing the fact that I did not have on any panties. "Bad girl, out playing on the jungle gym without panties," she said, before leaning down and licking my cunt. Then, resting her cheek on my thigh, she added, "Who knows what could happen to you out here in the dark without panties." Then she added, "You're so wet. You smell like sex."

She slid her face up my thigh, and the tip of her tongue ever so lightly searched the folds of my outer labia, grazing over my clit hood, and then finally plunged into my wet pussy. I moaned as her tongue entered me and pushed against the opening of my vaginal walls. I spread my legs farther apart—to give her better access to my cunt—placing one foot on either side of the edge of the platform I was sitting on. I laid back so I could see the cloudy sky above us.

Adrian licked straight up from the opening of my hole to my clit. "Umm, you taste like sex, too." Then her mouth encased my mound, her tongue centering on my clit and working it in tight circles. My body involuntarily jerked and she moaned.

I groaned and began to move my hips counter to her tongue strokes. She slipped two fingers inside me. I shifted to a back-and-forth pumping motion, and her free hand grasped my left hip. Her fingers dug into the flesh, forcing me to remain still—intensifying the sensation by restraining my movement.

Adrian slipped a third finger inside me and concentrated the friction of her strokes against the top of my vaginal wall. She increased the force of her tongue work. I closed my eyes, grabbed her short, blond hair, and allowed the waves of orgasm to flood through me. My hips jumped forward as I came and she captured the flesh of my labia between her teeth. I was suspended in time. My heart raced, but I felt as if I were outside of time—moving between the lines that make up reality.

AMIE M. EVANS

The muscles inside my vagina contracted and spasmed as my mind exploded with pure pleasure. Then it was gone, over, done.

She took a final lick of my sweet juices before pulling herself up. I smoothed my skirt down over my legs. Adrian leaned over to kiss me softly. She tasted like me.

∘   ∘   ∘

I WOULDN'T WANT anyone to get the idea that I've spent all of my time letting Adrian fuck me and not reciprocating. That wouldn't be entirely true. Of course, this is a bottom's confession, so I must confess that more of our sex time has been spent with me being fucked rather than me returning the favor. I'd much rather be the fucked than the fucker. It stands to reason, then, that my confession is about Adrian fucking me, while I skip over my servicing her. And while I acknowledge that it makes for a one-sided tale, when I think of our sex life, the images that come to mind are of her doing me. I almost never think about the reverse. I wonder if that is because I am a bottom or if I am a bottom because of that.

I try to imagine myself as a top. It makes me giggle. I like being done way too much for me to be of any good as a top to anyone. I like sinking into The Fuck too much to orchestrate what's going on. There is something magic about what tops do. How they take next to nothing and create so much pleasure and gratification. Turning the body into a vessel of such pure pleasure. I wouldn't want to ruin the enchantment I have with their magic by studying their craft. I'd much rather be left in awe by them.

∘   ∘   ∘

152

WHATEVER ADRIAN DOES must fill that empty space inside me that had started as a small yearning but has grown into a loud, insatiable demand that must still somehow be satiated. She must overcome, subdue, master, and fill my consuming hunger. It is beyond my control. It threatens to consume us both.

The hunger grows. It spreads away from my body and reaches toward her with its teeth exposed to rip into her flesh. I push through the hunger, and as she comes near me, her hand extended to grab my breast or neck, I flip onto my stomach and attempt to get on my knees. I will undo the chains from the O-ring and free myself. My upper body hits the mattress hard, facedown. My arms stretched in front of me, my weight on my knees, my ass in the air. I feel my dress slide up and expose my bare ass. Adrian licks between the crack and pushes hard with her tongue. The palm of her hand impacts my ass. I tighten the muscles at the second blow. I clasp my hands around the chains, and the stinging begins. Her hand comes down again and again against my bare flesh. Her free arm is around my hips, preventing me from sinking onto my stomach; forcing my exposed, quickly reddening ass to remain in the air, accessible and vulnerable. She stops. My ass stings; my cunt throbs. My resistance has been consumed and replaced by the hunger. Every part of me will submit to her touch. There is no resistance, no desire except for the desire to be molded by her hands and tongue. The cells of my flesh will yield to her touch and transform themselves into whatever she desires, as long as she touches me.

I feel pressure against my cunt lips. My own wetness has spilled out of me, betraying my desire. Adrian does not use her other hand to separate and open me; there is pressure—intense and concentrated—against the lips of my cunt. I feel the head of the dildo slip forward and slightly enter me, forcing my cunt to accept its size. I feel the stretching, the pulling of my pussy as the pressure continues. I moan. She pushes the head into my cunt, and the slightly smaller shaft plunges in afterward. My cunt is full. My body rises in an arch as the surge of pleasure rushes through me. Adrian moves her hips slowly, working the shaft in and out of me. My cunt relaxes, submits to her invasion, to the satisfaction of the fullness. I slide into The Fuck. After a few full strokes where the cock's shaft is consumed entirely by my cunt, Adrian's hips skip the steady climb and go from slow probing to slamming. Hard. Fast. She plunges into me. Pounding away. Nailing me. Her sweat and the juices from my cunt are all over us like baptismal water. The nerves in the soft flesh of my vagina ache with sensation. Her thighs slap against the backs of my thighs, her hand clutches my red ass as she slides hard and fast in and out of me. She pulls my ass toward her with each thrust.

I feel a popping sensation, followed by a severe emptiness deep inside my cunt. My body is outraged. My hips stretch to follow her cock, but it isn't there. I groan with displeasure as Adrian flips me onto my back, pushing my legs apart with her knees. There is no resistance in my muscles. Her hand pushes down on my pelvic bone. She reenters me with one strong, full stroke. She fills the empty void. There is no resistance left in my cunt. I am on my back, my legs are in the air, and my arms are chained over my head to the wall. I can see the top of her head, the white-blond spikes sagging under the weight of her own sweat; her face is pressed into my chest. I see my own legs in black silk stockings, my six-inch fuck-me shoes bouncing on either side of her ass as she rams into me. She clamps her teeth on my nipple, pulling on the ring, biting into the flesh. I reach for her upper arms, but the chains stop me, preventing me from touching her. I want desperately to sink my nails into her flesh, to draw the blood to the surface, to free it as she frees me. The chains clank against each other. She thrusts deeper into me.

I dig my heels into the flesh of her sides. She is a horse I am riding. I want her to fuck me harder. I want her to fuck me so hard that her cock breaks through my organs, tears through the muscles, rips through the soft tissue of my belly, popping out in a bloody fountain. And still she would not stop ramming into me.

I know she can do it. I have faith in her ability to fuck, and I have felt the pure, raw animal in her. Her sexual desire is fused to my sexual need. Adrian will do anything to push me into that blue, bottom space, to push me to the edge, to make me give her my orgasm.

o   o   o

IF SHE'D LET ME, I'd do everything in one night. Everything. I'd push my mind and body far past the breaking point. I'd expose my every weakness and vulnerability, until I was consumed completely. An evening of everything would leave me a lump of raw flesh. If we did everything at once, I would be left hollow, wanting. It is the mixing, the infinite combinations that succeed in filling my needs, answering my wants. The waiting. The anticipation. The wondering. These allow me to move from one desire to the next. I *want* every-thing, now. If I was given it, what would I be left to want? Wanting is the thread that creates the fabric of my identity as a bottom. If there is nothing left to want, who would I be? This is the ultimate need of a bottom—the need for a top to pre-vent her from fulfilling her truest desire, by filling only the barest of her immediate needs. Controlling the drug to prevent an overdose—to prevent the end of the bottom herself.

o o o

"HARDER," I GASP.

And she responds as if the idea had been her own. Perhaps it was. I am not sure where either of us ends or begins. Right now it doesn't matter. At this moment, all that drives us is The Fuck. All that exists is The Fuck. I look into her face. Her eyes are closed. Her arms, tense and fully extended, hold her upper body above me.

"Fuck me. Own me. I am yours to do with as you wish. Possess me. Consume me. Desecrate my body. Stab me there in that soft, sacred place, over and over. I will not resist you now. I will not refuse your request. Any order. Any demand. Any desire."

We are not two lesbians exploring each other's female bodies. We are not two individuals. We are The Fuck. One consuming mound of carnal desires, impulses, raw primitive animal urges. Perhaps the desire to fuck harder, to plow deeper inside my wet, greedy cunt was hers, and I am merely the vessel that gives voice to her need.

Harder.

Perhaps the want to be fucked harder, deeper, faster was mine, and the word never crossed my lips. It just issued from deep inside my snatch to her mind or muscles. I want her to fuck me, to fill my whole body with her cock. Plow into my liver, kidneys, stomach. Push her cock through my uterus into the lungs. I want her to fill my whole body with the length and thickness of her cock, to spread the aching, throbbing pleasure that she is creating in my cunt throughout my body with each stroke into me. I want her to pierce my heart and impale it on her cock—matching the rhythm of her fuck to the beats of my heart. I want her to fuck me until my eyes pop out and blood runs freely from my ears, nose, and mouth.

In one motion, Adrian's arms press my shoulders as she grabs me for more leverage, and her next downward stroke into my open cunt is harder than I had imagined possible. Her hips smack against the back of my upper thighs, her cock slides roughly in and out of me. The fake, stiff balls bump against my asshole, stirring a new emptiness, a new need inside me, a new hole demanding to be filled. I clamp my legs around her, locking my ankles across her back. I shall never let go. My cunt and clit throb, my asshole stirs, demanding to be included. I want her to make me come, but I am a greedy slut. I don't want her to stop ramming her cock into me. I want to stay here, used and possessed by her hunger, locked together. I want to come before the fucking makes my clit explode, my mind implode. I want her to fuck me until I break, fuck me through the come, and not stop fucking me, fuck me until I die, fuck me until there is nothing left of me but a shell.

o o o

I AM A BAD BOTTOM. I am undisciplined. Bratty. Willful. Disrespectful. Greedy. Adrian would have it no other way. I am a tease. A tormentor. A flirt. I purposefully drive Adrian to distraction at the most inopportune moments. I am loyal. Devoted. Committed. Qualities Adrian demands. Adrian is Adrian. She indulges, spoils, and encourages me. I am June Cleaver, Bettie Page, Princess Grace, and a common street whore on demand. But I am nothing without her.

o o o

ADRIAN REMOVES the dildo from its ring, fucking me with it in her hand, as her mouth engulfs my clit. Her tongue licks the engorged mass, flicking, pulling, putting pressure directly on it. I come, clamping her head between my legs, her mouth on my clit, her cock still slamming inside my cunt. She doesn't stop until the last spasm passes. My cunt and clit fuse. All that I am is condensed to that one single point. She creates the moment of my consumption, erasing me completely. This is the moment she unravels me, undoes me, releases me. This is the moment I exist for; this moment is the only reason I am alive. This orgasm she has ripped from me— she owns it as much as I do. At this moment I do not exist. I am a nerve ending, an extension of her sexual desire. I am one large cunt and clit. Adrian has forced this orgasm from me. She has created it from my resistance. She has reached deep inside me, letting my blood cover her hands as she tore through my liver, stomach, and heart; grasped my want, my sex, and my power; and pulled it to the surface—freeing it. Freeing me. Even in this moment, my mind wonders what we will uncover inside me next, what is to come in the future, and what intense methods will be required for her to cut through my flesh, dig in my organs, unearth the rest of me, release the rest of my power, and for her to give me her power. For this moment is small, these acts merely touching the surface of the dark we are standing next to. I know there is much trapped inside of me.

o o o

THAT FIRST KISS in the stairway of my apartment happened nine years ago. Since then we have had sex in parking garages, at play parties, in bathroom stalls at dance clubs, and, yes, even in our home. My body is a playground for her to explore. Sex is not just an expression of physical need and love but the path to finding our souls. It is a muse for tapping into our creativity. Sex is the physical language we share. The landscape of our world together. My body is the canvas onto which she paints portraits of deep desires and landscapes of profound dreams. Desire is the darkness into which we peer and wonder what is hidden there just outside of our vision, just beyond our reach.

Exuvia (1977–1980)

ROB STEPHENSON

I STARED at the brown bottle in my hand and took the last swig of beer left in it. I was still nervous and pushed the shirtless guy in front of me. My hand came away drenched with his sweat. I slipped past him and bumped into many more like him. Some of them had mustaches that would be more to scale on faces larger than theirs. Some had longish beards and hair down their backs. A few were in their underwear or skimpy shorts.

I was younger than most of them. My fear of being looked at was about equal to my desire for it. I wore baggy jeans, a purple pullover, and dirty high-top sneakers. I bravely faced the bartender and this time, I smiled. He had a frosty one open and waiting me for on the bar.

"Do you wanna dance?" The question boomed from behind me.

Unnerved, I swung around. His straight brown hair hung down to his shirt collar. He was stunning and so much older than I was, mid- to late twenties. The beer and his easy smile calmed me enough to look into his eyes. I nodded. He grabbed my hand and tugged me into the crowd. I left the beer on the bar. We swirled into the laser-light beams and danced nonstop until we were soaked in ourselves. He hugged me again and again. I tingled with anticipation under my clothes. His traveling hands vacationed around the skinny world of my body. I just stared into him, fingertips digging into his shoulder blades.

"Do you wanna leave with me? I have a car."

I nodded again. He pulled me toward the door before my head stopped moving. It was then that I noticed and immediately loved the thick purple suspenders that wedged faded denim tight up his buttcrack.

Outside the club, the erratic roars of cars and trucks rushing past us on the freeway above merged with the disco bass throbbing through the heavy wooden door. He pulled me to him and our tongues swirled around in a double spiral. It was a sweet prelude to the next three years of our lives together. I felt the startling difference between the light wetness of his skin under my fingers and the dense fluid we were creating in our mouths.

Once inside the mint-green metal of his old Cadillac, we fondled each other through our pants as he drove us to an empty parking lot somewhere in the city I'd never imagined, with my suburban head full of shopping-mall fantasies and hundreds of science-fiction stories. There was more tongue play, but he licked down my neck and smooth chest to spend a while moving back and forth between my nipples. Now I knew why city boys didn't wear drawers. It was only partly for show. My favorite appendage was trapped in a one-hundred-percent-cotton bondage hell. I squirmed. I moaned, squished and ecstatic in the corner of the backseat.

He was tireless and thorough once he freed me from my

Looms. I gushed three loads into him before he drove me all the way back to my parents' house in the East Bay, his right hand keeping busy in my lap.

For the next couple of weeks, Donny drove that Cadillac out to the self-serve gas station where I worked every night. After closing time, he would drive me to a deserted back road in the hills behind my parents' house. Once parked, we went at it.

After a mere two weeks of messing around in Marge (Donny's name for that old tank), he suggested I move to San Francisco with him. We'd already left a complex pattern of stains on that worn upholstery.

o   o   o

INFATUATED, SEX-CRAZED, Donny and I made room for me in his classic Victorian one-bedroom apartment on Van Ness and Union. For one hundred seventy-five dollars a month we had shiny parquet floors, French doors, twelve-foot ceilings, and an Italianate bay window crammed full of potted plants.

Donny had two best friends his age. Doug lived next door to us, while Jeff lived in Oakland. Doug was a common variety of slut: shameless, brutally frank, and utterly charming. The afternoon I met him, he had a joint in one hand and a drink in the other. Over the next year, I saw every sort of male come up the stairway with him and enter his apartment. After a half-hour to two hours, they would exit, never to be invited back again.

Doug carried a purse at all times, but otherwise dressed in jeans and brightly colored Hawaiian shirts. He was a waiter in an upscale dinner club a half-dozen blocks from our building.

Naturally blond Jeff was a steward for an airline. His flying schedule was erratic. That plus keeping an apartment across the bay in Oakland prevented him from hanging around with us much.

One night Jeff came back from Maine with a cardboard box full of lobsters and invited us over for his demented imitation of an Olympic seafood event. He had a huge pot of boiling water on the stove and a pan of melted butter on the table. He put two of the lobsters at the edge of the kitchen floor where the living room carpet ended and the kitchen tiles began. This became a starting line. They were released simultaneously and whichever ambled across the floor first was tossed into the boiling water instead of receiving a gold medal. It was an unforgettable sound: the *clackity-clack* of the unlucky winner frantically knocking its claws against the side of the churning pot of water for the few seconds before its death.

Donny worked downtown in a tall building. He'd had the same job for eight years and looked fantastic in a suit. He always looked good. He modeled part-time for magazines.

Since I had no job yet, I wandered our neighborhood, amazed at the stores and the people but always anxious for Donny to get home from work. We lived not far from the very first Banana Republic shop. At that time, it sold safari clothing, or at least a line of clothes based strictly on the torrid jungle look.

I found a job at a dessert place in the Cannery near Fisherman's Wharf that was no longer a cannery. It had been remade into a complex of shops and restaurants. I worked on the third floor. All day I looked out of the panoramic windows at the bay. The view was never the same, the water and sky always changing, always capable of surprise. Alcatraz sat alone in the middle of it, hoards of out-of-towners going to and from the island on scheduled tour boats.

One of my coworkers was a painter who loved Vincent van

Gogh and Egon Schiele. I bought books about them. I was fascinated with the short, intense Austrian life of Schiele and the emaciated economy of line and color in his work. I enjoyed how his stark nude renderings turned his subjects inside out and revealed their sharp, tragic cores, unlike the work of his more famous friend Gustav Klimt, whose pretty, gold-tinged surfaces were exquisite but rarely dug to deeper depths.

I let my hair grow out. I was determined to do all the things I had never been allowed to do while living with my parents, who, on religious grounds, no longer spoke with me.

We made friends with Toni and Thom, who lived on the same floor that we did. A delightful couple in their early thirties, they were graduates of Kent State and worked downtown as graphic designers for a small company. Their apartment was full of unique objects and seemed like a little wonderland to me. They were ex-hippies, now gravitating toward the punk and new-wave scenes. They had mountains of LPs, and through them I discovered all sorts of music I didn't know existed.

Thom smoked pot like many smokers smoke cheap cigarettes. Toni took a hit only on rare occasions. Donny had smoked pot off and on for years. It wasn't hard to get him going again.

Cautiously, over the course of a month, I inhaled huge tokes of the stuff, but it never made me high. I was so disappointed. It looked like so much fun. Thom and Donny would be giggling, childishly joyful in a world of their own. Toni and I were left behind.

One afternoon, we were all sitting on the floor in their living room. Thom said he had some killer weed called Panama Red. He rolled a joint in a few seconds and lit up. He said I had to try this one. I sighed and slowly inhaled the thick smoke into my lungs. I passed it onto Donny. Thom put on *Animals* by Pink Floyd.

From the first acoustic guitar strums, I knew something had changed. In a couple of minutes, I had to lie down on the floor. Thom cranked up the stereo, ignoring Toni's protests. She didn't like Pink Floyd. She wanted to hear Blondie or the Dead Boys. I turned my head and saw mysterious scribbles on the underside of their coffee table. It was suddenly profound that the table was made out of an unfinished wood door. There were lines and lines of writing under there, shooting off in all directions.

Thom handed me a purple felt-tipped pen and told me I had to sign the table. I tried to read the words. I recognized them but I couldn't make sense of them a moment after I had read them. All meaning just slipped away. That one side of the LP seemed to last for hours.

Starting that evening, Donny and I had a new surge in our lovemaking. We still went to the bars, but now we would get stoned at home and stay in half the time, screwing.

Donny brought home a leather body harness, and we took turns wearing it. Having that metal cock ring held firmly in place around my prick made my orgasms stronger and longer.

I was inside Donny's ass whenever I had the chance. I just knew he was the one for me, the one I would love forever. Funny how such fleeting sensations can inspire notions of the eternal.

Toni and Thom showed us the backside of nightlife. Instead of the disco clubs, we started going to concerts. We saw all sorts of bands. Mabuhay Gardens in North Beach became our hangout: a cheap Filipino restaurant by day and the hottest punk club in the city at night.

We must have seen a hundred bands there over the course of a year, many were local, but some big-name old-timers would show up there. Druggy Iggy and Bleary Bowie made a surprise appearance during the Idiot tour. Devo, before they had an album out, sporting yellow jumpsuits, ran amok amid projected super-8 loops of animated bouncing microbes from fifties instructional science films, singing "Mongoloid."

After seeing Patti Smith at Winterland, wrapped in the American flag atop a grand piano, her fingers bleeding as she sang a levitating rendition of "You Light up My Life," she showed up at Mabuhay and jumped up onstage with the Zeroes. She played one note on an electric guitar over and over, which didn't go too well with the Zeroes song, but she carried it off with the steely force of a lapsed Catholic pugilist.

I managed to say a few words to her afterward. She smiled and blinked at me. I'd had her sign a copy of *Babel* the day before at a bookstore, but she didn't recognize me. Without asking my name, she handed me an ivory-colored plastic bead with an R on it.

Perhaps the most memorable concert I saw there was a heroin-singed Nico accompanying herself on the harmonium. She pumped out tubercular organ drones with her feet, while she half spoke, half sang out of tune through rotting teeth. Her cover of "The End" by the Doors was a Teutonic nightmare, a subzero lunacy that carved its warped shapes exactly into the brain. Yet even she couldn't rival the freaky audience of outsiders that she drew into her malformed sonic sphere.

Donny sold Marge and bought a tan van, and we drove up and down the coast, blasting the Talking Heads, and ferociously humping at every beach and rest stop. We saw the Rolling Stones on the Some Girls tour in San Francisco, had such a good time that we bought tickets for the show at Anaheim stadium and vanned our way down Highway 5 to see them again. We took a bag of pot and a bunch of prerolled joints as well as a batch of potent magic brownies. The Stones were an hour late coming onstage. We were flying high. Donny took photos with an enormous zoom lens that he'd sneaked into the stadium somehow in a gym bag.

We were dragged off into the men's room by several young leather-gloved cops in matching uniforms. They frisked us and made us flush the bag of pot and the joints. They were nothing like the tolerant sort of cops we knew in San Francisco. These guys treated us like garbage. I was terrified, and for a few moments I was made aware of the pathetic aspects of my drugged stupor. They threatened to confiscate the camera and throw us out.

After watching us max out on paranoia, they decided that we had suffered enough and let us go back to our seats. We considered ourselves very lucky, because we still had the camera and the brownies, but even more so because the cops hadn't noticed the antique silver pillbox wedged under the cardboard bottom of Donny's bag. It had two quaaludes inside. Had they found them, we would've gone to jail.

o   o   o

DONNY INTRODUCED ME to his ex-boyfriend. He had a fantastic house a few blocks off lower Haight Street, and that night concocted the first of many sumptuous feasts for us in his overstocked kitchen.

Stan was in his fifties, wisps of gray hair combed over his balding head. A sort of entertainment jack-of-all-trades, he loved to talk in his radio voice and would burst into spontaneous phrases from opera arias if I provided more than a yes or no to one of his many queries. I had never encountered such a bombastic personality.

While nibbling a stalk of celery plucked from his third Bloody Mary, he told us how his recent circumcision was finally healed. He'd been jacking off hourly for a week now and was grateful to be rid of that constrictive scaffolding. Seconds later, he admitted that he couldn't get enough of creeping about in nearby Buena Vista Park, teasing around under the damp hoods of dark strangers.

He invited us to stay the night, but Donny refused before the question was all the way out of Stan's mouth. At the front door, Stan hugged me with hands roving in all directions. He took something from his pocket and pressed it into my palm, closing my fist around it. I thought I knew what was inside.

Months before, I had sniffed cubits of cocaine off a black porcelain tray with Donny, Toni, and Thom on Christmas Eve. We'd played poker all night long, rubbing our gums numb. By morning I'd won sixty dollars.

When we were home from Stan's, I carefully unfolded the little piece of shiny paper. But instead of chunky white powder, there were two tiny squares of blotter paper with a cartoon orange sun printed on each one. Donny told me it was LSD. He assured me that Stan always kept the purest stuff available in his freezer.

After a good night of sleep, we each took a whole tab. Nothing happened. I figured it was like pot, I would have to try it several times before I would leave the launching pad. I wanted to go outside; it was an unusually warm day. Donny convinced me to stay put and listen to some records.

It was less a launch than a step-by-step ascension. For the next twelve hours, we were tripping. There is much that I can't remember, but the parts I do are as clear as if they happened moments ago.

At first the world became transparent to me. Many connotations that formed the basis of perception were severed, and I was forced to find new ones. An electric clarity disrupted entrenched patterns of thinking. There were moments when this was difficult, but I did not have a bad trip.

At one point we put on all the coats and jackets in our closet and went up on the roof of our building. The sun was setting, and the Mobil gas station sign blinked on across the street. It was very important, the bluish aura that emanated from that sign. We both stared at it for a long time.

When it was fully dark, we went down to our bedroom and undressed each other. We were the most familiar strangers in the world. I touched the inch-tall symbol that was tattooed on his thigh. Ever more Pollux than Castor, Donny was proud of being Gemini. He bathed himself in the dimwitted light from the stars that shone daily in the astrology column of the *San Francisco Chronicle*.

Now under the spell of stunned dendrites, the mark of the twins on his flesh became an alien character that pulsed like a double window. I marveled at the halo that danced around us as I penetrated Donny. I found myself pulsing deep inside a jaguar, a young girl, a handful of mythological creatures, an old man. At times, it seemed as if I were fucking him into all these entities, there were fifteen or so of them. Sometimes they were changing me into strange complementary forms. Perhaps we were mirrors or mediums for the figures that were rushing through our minds, forming a psychic loop that was impossible to build during our usual consciousness. Or perhaps all of it was just a more spectacular set of illusions created by this temporary reconfiguration of my brain's switchboard, a glitzy circus of illusions that could easily replace the comfortable, threadbare ones I'd carried around for too long.

I felt no rush toward orgasm, just a high concentration of unfamiliar pleasure throughout my entire body. Sexual feelings lost their selfish edge and veered toward the mathematical.

Some acid trips have terrifying aspects. I experienced little fear. We were fortunate, although the tail end of it was unpleasant. Eventually, one gets tired during an endless stream of cosmic revelations to which there is no off switch. We didn't sleep much for thirty-six hours. And then I called in sick for two days as we recovered.

o   o   o

AROUND THIS TIME, Donny suggested we go to a bathhouse. He promised me it would be great fun.

At the entrance, a bored young man my age sat behind a window. He spoke to us through a microphone and asked if we were members. I felt as if he was trying to decide if he should let us in or not, though I'm sure he was instructed to let anyone in who would pay the steep nonmember entry fee, as long as they weren't a complete mess.

After we paid, he buzzed us in through a thick red door. Through another window, he handed us each a stiff white towel and a key to a locker. The key was attached to an adjustable elastic loop. It had a metal tag with a locker number stamped into it.

He smirked and told us to have a good time as he buzzed us through a second red door to the locker room. In minutes we were walking through the dimly lit hallways, clad only in our towels, our keys strapped to our ankles. We peered into little cubicles at nude and seminude guys in various suggestive poses in the little rooms. Some ignored us completely and others beckoned with a wink, a hard cock, or the flex of an ass cheek.

Donny seemed at ease and knew his way through the labyrinth of corridors. We sat in the wet sauna awhile, watching a young man with a soggy Afro being worshipped by five older white guys. His eyes were clenched shut and he was moaning softly. It was the perfect number of mouths for complete service: one kissing his mouth, two licking a nipple each and sometimes moving over to an armpit, the forth swallowing the fat prick that stood between his held-up legs, the last one rimming him.

I wondered how he kept from shooting with all the stimulation. He must've already shot several loads by the time we'd arrived. His wet skin was the color of the corkboard on the wall in our bedroom, where I pinned photographs of men from the magazines Donny brought home for me.

Donny grabbed my hand and pulled me away from them and back into the maze. After a few turns, we were in total darkness. An upbeat Bryan Ferry spurred us forward, singing "Come on, come on, let's stick together." The air was saturated with sweat and popper fumes. Lighting a single match would've set the whole place ablaze. I felt hands linger on my chest and under my towel, but Donny tugged me around a pile of writhing bodies.

And then I glimpsed flickering movements of light in front of me. I was looking through a small portal in a wall at blurs of light moving back and forth in a furious rhythm. I knew it was a porno movie, but the tiny portal let me see only a fraction of the screen that was on the other side of the next room. I couldn't make out exactly which parts of the bodies I was seeing, yet I kept staring at the frenetic abstraction, entranced.

At that moment, Bryan Ferry ended his song and I heard the grunts of the men I was now alone with in the dark. I felt a pang of terror as I turned toward where I expected Donny and saw only the black void of the room.

I ran my fingertips against the wall and moved along it until I found an opening I could pass through. Down a short hallway, I emerged into a room lit with a dull, reddish glow that emanated from little lightbulbs set under a transparent surface I walked above.

To one side of me was a row of smaller rooms with doorways but no doors on them. Each one had a red lightbulb in the ceiling. A guy was on his knees in one of the rooms, facing a wall.

I turned a corner and saw more of these rooms. I walked into one of them. My bare feet sank into thick foam padding covered with vinyl. Ten-inch-tall by four-inch-wide oblong holes were cut in all three of the walls at crotch level. These were specially designed glory-hole rooms, much more comfortable than the makeshift restroom varieties around the city.

I was considering whether or not to stick my prick through one of the holes when the largest penis I'd ever seen outside of a magazine poked its knobby head at me. It was already fully erect and bent up toward me through the hole.

I put my hand around it and squeezed. The whole thing pushed its way into the room with me. In the red light, I wasn't sure what color this cock really was. What did the man attached to it look like? Was he handsome?

I decided it didn't matter at all. Something like that doesn't just pop into one's face that often. I had to put it in my mouth. I wasn't even sure how it would ever fit, but the challenge of it made me hard. I let go of it, knelt down on the soft padding, and put the head in my mouth. It tasted mildly of chlorine. I took in another couple of inches, and it was already pressing against every surface inside my mouth. I didn't want to scrape him with my teeth, but it seemed inevitable. He didn't seem to mind and pushed in slowly. I tried to accommodate him and started gagging. I backed off and heard him whisper in an unfamiliar language. I tried again, a little more relaxed, but my enthusiasm didn't help much.

I heard Donny snicker behind me. I pulled off again, and he squatted down next to me.

"I'll show you how," he said low in my ear. I moved over, and in moments the whole length of it disappeared inside Donny's mouth. The guy attached to that monstrous thing started moaning and pressing against the wall that separated him from us. Donny slurped and sucked, cradling it in his mouth just as easily as he did mine. Flabbergasted and more than a little jealous of his ability, I sat back and started jerking off. Donny already was. I saw that he'd lost his towel.

The vinyl was slick with Donny's drool. The foreign man's muted moans cross-faded into unintelligible mutterings as he pounded a fist on the wall. Donny kept that thing in his throat and moved slowly back and forth. Not more than an inch of it came out of Donny's mouth before it was shoved back to the hilt. Donny never choked once, but I saw tiny tears form in the corners of his eyes and drip down his cheek. It was the only time I saw him cry.

Donny braced himself by placing his palms flat against the wall on either side of the hole and bobbed his head up and down like an epileptic porn star or one of the underage headbangers at Mabuhay Gardens. A low groan lilted upward from the other side of the wall. Donny tensed up, and I knew the man's warm sperm was on its way down into Donny's flat belly.

Did it shoot in discreet jets or did it dribble? What did it taste like? Was it pasty and white or thinner and translucent?

I spurted all over Donny's thigh while he jettisoned on the wall underneath the hole. Donny had some trouble backing off the fat tube still lodged in his throat. Finally, he gagged as he disengaged. I wiped his leg off with my towel and we strolled back to the lockers to dress in silence.

We exited through the last red door and deposited our keys in the little tray under the window. The smirking boy behind the glass had the same superior look stretched across his face, so Donny initiated a cinematic kiss with me before the little snot could turn away. I inhaled the foreign man's pungent crotch musk on Donny's lips. The light, nutty flavor of his ejaculate lingered on my tongue long afterward.

Donny loved the baths. He wanted to go all the time. And we did for a while.

Because I went with him, he felt he had carte blanche to fool around with anyone there. Of course, so did I.

I remember less of the fooling around than I do sitting in the dim, bluish light, watching a third-rate porn flick the third time through while I waited for Donny to finish. The newness had worn off and, over time, the desperation of many towel wearers became a more persistent memory than the occasional fantastic encounter.

We had a few threesomes, but somehow I always ended up lying down alone in a corner, trying to sleep in spite of the loud music that was piped in everywhere. I was always one of the youngest there and tired quickly of the pushy older men who were always after me.

After a couple of months of this, I told Donny I didn't want to go anymore. He shrugged and said okay.

Soon, he was going off to Oakland to visit his friend Jeff a couple times a week. He knew I didn't like Jeff much and would stay home.

° ° °

FUELED BY PUNK ROCK and Toni and Thom's post-hippie cynicism, Donny started to complain about his corporate office job. The tedium and the politics there were oppressive.

One afternoon Thom and I smoked a wicked joint with hash oil and a sprinkling of opium rolled into it. I abandoned Thom and cut off my long hair with a pair of drafting scissors in the bathroom, leaving a jagged fringe that I spiked up with some gel. Donny was amused but didn't feel inclined to follow suit. He kept his outdated pageboy shag.

I latched onto the idea that Donny should quit his job. That simplistic mantra kept coming out of my mouth: Life is short, do what you want to do.

° ° °

OUR NEIGHBOR DOUG had surgery to remove a colony of warts from his rectum. Afterward, he claimed to have lost all feeling there. He became reclusive. We seldom saw him except when he slipped out to work a shift at the restaurant. He didn't answer his door, though we knew he was home.

The few times we managed to get him to go out with us to the park or shopping, I noticed that the few sentences he spoke would trail off at the end. There were no more bitchy comments about the guys who passed us on the sidewalk.

There was no critique of women with fashion-impoverished wardrobes. He didn't remember things we told him from one encounter to the next, which became less and less frequent.

One afternoon I saw two guys carrying out Doug's sofa, the one he'd fought over with a shrill housewife in the back of a trendy antiques shop. That evening, he came by to see if we wanted his kitchen table and his record collection. He said he was leaving. He smiled as he told us he'd been in contact with them for a long time and now they would meet him in a location known only to him. They were coming in their spaceship.

We didn't laugh. Doug's omniscient smile sucked the humor out of us. He said they were going to take him far away. He no longer belonged here. We could go with him, but we had to leave very soon. We said nothing to fill the eerie silence that followed.

Two days later, I noticed his door was ajar. Doug's apartment was laid out as the reverse of ours. A tingling crept up my arms and across my chest as I walked through immaculate vacant rooms. There were no marks on the walls, no puffs of dust on the parquet floor. The windowpanes had no streaks. Filtered midday sunlight illumined the surface of every wall and appliance.

I opened kitchen cupboards and drawers, intent on finding any overlooked patch of grit. Everything was pristine. The bathroom was a sterile field. Even the old tile grout popped out like the painted teeth of a black-and-white B-movie star in close-up.

The bedroom closet smelled of bleach. I ran my fingertips along the top of a shelf above my head, dislodging a chalk-green rectangle of paper that fell to the floor. The face-up side had a cluster of lavender stars. The words *Space is the place* floated above them in a flabby psychedelic font. The other side had a phone number scrawled in pink ink, smeared and illegible from contact with the bleach.

o   o   o

THE FOUR OF US were sitting on the floor in Toni and Thom's apartment, listening to new records. Donny and Toni were arguing that age-old question about who gives better blowjobs, men or women? I suggested that we have a contest. Thom and I, both completely impartial, would be able to tell.

The contest, which Donny won hands down, literally, didn't last long. Ladies first, so Toni gave it a go. She had no idea what she was up against, as well as no technique or stamina. Donny vacuumed both of us dry in record time and then consoled the loser by eating her out. Thom was impressed. I expected nothing less from Donny.

I knew Donny was once married for five years to a nice Mormon girl from Salt Lake City. They had moved to the Bay Area and split up three years before I came along. Between her and me, Donny shared a couple of years with Stan.

o   o   o

ONE SATURDAY, Donny and I were walking near Dubose Triangle. A cheerful middle-aged man stopped us and introduced himself as Ray. He recognized Donny from some fashion layout in a local magazine and invited us to a party that was already in progress. Ray led us to his restored Victorian three-story house, all lavender and violet with deep-purple trim. A healthy crowd stood around, munching goodies in the frilly dining room.

Ray told us the real party was just getting started upstairs. We skipped the food and bounded up the creaking stairway. The ornate master bedroom was full of naked guys standing or laying on a row of mats spread out across the floor. Pillows of all sizes were within easy reach. Tiny plastic bottles of lubricant were plentiful.

The mood was jovial and shameless. Everyone was watching and egging on a bulky young man on his knees, sucking an older guy with a salt-and-pepper ponytail.

We took off our clothes and set them in a pile against the wall. Donny whispered that the guy standing by the bed couldn't keep his eyes off me. "And," he added, "he's got the boner to back it up."

"That's more up your alley," I suggested.

"Maybe so," he came back, "but he's not cruising me!"

Donny nudged me, and I walked over to the guy. He had haystack blond hair and was proud of his body. I was too nervous to say anything, but he immediately put his hand on my shoulder and said, "I'm Mike, g'day."

He was from Sydney on vacation. "You're fuckin' beautiful," he said, loud enough for the whole room to hear.

I blushed. I wanted to believe him. His tongue was in my mouth. I tasted whiskey and pot.

There was a lit joint in his hand. We blew a couple of large hits back and forth into each other's lungs and started kissing again.

A finger poked between my legs and found its target. I jerked my head to the side.

"Don't worry." Mike giggled. "That's just my cousin. He likes you, too."

A disorienting wave washed over my senses. Mike's pot was more powerful than I liked. I felt like a bag of Jell-O.

I was on my belly on the floor and tongues were licking me all over. I heard the farting sound of someone squeezing a lube bottle and a wet finger slipped into me.

"This is gonna be something," Mike muttered. I could hear the smile in his voice, and I loved his accent. Still, I panicked and struggled to free myself from his muscular embrace. Donny was the only one who'd been up my ass since I'd met him, and that wasn't often.

It didn't hurt much after the initial slow thrust. Mike wasn't in a hurry. His considerate pace brought me pleasure I hadn't known with Donny, but it was unbearable. I wanted to be swept away by the sensations, the way Donny could be completely caught up in being fucked when I was inside him, but I was having trouble remembering who was doing this to me.

Again, I struggled to push myself up and was held down. Someone was beside me on the floor. I turned and saw Donny's face inches from mine. I kissed him and he laughed into my mouth. For a few seconds I thought we were alone together, but the Aussie voice behind me said, "Here it comes!"

Donny kissed me harder and bit my tongue, breaking the skin. I tightened up all over and Mike gushed into me. I came a moment later as he slowed to a gentle rocking motion.

The sour smell of Mike's soaked armpits filled my nostrils, and I tried to pull myself up once again. I noticed Mike's cousin crouching behind Donny, who was now on his knees, his ass in the air.

Mike pulled out and rolled off me. Donny bent his head down again for more kisses. Mike's cousin murmured a monologue into Donny's butt, and Donny jerked himself off.

The smell of Mike's sweat had broken whatever spell I'd been under. I was staring at Mike's cousin as he licked his own juice off Donny's calves, nodding to whatever Mike was telling me as he rubbed my shoulder, but my thoughts raced in little boomerang trajectories, somewhere far from this orgy.

I stood up when I realized Mike was telling jokes and everyone in the room was laughing at them, even those who were still fully frolicking. Donny helped me dress. I had to get out of there.

o   o   o

A FEW MONTHS LATER, Donny brought home a wad of severance pay and a couple plane tickets to London. Off we went to stay with a schoolteacher friend of an English guy Donny knew from somewhere.

Nigel lived in South London. It was a big house in a row of big houses surrounded by rows of other big houses, all smashed against one another. Most of the bedrooms were rented out to young gay blokes who were working shit jobs or unemployed. Nigel was a bit of a housemother.

Donny managed to score some killer pot hours after we'd arrived. Everyone in the house was stoned for the next two weeks. Nigel blasted his old Donovan LPs and invited more local young men over for tea and bickies. We assembled quite a list of things to do after talking to them.

We hit the recommended bars and downed legally meas-ured gin and tonics, which were much weaker than the cock-tails we were used to in U.S. bars. The punks here were fueled by a deep-seated disillusionment with everything around them. It seemed that a majority of American punks were often spoiled brats who could afford to buy their ripped-up fashion accessories from a boutique.

Yes, the Brits had Vivienne Westwood, but most of the punks we saw were twelve to fifteen years old and wore mangled thrift-store clothing they'd altered themselves. This surprised us. The punks in San Francisco were anywhere from sixteen to forty and blended in with the city's enduring nonconformist flavor.

We told people at clubs that we were from a punk zine in San Francisco. It wasn't hard to get the fans of a band to interact with us. Donny photographed them while I pretended to record their answers to questions on a broken tape recorder of Nigel's. I don't know why they believed us. Perhaps they didn't and just didn't care. Maybe they were higher than we were.

We saw many of the big-name punk bands perform during the month we were there. Wire's *Pink Flag* was just out. They were right to point. Every song lasted less than a minute.

On the train to Windsor to see the famous castle, I had Donny every which way in our compartment between stops on the train. We were pleased with ourselves and left a greasy mess on the seats. Queen Elizabeth II was staying at the castle that day, and all the blinds were drawn on the second floor. We expanded our shenanigans on the train back and were caught with our trousers down by a train employee who made us feel like shit while feigning indifference. As soon as he was in the next car, we were back at it.

We took many train trips from London to the surrounding areas. Finally, I insisted on seeing Stonehenge.

A few other brave adventurers were on the bus that took us the last ten miles in the grayish countryside. We were allowed inside the fence that surrounds Stonehenge and protects it from the graffiti monsters and rock chippers. This was a rare thing. The guides must've felt like we deserved something for our efforts on such a dark drizzly day.

I was disappointed at first. I expected the stones to tower over us, to dwarf us into respect for the miracle of the ancient ways by their enormousness alone. But compared to modern urban architecture, they were dwarf-sized.

As I sat on one of the stones that was lying on its side, Donny and the other tourists were silent. For a few moments they were all out of sight on the other side of the circle. I took many slides with my crappy Instamatic camera, making sure no one was in them and that the fence wasn't visible.

I considered what kind of minds had felt it necessary to orchestrate the collection of these stones into some kind of monument or temple. It took lifetimes of dedication to gather the stones and assemble them. Although there are many theories of why Stonehenge was created, there has never been a convincing conclusion, but it is certain that the necessity for it to exist lasted centuries, long enough to complete most of the gargantuan task.

We stayed the night at the Salsbury Inn. It was a grand old hotel. We had some beef roast and Yorkshire pudding for dinner in the stuffy dining room. I didn't take much to the overdone meat, but Donny wolfed it down.

Our room had an old radio built into the wall over the bed. The volume and channel selection knobs didn't work. When we turned it on, caustic punk music rattled the tinny speaker. We left it on and passed out fully dressed, holding on to each other on the lumpy mattress.

The next day we visited the cloisters of the cathedral in Salsbury. Its spire is the tallest in England. The rest of the day, we strolled around in Bath, visiting the famous St. George's baths there. Once used by royalty, they had fallen into disrepair. I envisioned kings and princes frolicking with one another there, away from the prying eyes of their families.

I lingered at the rose garden by the Avon River. Each bush had a metal plate on a stand in front of it delineating the type of rose on it, written in flowery scripted English and in braille. I couldn't resist running my fingers over the brass bumps as I inhaled the few winter blooms with eyes closed.

Later that night, back at Nigel's, I awoke out of sound sleep. I was alone in bed. I fumbled my way downstairs in the dark, led forward by the pervasive odor of pot. I flicked on the kitchen light and found Keith, the youngest lad in the house, sitting on a kitchen chair with his head thrown back, blinking at the sudden illumination. The table had a half-eaten sandwich on it and a joint burning in an ashtray. Donny was on the dirty linoleum between the boy's legs, gorging himself on Keith's uncut cock.

Keith squinted at me and said, "Hehhhhhhhhh." Donny turned an eye in my direction, but kept up the rhythm.

Keith looked down at Donny. He said, "Nuhhhhhhhh." I turned the light off and went back upstairs. Clearly, Donny did love that overcooked English meat.

An hour later, yelling at each other, we woke up everyone in the house. I don't remember what we said, but I know that I was angrier than I'd ever been with him. Did I feel betrayed by his little infidelity? Did I wish I was the one that had had it off with the skuzzy little bugger? Was I embarrassed because everyone in the house would know Donny was a slut and that we weren't exclusive? Or was it a combination of all of these things totaling up to the feeling that I was losing control of what I thought should be happening in this relationship, a relationship whose boundaries we had never once discussed with each other?

I had several ideas coexisting in my mind of what I thought should be going on with Donny. I wanted a special sexual relationship with him, some kind of exclusive thing, but I also enjoyed the same freedoms he did with other people, though to a lesser extent. Since neither of us directly verbalized what we wanted, it was unclear to both of us where we were in agreement, not only with each other but within ourselves.

The next day on the train to Wales, I had a couple of gin and tonics. Donny was surprised to see me drink in the early morning. I was silent. The rushing landscape outside the train window exhilarated me, almost as if those spindly trees were scraping the sadness and anger away as they passed through my reflection. I thought of how good it was to slapfuck Donny's butt after the verbal part of our fight was over. Both of us had lost that argument, but we'd had a good time once we'd moved beyond words. He sure didn't complain.

By the time we were walking among a muster of peacocks at the Cardiff Castle, I was determined not to sulk any more on this trip. I would distract myself with pot and booze and experience as much as I could while we were here in the UK.

o o o

BACK HOME in San Francisco, I decided to continue studying music. In spite of my punk/new wave obsession, my mind still longed for the complexity of the classics. I had taken piano lessons for twelve years. Donny was supportive after I played some Chopin preludes for him at a friend's house.

I bought a used upright for eight hundred dollars and found a teacher through a music school. He invited me to his apartment so we could see if we liked the idea of working together.

Micah was in his late thirties and kept in shape with a vigorous schedule of playing tennis and swimming laps. He further impressed me by playing a few of my favorite pieces from memory. Seconds later, he leapt up from the piano bench, grasped my hands in his, and said, "Schumann."

He said I had large hands and could stretch to handle the sweeping chords in Robert Schumann's scores. We began immediately.

Micah's enthusiasm for Schumann became mine, and I read everything I could about his life and his music. I struggled every day to master the enormous difficulties of playing these intricate pieces.

I had my lessons once a week, first at Micah's apartment and then later at the glitzy apartment of his wealthy boyfriend. Michael's place was chock-full of Jasper Johns's and Robert Rauschenberg's lithographs, hung across from one another in the living room. Except for the art, everything was radiant white. I didn't dare to sit down anywhere. The Steinway grand was on an elevated floor near a wall of glass that looked out over the city skyline.

I preferred the frowsy spirit of Micah's place with its uneven stacks of music scores under the chairs and sprawling open closets piled high with crumpled clothes and banged-up cardboard boxes. It smelled like someone lived there.

Micah didn't want to admit that Michael was his sugar daddy, though I reminded him about it sometimes. He would grind his teeth and say that this was a ridiculous idea. I could sense the rumblings of discontent, like a bad case of heartburn after eating raw onions, recurring at regular intervals. He couldn't stand the idea of being owned, the idea of being a handsome man in his prime, somewhere close to forty, a favored student of many famous pianists, not famous himself yet capable of cranking out the piano's greatest hits of all time at dinner parties. And there he was, all bought and paid for by this older, sexy American who oozed old family money.

I made the mistake of confiding to him that Donny was cheating on me. I was sure of it. Micah thought Donny was ignorant and didn't care about me. He told me I should leave him. But I defended him every time and refused to see that as an option.

He gave up after a while, and we concentrated on the music. It was the way we expressed our mutual passion for something outside ourselves. He praised my playing, and I tried ever harder to make Schumann come alive through my hands.

o   o   o

FOR A TIME, Donny talked nonstop about opening a punk boutique called BRATZ. He'd registered the name and had some tacky T-shirts made. Nothing came of it.

Speculative realtors from China bought our building and jacked up the rent. We left Toni and Thom behind and moved across town to 16th Street, with a view of Mission Dolores across the street, famous for hosting an unsettling scene in Hitchcock's peerless masterwork, *Vertigo*.

Donny splurged and a water bed was delivered to our new apartment. We put the heavy oak frame together and watched the rubber sack swell up with water. We were in such a rush to test it out that we didn't fill it to capacity. We smoked a joint and started humping away. I discovered that by tucking my feet between the mattress and the frame, I had a bit more control over the liquid motions of the bed's surface.

The needle skidded across the Santana album playing on the turntable. Everything started rattling around us.

"Earthquake," Donny yelped and plopped me out of his ass.

We both had in mind to reach the door frame, but a mini-tsunami swept through the mattress. By the time we maneuvered our way out of it and stood in the doorway, the earthquake had passed. We laughed and hugged each other for a minute before starting up again on the bed.

o   o   o

DONNY FOUND A JOB managing a café in Sausalito. He hired me a few weeks later. I learned how to make authentic Italian cappuccinos and caffe lattes from the owner. I mastered the subtleties of steaming milk and was able to make multilayered coffees in slender glasses that made them look like parfaits.

On weekends, the line of tourists went out the front door all day. Buzzed on espresso, we'd grin while insulting them. We excelled at caffeine-based sarcasm.

On weekdays, local artists would stop by. Photographers, painters, and pop stars made the occasional visit. An exhausted Van Morrison would come in midday for a grande. He sugared and downed it in a minute, but it had no effect on his bitter mood.

I did a few snorts of coke with another popular singer in the ladies' room. Her band's last album was played nonstop on the radio for a whole year right after Donny and I met. Witchy and weary, she held a miniature spoonful of the stuff under my nose every time I started to ask her a question. She scooped it out of an antique jade perfume bottle. I found her chatty, batty, remote, and spoiled. She probably thought the same of me.

For several weeks, a twitchy guy with a scraggly, graying beard came in late and sat scribbling on a pad, downing cheap white wine and double espressos. Years later, I saw a photograph of the man on a website. He was Philip K. Dick, writer of many sci-fi novels I had greedily devoured years before he was my customer.

Donny spent time with various customers, both at the café and elsewhere. For more than a year we had a great time making friends and establishing ourselves in the center of the café life. We still went to concerts with Toni and Thom.

While channeling Andy Warhol one Saturday afternoon, we covered everything in our apartment with aluminum foil and called everyone we knew to come over for a party. More than a hundred people showed up, and it lasted well into Sunday afternoon. We found four leather dykes floating in our waterbed at the end of it all. The spikes from a collar had punctured the mattress. After cleaning up that mess, we happily bought a waterless bed.

o o o

TWO IRANIAN SISTERS began to frequent the café. They captured Donny's attention and held it. Not only cousins of the infamous and wealthy Shah, they were the kind of women that men became idiots over in public places.

Venus was addicted to substances. She didn't talk much. I think she was embarrassed about her accent, but perhaps she had little to say. She had a high-class call girl's wardrobe. Most days she was blond.

Honey had a less radical look, but she was the talker. She had Donny's head filled up right away. She gave him expensive drugs, though she didn't seem to have a drug problem. She knew how to get what she wanted. I'm sure both sisters had been educated in the best schools. I never saw them wear the same outfits twice.

Soon Donny was with Honey whenever I was working and he wasn't. Café gossip said they were having one heck of a wild affair, but I didn't want to listen to that. After all, I was still getting a surprising amount of action in the sack with Donny.

When he did confess to me that the rumors of Honey and him were true and that he intended to continue, his words were like quick-setting cement poured into my brain, I stopped listening.

Toni and Thom suggested I leave him. They were furious. It would have been a wise decision, but I didn't know how to leave him. I had never lived by myself or counted on myself to function in the world. I was dependent on Donny in many ways, some I didn't know about yet. He was my new family.

He continued with her in the café and elsewhere as if nothing had changed, while I sulked into depression. Though I was still working for Donny, we didn't work the same shifts.

I quit smoking pot. It was making me anxious and lethargic. I went back to reading books and continued practicing the piano for hours a day.

I never knew if Donny would be home. We avoided each other for the most part but managed to go at it quite savagely in bed a couple of times a week, the last vestige of our failed communication. It was my desperate attempt to keep him coming back home and his ambivalent appeasement for the affair with Honey.

Meanwhile, Venus, the headless blond beauty was looking burned-out. She stopped coming around. Honey stopped coming in, too. They had left the country.

Now Donny was depressed, too. He came home every day for a week. It was evident that there was little left between us. The skeletal mechanism of our convenient living situation was grinding down.

Three months later, I came home to a living room full of boxes. Donny had packed most of his belongings and said he was looking for a place to live. He couldn't live here anymore. He was having a new affair with one of the girls I worked with at the café. She was no Honey, but she was pregnant with Donny's child. They were planning to get married in a few months. I considered ramming our serrated bread knife through his head.

The next month was the worst. He had trouble finding a place to live, but he wasn't around the apartment. I had to pass those boxes every time I went to the kitchen.

I started going out to the bars to do whatever with whoever was available. This drunken barrage of sexual encounters had little of the rapture I'd known when I was a few years younger and exploring the wonder of my ability to have carnal pleasure and inspire similar sensations in others.

The last night Donny was at the apartment, now emptied of his belongings, I demanded that he let me fuck him. By the end of it, I was screaming at him about his lies and infidelities. He listened patiently to what I should've made an issue of two years before this. The next morning I realized that I'd given him both gonorrhea and crabs that night.

A week later, the café owner fired him. Nicky, the tough, Sicilian son-in-law of the owner, tossed Donny right out of the place on his ass when he started to mouth off at Papa. His new fiancée stomped right out of her job the same night.

∘ ∘ ∘

THE WEEK DONNY LEFT, Micah was the first to console me. I didn't go into much detail with him. He was pleased that Donny was no longer with me.

When I stumbled in the same difficult passage for the third time, he grabbed my jaw and turned my face to his. He paused a few seconds and kissed me.

Although aggressive with his tongue and his hands in the beginning, Micah quickly lost his momentum and floundered, perhaps hobbled by some disabling guilt about what men like to do with each other, or the image of Michael's grinning face flashed into his head for a minute.

I, however, had no inhibitions whatsoever. Since visiting the clap clinic, I had kept to myself, even though two guys gave me their phone numbers while we were waiting to get our paper cups full of pills.

Micah fumbled with his clothes. I was already stripped and pushing him down on his bed. His jockeys were still around his knees, so I pressed my knee between his to pin him. Without ceremony and a generous glob of spittle, I pressed into him. He writhed beneath me, begging me to go slower. He was physically stronger than I was, but I had the advantage of confidence and experience.

I chewed on his ear and muffled him with my hand. His resistance faded as I inched into him. I knew it was hurting him initially, but I went ahead and gave him something a dead Romantic composer couldn't and his aging sugar daddy probably had no interest in doing.

His sweat was heavy as I licked the salt off his hairy neck. I could tell he wasn't used to having much up his bum, so I squirted into him as soon as he creamed up the bedspread. Over and over he croaked, "Gingie, Gingie, Gingie."

o o o

I DIDN'T HAVE TO look hard for a roommate. As soon as Donny moved out, Kirk, a neighbor I barely knew, moved in from upstairs. He didn't want to live with his boyfriend anymore.

Kirk painted his room turd brown and canary yellow with steel-gray trim. He was an art student. With anarchistic flair, he indulged in an extreme mode of living.

We went out together to exhibitions, films, parties, and clubs. We discovered Bombay martinis, very dry, up, with a twist.

Kirk brought to me an awareness of the currents of contemporary art. He checked out dozens of books about avant-garde artists from his school library. I read every book that came into our apartment. I became as promiscuous in my reading as I was with sexual partners.

I was stunned by John Cage's "Silence" and found myself more connected to the noise of the traffic outside my window than to the Beethoven sonata I was memorizing. I questioned my compartmentalized interest in the art, music, and literature of the past. Modern radical art was so vital, so much about being alive this moment, and in many ways geared more toward having good ideas than toward a solid traditional technique.

o o o

MICAH WAS EDGY now when I came for my lessons. He would slide close to me as usual. His hand would snake over to my leg and then jerk back after a few seconds of contact. He was never shy about touching me before we'd done it.

He invited me to come with him to the wine country to spend the weekend at Michael's summerhouse. He said it had one of the largest swimming pools in the neighborhood. Michael was out of the country. I agreed to go with him.

The trip to Napa was not what I expected. It certainly was not what Micah expected, either. We had a fight about something trivial on the ride up.

Once there, I swam nude in the big pool. Micah watched every move I made. And I watched him watching me.

He cooked. I drank too much wine with dinner. We slept in the same bed without touching.

We didn't speak on the way back in his brand-new compact car. Michael had bought it for him the day he left on his trip. Between my legs, I gouged a hole in the synthetic seat cover with a pencil.

When I showed up for the next lesson, he answered the door with his body covered in lather. He said he'd be back in a minute after he washed off.

He came back draped in a fluffy towel, no doubt part of a gift set from Michael, dark hairs curling up over the edges of the stark whiteness of the towel. His legs were sturdy from all the tennis, but I saw the softness Michael would always exploit in him, to keep him as a precious object. I didn't know how to say it, but I thought he still had time to turn things around.

Hoarsely, he asked me if I had given him crabs. I burst out laughing. I told him I'd had them a couple of times in the past but not now. I would know.

He asked again with a tone that was more implicating than inquiring. I said no again and said he must be fooling around with other guys.

He cleared his throat, looked down at the floor, and went back into his bedroom to dress. I sat down at the piano. I had been working for months on "Fantasiestücke" by Schumann. As I played one of the most troublesome passages, he began walking back and forth in a short line behind me.

When I was nearly finished, he bent down and said to the back of my head, very slowly, "You will never be good enough to play this music. You don't have it in you. That fifteen-year-old girl from Saint Petersburg who started with me two months ago can play this right now ten times better than you will ever play it. You don't work hard enough. You don't perform in public well. You should stop wasting your time."

I knew he was right, even if what prompted him to say this was not right. I never had another piano lesson. Eventually, I sold the piano to a young man my age. He was elated that his eight-year-old daughter was going to take lessons.

o   o   o

DONNY AND HIS FIANCÉE started to come regularly into the café during my shift. They giggled and held hands while drinking their coffee.

I started to lose weight, but I needed that job. I was just making ends meet. My rooms in the apartment were empty except for the piano, a stereo, my books and records, and the floor-to-ceiling yellowing Victorian lace curtains that were hanging in the bay window when we moved there.

I wasn't sleeping much. I read book after book, hoping to drive the black thoughts away that repeated in vicious patterns whenever I relaxed. Unreasonable fears of hell crept back from childhood into my dreams. I knew I could never return to the religious world of my upbringing, no matter what happened.

Eventually, I swallowed a full bottle of heavy-duty tranquilizers that Donny had left behind in the medicine cabinet. I washed them down with vodka, puked them up into the toilet ten minutes later, and headed out to the bars.

Outside the apartment, I found a batch of finger paintings swirling around my feet in little whirlwinds. I collected them and brought them indoors. Kirk and I laid them out on the kitchen floor. They had brightly colored human forms, sunny skies and puffy clouds, friendly dogs, and tables heaped with food. Each one was signed *Giselle* in large purple letters.

We tacked them up all around us on the kitchen walls. We invited our friends over that night for Giselle's opening exhibition. It was a great success, except that Giselle did not attend. We wished we had known where she lived.

About four a.m., the last guests left and Kirk went with them, bombed to smithereens and tempted by the prospects of another party. I knew I would be cleaning up everything with a hangover the next day.

When I saw Kirk again, pale and hands trembling, he said, "Wow, that exhibition party was something last night."

"Kirk, you can't be serious," I replied.

"Yeah, it really was. You sure cleaned it up fast."

"Kirk, that was three days ago!"

He didn't believe me until I showed him the newspaper. He shrugged and went back to bed.

After his lost weekend, I drank little booze. I'd nurse a beer or two, but I didn't want to become an alcoholic. I knew now that Kirk was out of control.

After a few weeks completely sober, I expected my sex drive to dwindle. I was wrong. In fact, I found it easier to pick up guys, not that it was ever difficult in a city like San Francisco. But I was bolder now. There were few unrewarding encounters.

o o o

I WAS AT Headquarters after the bars had closed. Public Image ripped through damaged speakers into the dark room.

Kirk had just headed out the door with a coked-up, middle-aged guy who lived up on Twin Peaks. I was about to leave myself, when the lead singer of a local punk band strode into the place. I had his picture at home on the cover of an underground music magazine.

He ordered a beer and walked right up to me. He knew I knew who he was. He wanted to go home with me if I had a place to go. There must have been no doubt in his mind that I would take him with me.

We didn't say much on the way to my apartment. I thought he might change his mind, but he came up with me, took off his clothes, and headed for the bathroom with his little black satchel.

A minute later he came out with a syringe and asked me for a spoon. Did I want to do some heroin with him?

I didn't. I'd had my one mind-bending LSD adventure, and I thought I should leave it at that. Besides, I'd heard such nasty things about junkies.

I watched him prepare for his injection. He didn't seem to notice that I was in the room with him once he'd begun. I would've told him he couldn't shoot up in my place, but I thought there would be a chance for sex if I let him. His floppy penis had great potential, and his runt of an ass was charming.

Of course, as soon as he was zooming around inside his pretty head, I might've been a pillow or a beanbag chair. He was useless to me now and losing what little color his skin had. Surely, he'd never seen the sun except on TV.

At one point he turned so bluish, I thought he was going to pass out or drop dead, but he just lay there on the floor, humming to himself. I imagined his shrunken corpse in the

Dumpster out back. He was more and more cadaver-like. The limp creature at my feet bore little resemblance to the punk god I had seen onstage a year ago or even an hour and a half before at Headquarters.

I waited around a few more minutes and went to bed. When I fell asleep, he was sitting on the floor six feet away from me, holding his pants over his face, mumbling to himself.

He woke me up and asked me to help him shoot up again. I told him he had to leave. I wanted to sleep and was convinced he wouldn't survive another spike. I dressed him the best I could without his cooperation.

Holding him in front of me by his bony shoulders, I walked him down the two flights of stairs to the sidewalk. As soon as I shut the metal gate with him on the other side of it, he sat down on the bottom step and sagged back against the flaking gray diamond pattern.

Hours later, when I looked out the window, he was gone. I went down to check the mail, and there on the oil-stained concrete were his scuffed-up shoes, one black, one brown, similar but not the same style.

Two months later I bought his band's new album. He looked better than ever on the back cover. There was no trace of the beached jellyfish I'd spent a few hours babysitting.

o   o   o

THE PHONE RANG on a rainy afternoon while I was submerged in a Yukio Mishima novel, perhaps *Forbidden Colors* or *Runaway Horses*. In those days, I could read most of a prolific author's works in the course of a few months.

It was Honey, calling from Paris. She wanted to apologize for the way she had behaved with Donny and for hurting me. I told her I wasn't angry with her. If she hadn't started up with him, it would've been someone else, and, in fact, it was.

She said she was happy. She had just married the prince of some tiny country I didn't know existed. She rambled on about him for a while and then hung up abruptly, never having asked me a single question about how I was doing.

○   ○   ○

I PLAYED A LOT of pinball at the Stud bar. It was a good way to be out in public but not in the thick of things.

One night, I went home with a quiet, friendly pinball ace after he'd let me win a few games. He lived in a big apartment building on one of the top floors.

He rushed me into the bedroom, took off his shoes, pants, and T-shirt, and from a dresser drawer pulled out and handed me a pair of handcuffs. I felt the cold metal in my hands and looked at him, puzzled. I knew I wasn't going to wear them.

I told him so and added that I didn't know him well enough. He laughed and told me to cuff him to the brass bars at the head of his bed. He knelt in the middle of the bed and put his hands through the bars.

He was still wearing a wife-beater. Threadbare Jockey briefs hung loosely over his posterior, yellowish from repeated washings. I could see pink flesh through the holes in the bottoms of his once-black socks.

He shivered when I touched him. He bent forward and put his head on the pillows. This pushed his backside toward me as I stood by the side of the bed.

He whispered that I should look under the bed. There I found a dented cardboard box with lengths of clothesline, some small whips, and an assortment of paddles, dildos, and some items I didn't recognize.

I wanted to look through the box carefully and examine each object, hold it in my hands, and envision its exact use, but he was pleading to be hit. He rasped on about how he had first seen me playing pinball and was attracted to me. That made me smile. I knew that I could be quite physically innovative with the pinball machine. I'd involve my whole body, coaxing every ball into giving me the most points possible.

I selected a wooden spoon, one of the heavier ones, traditionally used for stirring big pots of thickening stew. I tapped his butt with it. He became still, silent. I hit him a few more times, harder. He had a meaty ass. I pulled down his drawers and saw red flaking patches of skin on his cheeks. I recognized it as eczema, yet I reacted inwardly as though it were leprosy. I felt as if I'd been persuaded by a seasoned con man to purchase inferior goods at the store. It wasn't the first time I had this feeling, and it would not be the last.

"You have to make it hurt," he said, and moved his backside as close to me as his situation allowed. The whining, impatient tone prodded me, and I made it hurt.

I hit him hard enough to make him yelp, though he remained frozen, an unlikely statue in his awkward position. I sensed him challenging me to act in a way I had never before dared to act.

I hit him a few times, harder, testing him, making him yelp. It wasn't my apartment, and I wanted him to make some noise.

A wave of intensity washed over me, much like the feelings that could arise when I was in the middle of fucking someone hard, that unstoppable gush of chemicals in the brain that push toward the impending climax. This was stronger, and I was uncertain of where a wave of this magnitude might carry me. An unvoiced rage pulsed in my temples, and I started smacking the fleshiest parts of both his cheeks with a strength I had at first not decided to use. I answered his cries with renewed vigor and turned his ass purple in minutes.

Through his tears, I heard a new kind of begging. He wanted me to stop. The raspy, whining character of his voice was gone. It was a request, not a directive.

Eventually, I lightened up, but I took my time before I delivered a last brutal *thwack*. He was shaking and shivering in his own sweat, while I became utterly calm for a few moments, until I heard the spoon land on the parquet floor. I ran my hands over the bedsheets, looking for the key so I could unlock the cuffs.

I was afraid to touch him. I wanted to run out of the room, through his front door, and never look back.

"You didn't stop when I asked you to," he mumbled. He sobbed as I released him from the brass bars. I wondered if I should apologize to him, not sure of how all this had happened.

"I like that about you. You can come back anytime," he continued. "Do anything you want to me."

He clenched the brass bars tighter and remained in his prostrate position. He looked at me with bloodshot eyes that sparkled with hope. His face was radiant, his words heavy with gratitude for what he had wrested out of me just minutes ago.

I hurried home, mind racing, heart pounding. How could something so powerful and sexual come to pass between us when neither one of us had even ejaculated? I hadn't removed my clothes. Before that night, I'd always thought that successful sex had to result in an orgasm (my orgasm specifically, but even better if my partner had one, too). And the ultimate sexual act had to involve a physical merging. Moving inside another had until then been a literal concept.

o   o   o

THE SAME WAY my views about art and life in general were changing, so my sexual outlook began to change, to shift into areas I had never dared to look at closely. I had no confidence in whatever mythical love I had hoped to find through a relationship with Donny. For me, no simple notion of the interconnectedness between love and sex would exist again. Old ideals seemed shriveled and empty, something like the shell of dead skin a dragonfly nymph leaves behind after it leaves the water for the last time and its new unfolding wings fill and harden with fluid. It still has the same body, the same shape, but it moves through the world differently because it has wings.

I began searching for new ways to interact with sexual partners and the world at large. And, of course, I found them.

Confessions
of a Spankaholic

RACHEL KRAMER BUSSEL

I DON'T REMEMBER who the first person to spank
me was, but I can tell you I liked it almost from the start.
Something about having a firm hand land a resounding whack
against my upturned ass while I shuddered in equal parts pain
and pleasure made me want more right away. I longed to get
spanked by anyone and everyone but took my time observing
and mentally taking notes. I knew I was on my way to becoming a spankaholic, but wasn't sure just how far I wanted to go
with it. Here are some stories from my spanking files, the highlights of my memories of many pretty hands, asses, and
whacks that left more than a momentary mark on my skin.

In my early twenties, well before I really became a spanking
aficionado, I witnessed and was part of one of the hottest
spankings I've ever seen before or since. I'd brought a beautiful tall, thin, curly-haired girl with a mouthwatering accent,
the kind who could say any word and make it sound like a
come-on, with me to an all-female play party. We'd had one

date where we wound up making out on the dance floor of a local bar, and I hoped we'd have more dates in the future. Still, I wasn't really sure where we stood. I was willing to see where the night would take us. As we got off the elevator and entered the dungeon—with its reception desk masking, for the moment, the kinky accoutrements that lay within—we were greeted by women in corsets, chains, hobble skirts, leather, and uniforms.

We each saw people we wanted to talk to, so we separated in the small space to chat and explore. A friend and I made our way into one room where there was a pulley, and she experimented with it, asking me to raise her up in the air. Then I tried it but felt too out of control with my feet off the ground. We wound our way back to the snack room, where we proceeded to catch up, when my date came running into the room. "Tina's going to spank me," she said breathlessly, her face lit up. "I wanted to let you know, in case you want to watch."

Of course I did! Tina was a sexy butch who easily caught the attention of almost every woman she passed. I rushed back into the room I'd come from earlier to find an audience of seated kinky dykes looking on as my date clambered up onto a padded bench and spread herself out facedown. She pushed her jeans and panties down to her knees, her most prominent feature now bared for all to see. I approached and was granted permission by Tina to sit and watch as my date got the spanking of a lifetime.

Somehow, even though I wasn't the one delivering the smacks, I felt like I was. I learned a lot from watching Tina, who went about spanking my date's small but perfectly proportioned ass with total concentration. She was into it, but she didn't waste words and seemed extremely focused, watching where each slap landed in order to cover every inch of my girl's ass. At one point, when her skin had gone from tan to bright pink, verging on red, Tina motioned for me to touch her skin, and I did, aware that we had a roomful of women watching our every move. Then Tina asked my date, who I was beginning to realize was probably no longer solely "my" date, if she wanted to get fucked. "Yes, please," was her response, and again, Tina very ritualistically slipped on a glove and proceeded to sink two fingers into her pussy.

I don't know if I was holding my breath, but I know my eyes were glued to the sight in front of me. I wasn't sure if I was jealous of the treatment my date was getting or that Tina was giving—I wasn't sure what to think. But I knew that I was overwhelmingly turned on and grateful to be a part of their games. I learned that night how to take spanking seriously and how to be stern but kind, how to take something that could be a public spectacle and make it highly personal. I learned how to say a lot using just my hands, and even though my date left that evening with Tina, I felt as though I'd gotten more than my fair share of pleasure from her company.

o   o   o

ONE MEMORABLE spanking session occurred early on in my spanking career, with a woman who shared my name. She was a little larger than me, with a voice and personality to match, and scared me slightly; she had so much kinky experience, it was like she came with a pedigree, while I was practically a spanking virgin. And yet, even though we came from different countries (she was British but visited New York every few months), we shared not just the same name but enough similarities to set me at ease. If they say kissing someone of the same sex is like kissing yourself, being with a lover who shares your name is an even more profoundly odd, almost narcissistic, experience. But back then, in my early twenties, I needed lovers who could show me the ropes, so to speak, who could teach and show me new things, who could impress me with their dexterity.

Rachel was sweet, buying me a pair of shiny red shoes that even eight years later still hold pride of place in my closet, but she was also a little intimidating with her take-charge attitude. This was an awe-inspiring combination to a newbie like me, not because of anything she did so much as because I had never met anyone quite like her. Between her British accent and sweeping gestures, she was light years ahead of me in the cool department, like she could run New York with the back of her hand if she'd wanted to. I was a bit shocked that of all the women around us at the play party where we met, almost all of whom had more experience giving and taking beatings, floggings, whippings, and more, she wanted to talk to me. Still, she took a shine to me, and we made plans to meet up again while she was staying in town at a friend's house.

I was in law school at that time, a fixed, complex, confusing world in which I was becoming increasingly lost. I was out of my league and hadn't really made any friends, let alone found people to date. Most were settled down and I was only twenty-two, too young to be thinking along those lines. So meeting Rachel and the other kinky women I encountered in the surprisingly accessible local kink scene was a revelation. Here were women who didn't play by the usual rules; instead, they had their own codes, cues, and rituals that I wanted to be part of.

I kept taking one step forward into that world, then one back. I knew I wanted to try things, I just didn't know how far I wanted to go. I saw and heard about cutting, kicking, branding, wax and fire play, violet wands, spanking, caning, mistresses and slaves. I saw small dungeons tucked away on unsuspecting streets, and tried to fashion my decidedly vanilla wardrobe into something worthy of being there among the leather-and-latex-clad. But most of all, I tried to get over myself and my fears, to walk through that invisible wall separating them from me, leaping over the separation from fantasy to reality. I had to watch for a long time, though, before I truly understood the difference, especially when it came to spanking.

If I'd been intimidated by the scene at the play party, this apartment certainly kicked my nervous excitement into overdrive. The entire wall of her friend's very masculine bedroom was covered with intense-looking knives and other instruments of torture. I could practically hear the handcuffs jangling, and wondered which ones, if any, Rachel wanted to use on me. I felt the urge to run but an equally compelling urge to stay.

I spread myself across her lap, feeling almost as though I needed to pinch myself to believe that I, a formerly innocent yet intellectually curious law student, was actually baring her pale, white ass to be slapped by a woman with strong hands and a quick tongue. She laid into me from the get-go, causing me to cry out. I kicked my legs and knew I was getting turned on, but a part of me held back. I waited to see how much it would sting, and the answer was *a lot*. While I'd thought I was ready, I kept opening my mouth to object, so nervous about whether my body could handle the assault it both wanted and rejected, that I eventually, at the first slap that seemed to go too far, called the whole thing off. I was disappointed with myself, knowing that plenty of players could and did take so much more, but I knew the timing wasn't quite right for me to plunge butt-first into this magical world.

I realized that I needed to trust myself and my partner, to truly relax one hundred percent if I was actually going to enjoy my spankings, to let the pleasure in along with the pain. Too much fearfulness made my body stiff and made me unable to let go and get into that other world where pleasure and pain mix and mingle, stirring together to become something new and potent. It would take a few more years before I really got my spanking mojo going.

∘ ∘ ∘

ANOTHER WOMAN who helped induct me into the world of spanking a few years down the road was Natalie. I met her at a play party while on vacation in San Francisco, and she immediately intrigued me. I walked into a roomful of strangers, feeling totally out of place, especially because everyone seemed to know one another at this semiregular gathering of perverts and open-minded sex folk. I was there as the date of someone somewhat well known in that community. I clung to his arm at the beginning, ready to bury my face in his neck, should I need him for support or want to escape. But everyone there was incredibly welcoming to me, and by the end of the night I felt like a real part of their scene, even though most of them I'd never see again.

Natalie caught my eye right away. She was tough but had a sweet, girlish laugh, the giggling human equivalent of cinnamon bubble gum, sugary but with a hint of spice. She had blond hair and blue eyes, but other than that was the farthest thing from traditional you could get. I felt as though I'd stumbled into some fantasyland and couldn't keep my eyes off her. Still, I couldn't muster up the courage to talk to her beyond our initial conversation, which was filled with harmless talk about how long I was staying and what we each did for a living. Venturing into pervtalk with her seemed like too big a leap.

I went back to my date and asked him about Natalie, confiding in him what I wanted Natalie to do to me. "She's known as a pretty hardcore bottom around town," he said, giving me the impression that there'd never be anything between us. I made every excuse I could think of to talk to her at the party, playing with her golden hair, admiring her black bikini adorned with orange flames, and matching shoes. Though I'd never done anything like it before, I saw myself kneeling down before Natalie and kissing her feet, doing anything to make her smile and pet my head. (Little did I know I'd wind up huddled under blankets with her in her bed only a year later while on another visit to San Francisco, talking her ear off as we cozied together against the early-morning chill.) Then I proceeded to let my date spank me the way he'd been doing since we first got together, in front of a roomful of strangers, though most of them were too busy with their own couplings to really pay much attention to us.

It wasn't until I'd returned to the East Coast that I got an e-mail from Natalie that made me literally squeal with glee. I jumped up from my desk at my day job, then realized there was nobody there with whom I could share the fact that she'd said I was the only one at that play party she'd been interested in playing with. I also learned that she was actually a wicked top *and* that she was coming to New York. I had to keep my delight to myself, save for the huge grin I couldn't help sporting all day.

I couldn't believe it; whatever I'd done had worked, and she wanted me just as much as I wanted her. Even before the two of us did anything together, this knowledge made me feel, finally, like less of a newbie outsider observer and more like an actual member of the kinky community. Even though there was no official membership card, I felt like I'd had an N for newbie stamped across my forehead, perpetually staring into rooms and hearing cries of pleasure ring out as people got hoisted into the air, bound to crosses, and whipped until they almost bled at the parties I attended.

Natalie and I arranged for a spanking date while she was in town, but what wound up happening was even more exciting. I'd long been an avid sex-toy user, browsing at Toys in Babeland whenever I had a little cash to burn. I was well armed with vibrators but wanted to have a good paddle or two around just in case. A dominatrix friend had given me one she'd won as a prize, a black, shiny, patent-leather number with a star cut out in red on one side. She'd even spanked me with it, leaving my butt stinging. But I wanted something else, something special, and I settled on a paddle that had leopard-print fake fur on one side and firm leather on the other. I had both these toys for many months before they ever saw any use beyond hanging decoratively on my bedroom wall, where I'd see them and feel my body twinge with longing for an unknown top to come along and beat some rapture into me. I hoped that Natalie's visit would be the occasion for my paddle's deflowering.

I never could have expected, however, that our two-person date would wind up as a wild double date that culminated in an orgy with Natalie and some of my best friends. We started off at a local bar, drinking and being silly, after Natalie and I had spent the day holding hands and wandering around New York. She was so soft and curvy and beautiful, and I was both crushed out and in extreme awe of all the things she knew, like how to tie elaborate knots, and her penchant for peeing on

SUVs on the street to show just how much she hated them. Her spice prevailed over her sugar, but it was the sticky, swirly combination that drew me to her. She didn't care what anyone else thought of her, and it showed, not in a bad way but in a take-charge, kick-ass way that I wanted to emulate. Even though our lust for each other was simmering under the surface, there was also something very gentle and caring about the way we interacted, like we could kiss for hours and hours until we got to the good stuff and not feel cheated.

So we wound up out with my friends Jane and Sean, a couple I'd dabbled in with flirting and more, though his cock was off-limits when the three of us were together. They were plenty of fun and were my regular drinking buddies in my Williamsburg neighborhood, always ready to hit the local dive bar. I also got a kick out of the fact that long before Jane had moved to New York from Florida, I'd bedded her at a writing conference on a couch in front of whoever happened to be passing by. We'd morphed into a flirty friendship, with the flirtatiousness aided by copious amounts of alcohol. So between the four of us, things got extra-wild. Sean had just gotten a penis piercing, and Jane kept yelling for me to scamper off to the bathroom with him to see it. I did, and oddly, though I'd had the hots for him when they first got together, seeing this latest metal adornment didn't do much for me. Still, having a guy unzip and show off his cock at the behest of his girlfriend certainly got me in the mood, and we eventually took our little party a few blocks away to Jane and Sean's apartment. I still hadn't gotten the spanking I'd been craving from Natalie, and was prepared to get one in front of everyone, if need be. We even had the paddle with us, but for some reason we wound up going online, lured into looking at bondage photos of Jane taken by a local Internet porn photographer rather than tying her up ourselves. Somewhere along the way, I got it into my head to call my San Francisco lover, the one who'd taken me to the play party, wanting to tell him that I was with Natalie—and that she was going to spank me.

I was breathlessly recounting our drunken antics, with all four of us piled onto the couch in various formations, when Natalie none too decorously pulled the phone out of my grasp and shouted a good-bye before flinging it onto the floor. "You can talk to him later; we need you now," she said, before pulling my face to hers and kissing me lustily. Beside us, Sean and Jane were groping each other, and soon Natalie was spanking me, her hands just as powerful as I'd imagined them to be. Soon she got out the pretty fur-lined paddle, showing little mercy with its more tender side as the leather whacked my ass again and again. I rested my head against Jane's back as I got more and more turned on.

"I want to try," Jane shouted when Natalie took a momentary break from roasting my ass. My magenta-haired friend jumped up, then pulled off her skirt and settled herself across Sean's lap, leaving her in the perfect position to be spanked. While Jane was just getting started, Natalie had already warmed up her spanking arm on me, and brought the paddle crashing down onto Jane's ass with a resounding *smack* that made us all jump a little. "Ow!" Jane yelled, almost indignantly, even as she raised her pale buttcheeks into the air for more. I knew she wasn't used to such a vigorous pounding, and stared in delight as Natalie did what she did best.

I watched, and helped a little, mostly running my hands over Jane's ass to feel the aftereffects of Natalie's smacks. Seeing my friend get the punishment I thought had been my purview alone was a treat, and it felt as though the four of us were moving as one as Natalie spanked, Jane writhed, Sean kissed Jane, and I floated around the other three, stroking here, pinching there. Later, Natalie spanked me as Jane sucked on my nipples, the burn from one woman soothed by the tug of the lips of another.

All of us were slightly incongruous, our outsides not necessarily matching up with the inner perverts we knew ourselves to be. To the innocent bystander, Natalie, with her blond pigtails and sassy cheerleader look, could've been sweet as pie, as girly and feminine as you please, but once you dug deeper, there was a sassily sadistic streak to her that came to the fore when she really got into the spanking zone. To the rest of us, spanking was a fun diversion, but she turned things up a notch, knowing exactly where and how to hit, which words to murmur to set us off, and Jane and I were the lucky recipients of her perverted mind. We all wound up tangled in a heap in their bed, happily exhausted, not minding the debris we left in our wake.

o   o   o

MY RELATIONSHIP with my San Francisco lover continued for as long as it could, despite the distance. I found myself finding excuses to head to California, and was thrilled when I found out that I would be in Los Angeles for a family function. I asked my San Francisco lover if he would fly down to meet me, and he agreed, making the prospect of a boring family vacation into one now tinged with kinky fun. Looking back, I have no real clue what we were doing, only that I was desperate to be with him and would grab any opportunity to do so. He picked me up where I was staying with my family, and we were off to a hotel. The first thing we wanted to do, of course, was tear each other's clothes off. We'd been having steamy phone sex as often as we could get away with it, sharing all kinds of fantasies, and I felt closer to him than ever. We were ready, but there was one little problem: Each of us had forgotten to pack even a single condom. This was typical for two overworked, absentminded writers, but in the heat of the moment, naked and horny, we didn't feel like going back outside to get any. He came up with an ingenious solution to our momentary dilemma.

"Turn over and stay there," he barked, his voice turning from tender to demanding. Just hearing those words was enough to make me fall for him all over again. He didn't scream, and I knew that if I wanted to, I could get up and cross the room, but with him, the thing I most wanted was to have him tell me what to do, and then do it. I'd never experienced quite that same thrill before, that desire for discipline of the highest order. I turned over, offering up my backside, greedy, as I waited for him to return. I was willing to let him do things I'd only thought about before, things I hadn't been sure—before I arrived at our hotel room—whether I'd go through with. But when he slipped the blindfold over my head, I knew I wanted that darkness, wanted another chance to escape from reality into our own private, special world where only the sound of his voice and his touch mattered.

"Give me your wrist," he said, and I did, feeling him shackle me to the bed. He made me test the bond, and I truly couldn't escape. This was it, my moment of reckoning, and I chose him. I was nervous, my heart pounding, but excited as well, because I trusted him implicitly. And I knew he was about to spank me. The first night we'd been together, I'd lain on the floor across his lap, after he'd fucked me so hard and so well that I gushed all over him. He'd spanked me for what seemed like hours, though I'm sure it was much less, and still I wanted more. He got out a glove and some lube and did things to my ass that I'd always imagined I'd find unpleasant. But the way he spanked me made me want everything from him, and our hotel adventure was no exception.

He got out a paddle and began spanking me, the firm leather striking my bare curves until I couldn't think at all, could only take and take and take from him. It felt divine, and he kept on going while I shivered in delight. "I don't think that's enough for you, is it?" he asked. He was a pretty ordinary guy on the surface, but he had one of the most sadistic minds I'd ever encountered. When he spoke, he knew just the words to get me off. He could say, "You're my little whore, aren't you?" and I'd say yes, and mean it. One of the greatest compliments I've ever received came after I'd made him come, long-distance, during phone sex. "You're good at that!" he exclaimed, like it was a huge shock.

So while he told me alternately what a greedy slut and what a good girl I was for taking his smacks, still, a part of me wanted more, and he knew it. He always seemed to know what I wanted, often even before I did. I'd brought a modest collection of toys, none of which I'd tried before but ones I had been desperately curious about. He stopped spanking me, and I heard him rummaging through my toys. Then I felt that telltale first drop of lube land on my ass, followed by his fat fingers massaging my anus while I sighed in pleasure. "Do you want me to fuck your ass?" he asked, his voice calm and matter-of-fact even though I knew his cock had to be totally hard by then.

"Yes," I whispered, unable to say it any louder. There were still things I had to whisper, had to say quietly, lest the whole world hear. Then he gave me a small vibrator to use on my clit, placing it in my hand and turning it on. "Put that on your clit while I spank you," he said. I immediately moved the buzzing toy to my clit. It was smaller than the kind I was used to, but in this position, under these heady circumstances, it was just right. Then he proceeded to ease the small buttplug, no bigger than two of his fingers, a small purple bit of curved plastic, into my ass before spanking it all the way inside. As he used the paddle to pound the toy home, I bucked against my new toy. Once the plug was snugly between my cheeks, he returned to spanking my ass, a triple assault that soon had me crying out, not caring about the hotel's thin walls as he reddened my behind and got me so excited that the tiny plug kept threatening to slip out, making its exit by sliding along my slippery backdoor channel until he had to pummel it back in. We repeated this process over and over as the vibe buzzed against my clit. There was nothing I could do to escape, nor did I want to.

o   o   o

THERE WERE OTHER spankings after him, but none that stand out all that much. I'd started to experiment with the other side of the equation, meeting submissive men who took a while to reveal their true natures, but once they did, it was bottoms up. At first, I wasn't quite sure how to react. When you're used to getting spanked, to the mental and physical and emotional roller coaster that a powerful top can provide, how do you turn the tables and become who you once feared? I tried playing the domme to these guys, tried getting into their minds and being the one to lead us down paths unknown, but every time, something seemed lost in translation. I felt as though I was reciting lines of text, acting rather than truly giving them what they needed. And for my part, even when I did manage to talk the talk, I didn't feel that corresponding thrill deep inside. I could do it, but I didn't get off on it. Until I met Kerry.

It wasn't until I met Kerry that I really learned how to spank someone else. I'd done it before, here and there, but had never felt anything like the jolt I got from being spanked; it was something I could do but never something I *needed* to do. We'd been seeing each other for a few months before that need became overpowering. She was small, and often felt as though she was a doll or a girl, someone much more fragile and delicate than I. But instead of feeling overly big next to her, we complemented each other perfectly. She somehow brought out a side of me that wanted to protect, torment, and tease her all at once, and making up games for us to play excited me. One of which went like this: Two days before our trip to Los Angeles, I tell my girlfriend she's not allowed to masturbate until we arrive in the city of angels. I've never given her an order like this, and I'm not sure how she'll react, but I'm pleased that even though she is usually a once-a-day masturbator, she not only follows my command but delightedly tells her friends about it. After her parents drop us off at the airport, I pull her into an extra-large stall in the airport bathroom and make her close her eyes before fastening a glistening new magenta collar around her neck. We exit and both admire it, our eyes drawn to this simple addition that in a moment seems to drastically change our relationship.

We board the JetBlue flight, not caring so much about the multiple cable stations as the chance to get it on while in the air. She has the aisle seat, and I have the middle. I know she's scared of flying, but I intend to make sure she doesn't have time to worry about any disaster befalling us. After we're seated, I start playing with the collar, my hand automatically reaching for the hook. It looks so good on her, so natural, and I can't help but look up at it and smile every few minutes. We've been inching toward playing like this—me ordering her around, spanking her—but the collar has raised the bar for our play together. Since she likes to be choked, I know that every time I tug on the collar and the band digs into her neck, she gets excited, and I use this knowledge to my strategic advantage.

I have a surprise planned for her, and she is trying to guess but clearly has no idea. We have piled huge stacks of books and magazines in front of us, all the ones I've been meaning to read but haven't had a chance to. The flight attendants keep stopping to examine our towering media piles, picking up Ellen DeGeneres's book and saying, "Oh, she's so funny!" before heading on their way. When the drinks cart arrives, I ask for a water and a tomato juice, and some ice. When they ask Kerry if she wants ice, I nudge her and she says yes. I'm delighted when our drinks arrive with not one but two cups of ice each—perfect! She still doesn't know my plan, and is pestering me with questions, so I finally whisper her mission to her.

There is an "iced T-shirt" contest coming up at a local play party in a month. "I want you to enter it, and wear that shirt that clings to your tits, but first I want you to practice your nipple-icing skills, right here, right now."

She gives me a big grin and says: "You're fun," agreeing immediately. As quickly as possible, I grab a piece of ice and slide it into her bra, hoping that no one around us has noticed. I do the same for the other nipple and watch as a stain quickly spreads across her top. I don't linger and rub them into her nipples for fear of getting caught, but can tell by the way she squirms that the ice is having its intended effect. Every fifteen minutes or so I slide more ice into her shirt, and we try to cover our giggles. Even once it melts, her nipples are prominently visible through her shirt, the wetness giving her a look at odds with the rest of her put-together appearance.

Later, we spread most of the magazines across her lap strategically, so when I slide my hand under her skirt, nobody will notice. The guy sitting by the window is preoccupied with his computer, and the other passengers are watching their TV sets, so I have time to slide her panties aside and slip two fingers inside of her, while trying to move my arm as little as possible. The magazines teeter but stay in place, and I hope that I'm the only one who can hear the way her breathing has changed as she gets wetter. I bend my wrist as well as I can from my seat, not able to enter her as deeply as I'd like but teasing her nonetheless, stroking the entrance to her cunt and playing with her clit. I stop after only a few minutes, knowing that this warm-up will make her ready for much more later.

As we exit the plane, after gathering all of our stuff, one of the flight attendants gives us a knowing look and says, "Be good, girls," a twinge in her voice letting us know that she has a clue that we haven't been exactly "good" up to this point. We smile and exit. The plane ride is only the start of our public sex, but she doesn't need to know that, yet.

As it turns out, she's the one who ups the ante while we wait seemingly forever to get our rental car. We're New Yorkers, so this is completely out of my league, not to mention the fact that cars scare me. There are only a few customers waiting in front of us, and she takes the opportunity to flash her welt-covered ass at me, causing me to flash back to the night before we left.

I used to work the door at a women's play party for a few years, greeting all manner of kinky queer chicks. Some would come in proudly displaying ample amounts of cleavage, others wielding huge implements or having their slaves carry them. I saw a wide array of kinksters in my years of observation, but one of the things I didn't get to do very often was play. This suited me fine, as most of the time I was single, and generally don't favor public sex, especially for scenes of such an intimate nature. For me, spanking takes me to such a deep, intense, overwhelming headspace that I have little room while I'm giving spankings or getting spanked to ponder whether I'm measuring up as someone's entertainment du jour. I don't want to have to think about anyone else except me and my partner when I'm engaged in spanking, but with Kerry, I made an exception. I made lots of exceptions with her, somehow wanting to do anything and everything together. We had this magical ability to laugh our way through even the craziest schemes, willing to test out new scenarios even if we found they didn't suit our needs.

I have never been much of a belt wearer, probably because I invariably favor skirts or dresses. If you counted the total number of pants in my closet, you'd probably need only one hand. But with Kerry, I found that her belt could come in very useful—to spank her with, that is. Just holding it in my hand made me feel incredibly powerful and self-assured, never mind listening to it sing as it sailed through the air. That night, I arranged to get off duty early so I'd have a little time with her. We found a darkened nook that was still visible to other people but not in the middle of a huge crowd. I ordered her to take off her jeans while I doubled the belt over in my hand, feeling that same familiar rush of power and pride when she did as I said. Having ushered her into the world of S/M play, I'd been amazed at how quickly she went from merely curious to an almost insatiable bottom. She pushed me to think more creatively about what I wanted from her, and I was in turn awed that just by telling her to do something, she would. That kind of power was new and trippy for me, so seeing her bent over against the wall like that while I let the belt fly through the air and sear against her skin turned me on in a way nothing else had.

It was a different sensation from someone directly touching me, but no less exquisite. I could sense some prying eyes lurking around, but they just made me more focused on my task. In the murky light, I could make out the bare outline of her ass, so I knew where to strike, but I didn't see all the damage I had done to her delicate skin until the next day. At the car rental. She just laughed as she shook her ass lightly, letting her skirt fall back down. She egged me on and I stepped forward, forgetting momentarily about where we were and what might or might not be appropriate. I gave her ass a light slap, but part of me wanted to simply grab her right there, ignoring everyone else. That's how it was between us and continued to be until the end.

The last time we had sex before we broke up was the most powerful, and pitiful, and bittersweet moment of all. From day one, there'd been another girl between us, lurking, waiting to rush back into Kerry's arms. We all knew it but kept it unspoken, pretending we were in our own universe. Some of the time, we truly were, and even strangers could tell that we were in love, with or without the collar or any other adornments. But the previous week I'd found out for sure, and had been dreading her return from her vacation with the other girl. My stomach had flipped when I'd heard, and I could barely sit next to her on the train, heading home feeling weighted down, knowing I was about to lose the girl who meant everything to me. So, since the next day was Valentine's Day, I tried to keep things light. We met up in SoHo, and I bought a pair of Fluevogs, those delicately curved trademark forties-heel shoes, in magenta with lime-green piping. They were on sale, and they fit perfectly. We made it back to her place, and I sat there babbling. She handed me a box from Victoria's Secret, one whose contents I could predict before I'd even torn the first ribbon.

Months earlier, we'd been in a mall together and I'd tried on a delicate purple lace bra but had decided it was too pricey. Sure enough, what lay inside was the very same bra along with a matching garter. I wanted to hand it back, knowing I'd never be able to wear it again without thinking of her, wondering if the other girl had been with her when she'd bought it, but instead I just tucked it into my bag. We kissed like we'd never get the chance to again, which in many ways was true. I went about spanking her almost like a robot, wishing I could feel anything but what I was feeling, wishing we could somehow start over, go back to the beginning and discover ourselves all over again. But all I could do was move by rote, trying as hard as I could to bring us somewhere close to pleasure, even though I knew that was impossible. We tried to pretend everything was normal, but even though our bodies could respond, it wasn't worth it if our hearts weren't in it, and eventually I dropped my hand and we simply lay there with nothing to say, with a silence so deep no loud whack could fill it.

o   o   o

MANY MONTHS WENT BY when I didn't want to have anything to do with spanking. Every reminder of it just felt painful, and I wondered what I "was" in terms of kinkiness. Still a top? A bottom? A switch? My entire erotic identity had become so wrapped up in my relationship with Kerry, which had taken me to new heights I'd never experienced before. But then I slowly started to let in the possibility of trying again.

It felt as though it had been ages since I'd been spanked, and spanked properly. My body barely remembered it, which was compounded by the fact that I'd now edited a book of spanking erotica, so I felt I had to talk and think about spanking all the time, not to mention answer questions and field queries about the topic, but getting to do it was much more rare. I met Carl while giving a presentation to a local group about spanking. He was cute, bald, and muscular, and when he started flirting with me at the presentation, I got totally flustered. I was pretty sure he was top-about-town, and uncertain about what, exactly, I was getting into when I went to his house and agreed to meet him for a spanking date, but I was certainly excited. I barely knew him, though we'd exchanged a few e-mails in preparation for the day. His apartment was stark and clean, and we got right down to business. I was wet almost from the moment I walked in the door, but he didn't find that out until much later. We started out with his hand, and he was stronger than anyone who's ever spanked me before. He made me take off all my clothes while his stayed on, and immediately, that power imbalance tripped me up.

Before arriving, I hadn't realized he was involved with someone, though when he'd flirted with me, one of my first thoughts had been, *How can someone so hot be single?* So it made sense that he had a partner, even though I was quite disappointed when he told me that I'd be denied the pleasure of having his cock inside me. I didn't think about it too much at the time, though to me one of the most perfect sexual combinations comes from getting spanked as hard as I can take it, which inevitably makes me crave a good, hard fuck, and then getting that fucking, whether by fingers, a cock, or a dildo. One without the other is only half the fun, but I'll take half over nothing. Besides, Carl took his spanking seriously, just like Tina had so long ago; it's a rare quality I'd come to find in the people who are in it for more than a lark, for whom spanking speaks to them on a primal level. I've been with too many lovers whose idea of a proper spanking involves three, maybe four, halfhearted whacks, and then they're done. They think that's enough, rather than just a mean tease that almost makes things worse.

I agreed to Carl's boundaries, even though as his hand came down to beat my ass, I couldn't help thinking about him bending me over the very chair he was sitting on and taking me hard from behind. I was once again splayed across his lap, my long, brown hair falling to the floor while he made me count. After we were done there, we moved to the couch just as a loud, harsh thunderstorm struck outside. Getting spanked as the sky outside darkened made my "punishment" feel even more intense. "You should get spanked more often," he said, "since you're so good at it." He talked to me like what we were doing was an everyday occurrence, even though I wondered if I'd ever been spanked so hard. He had plenty of weapons to choose from, and he put them to strategic use.

He took a small but sturdy paddle and made sure to strike me in time with the lightning. My skin was starting to get hot, and I wiggled around on his lap, knowing that I was making his cock hard. "Stay still," he ordered, gripping my hair at the back of my neck. I moaned and tried to do as he'd said while he kept right on spanking me, a steady, thorough beating that seemed as though it might go on forever. I had come so far from that first, nervous spanking with Rachel, and this time, I could sink into the heat from his hand and surrender to the pleasure he was offering me, knowing both what I liked and what it felt like to be on his side of the equation. He let me suck on his fingers, which got me even hornier, and I was hoping that perhaps I could get him to stick them inside me.

Instead, he continued spanking me until my entire bottom throbbed. I was torn between wanting more and wanting a break when he decided for me, rubbing his warm, strong hands against my ass, pulling my cheeks apart as he examined me. Even though we hardly knew each other, between our e-mail banter and the way he seemed so enthused about spanking me, I felt totally at ease. He then grabbed me by the hair and positioned me between his legs. My pussy twitched, much as it does now, recalling what happened next. Nothing makes me wetter than being on my knees. He pushed my hands behind my back, then offered me his hard cock to suck, but only if I refrained from using my hands. I wanted more, and I'm sure a part of him did, too, but this was the agreement we'd both somehow made in this triangle, so I leaned forward and sucked his dick into me as my hot ass felt the aftereffects of his blows.

He guided me through the process, making me slow down. "Just the tip. I want you to only suck on the tip. Run your tongue along the edge," he told me, forcing me to pull away for a moment and look into his eyes. He knew exactly how horny this was making me, how much I wished I had his cock deep inside my pussy when I took him into my mouth. But I knew that he was having trouble staying in control, keeping his firm, stern, manly role while I was sucking him for all I was worth. I clenched my fingers together behind my back to keep them where they belonged, even though I would have much rather had them wrapped around the base of his cock and fondling his balls, yet something about knowing they were behind my back *for him* made it worth it.

I returned to my task, slowly swallowing him down my greedy throat while he occasionally moaned and murmured. He fondled my cheek, his fingers stroking lightly as I felt his hardness against the soft walls of my mouth and ran my tongue against his skin. I moved a little so my pussy was pressing against my ankle, needing any bit of relief I could get. I moaned against his cock, trying to speak but quickly finding that I couldn't. My mouth was wet, too, pooling with saliva as I rode back up, keeping him between my lips the whole time, forced to get creative as I got acquainted with the process of no-hands cocksucking. Then he helped me out, holding on to his dick while I started bobbing up and down, faster and faster, and—even though he was plenty big—wishing he were bigger. I liked the challenge of giving a blowjob as much as the act itself, the way I at first have to open my lips wide and momentarily wonder, even if it's someone I've been with before, whether his swollen head will actually fit between the O of my lips. The way I then steer myself down, wondering how my mouth will ever accommodate an entire cock but knowing that I need to keep going and find out. He again tangled his fingers through the hair at the back of my neck and lifted me off. The tugging made me wet all over again. Hair pulling sets me off like nothing else. I stuck out my tongue and he beat off against my mouth and lips while I tried to get him inside. I inched forward and he placed his cock between my breasts, where it rested like it was made to fit there in that soft, flesh tunnel.

I leaned down and did my best to lick his head as it rose up to meet my tongue while his legs pressed against my sides. I was trapped, and I loved it, wishing I could stay there forever, even though I knew I couldn't. Then he jerked himself off with

226

slow, assured strokes before coming all over my breasts, his cream dripping down my chest and stomach like a painting.

Then came the strangest and least satisfying part of our evening. I was so turned on from everything we'd done, I was practically climbing the walls with need. And, make no mistake, it *was* need. Spanking is not a one-act play with me; it's foreplay, even though I sometimes never want it to stop. But when it does, I need to get fucked. But that wasn't going to happen, even with his fingers. "I want you to come for me," he told me, spreading me out on the floor in front of him while he retained his regal position on the couch, looking down at me. I spread my legs but felt nothing but silly. Giving myself to him was one thing, but trying to re-create my masturbation rituals, which are not only private and so tied with my own bed but that also don't entail the most attractive positions the body can form, was another. I wanted to refuse, but I'd come this far, so figured I might as well continue.

At first, I looked at him. After all, he was the one who'd just seen inside me with his hands, read my mind as he spanked me just hard enough, then ever so slightly harder, than what I thought I could take, making me push my own limits in a way that set off a roaring ache inside me. But watching him watching me actually made it all worse. His eyes felt too strong for someone who I might never see again, someone whose partner was really running the show there. I shut my eyes and focused on my fingers, an unusual sensation since I'm much more used to a powerful, electric vibrator that can move faster than my fingers can ever hope to achieve (and I can type one hundred WPM). I tried my best, wanting to give him what he wanted, even though I had a sinking feeling that no amount of finger foreplay would make up for missing him ramming himself into me, for taking me the way he'd just taken my ass.

I was suddenly self-conscious about him seeing me so raw, waiting for me, asking me for something I had a feeling was impossible.

"Do what you do when you're alone," he said, then asked how long it usually took. We were encroaching on tricky, dangerous, personal territory. Dare I tell him that sometimes I can't even make myself come? That when I do, it's glorious and earth-shattering, but when I can't, like now, I feel like my body's betrayed me? We didn't know each other well enough for that, so after a few more futile attempts, I climb across his lap for my final good-bye spanking. As I leave, I'm of two minds about the whole encounter. He gets my need to be spanked, gets it inside and out, the head play and ass play, but is that really all there is? There's got to be more to life than just a spanking, even one from the best.

o   o   o

RECENTLY, I wound up at a small event that transformed into an orgy before my eyes. Some of the people there knew one another, some didn't, but the couple who caught my eye were new to me. I had observed their interactions, the way he pulled her close to him on the couch, the way they finished each other's stories. There's something about couples that gets me going, because I know that if I join them, it'll be for much more than a two-plus-one-equals-three equation. They bring more than their share of erotic energy because they know each other so well, and even though when I'd arrived I hadn't planned to play with them, later, when we were all piled onto one bed, my observation turned into participation quite quickly. I gave him a backrub, then we switched positions and his powerful fingers sank into my back, practically melting me against him. Hands started to inch their way up my legs and over my breasts. Who the hands belonged to I didn't know, but the harder he kneaded my back, the more I didn't care.

I wondered if Shira would be upset when her boyfriend switched his attention from my back to my breasts, but she soon joined him, and my skimpy slip came off. But once Shira slithered over to me, she was all I could think about. The others in the room seemed to fall by the wayside as she kissed her boyfriend and then me. Later, I found I was the first woman she'd ever kissed, but I would never have been able to tell. We were both wearing only our underwear, and somehow, that felt right. I didn't want to get totally naked, though I did enjoy grinding my knee against her panty-covered pussy. I put my arms around both of them, kissing her while stroking his arm.

She had large breasts, the kind that seem to pull me to them as if magnetically. I leaned down and sucked one into my mouth, her moan my reward. The more we kissed and fondled and sucked, though, the more I wanted to spank her. At first, I thought I'd keep quiet about this request; even in a group of perverts, it felt weird to ask out loud, to have everyone know that was what I wanted. Plus, I wasn't sure who to ask for permission—him or her? Finally, though, I just had to do it; her ass, straining against the confines of her panties, was just irresistible. She agreed, and so, with her lying on top of me, I reached my arm around and smacked her ass. Then I squeezed both cheeks, wishing we knew each other better or were alone so I could really explore her body. But I kept on spanking her, while her boyfriend joined in as she kissed me. She was clearly enjoying herself. I'd had no idea if she would even want to be spanked, but I was glad she did. It didn't go on for as long as I'd have liked, but that brief taste was enough to let me know that my time as a top wasn't totally over yet.

o   o   o

EVEN THOUGH I've certainly had my share of spanking fun, I'm not done. I have many fantasies that haven't yet been fulfilled, some scripted and some free-form, ones that keep me awake late at night, ones that haunt my mind, ones that keep coming back to me. I want to co-top a curvy, writhing, pretty young thing, a round, sexy girl who's used to getting her way, a naughty brat who needs to be taught a lesson. A girl who will really appreciate a spanking but one so wily and demanding that she needs two people to take her down. Someone to push me past my own limits to spank me harder than I've ever been spanked but then be there to hold me afterward, to whisper cruel entreaties and sweet nothings into my ear when I need them.

One thing's for sure: When I make good on these fantasies, I'll be writing it all down.

About the Authors

BILL BRENT is the author of *The Ultimate Guide to Anal Sex for Men* (Cleis Press, 2002). His fiction and essays appear in more than thirty anthologies, including *Everything You Know About Sex Is Wrong*, *Best American Erotica 1997*, *Best Gay Erotica 2002* and *2004*, and *Bi Guys*. He coedited the *Best Bisexual Erotica* series with Dr. Carol Queen, the second volume a finalist in the fourteenth Lambda Literary Awards. He coedited *Tough Guys* with Rob Stephenson, which was a 2002 finalist in the sex category of the Firecracker Alternative Book Award. His articles have appeared in the *San Francisco Bay Guardian, San Francisco Bay Times, Other* magazine, *P.O.V.,* and at GoodVibes.com. He has self-published several chapbooks of poems, short prose, illustrations, and photos. For details, or to subscribe to his e-mail newsletter, please visit his website, www.AuthorsDen.com/BillBrent.

RACHEL KRAMER BUSSAL is the editor or co-editor of over a dozen anthologies, including *Caught Looking, Hide and Seek, He's on Top, She's on Top, Yes, Sir, Yes, Ma'am, Crossdressing, First-Timers, Up All Night, Glamour Girls, Sexiest Soles, Ultimate Undies, Secret Slaves; Erotic Stories of Bondage,* and

Naughty Spanking Stories from A to Z, volumes 1 and 2, and the non-fiction collection *Best Sex Writing, 2008.* Her writing has been published in over 100 anthologies, including *Best American Erotica, 2004* and *Best American Erotica, 2006, 5 Minute Erotica, Single State of the Union,* and *Everything You Know About Sex Is Wrong.* She's contributed to *Bust, Cosmo UK, Huffington Post, Mediabistro, New York Post, Penthouse, Playgirl, San Francisco Chronicle,* and other publications. She serves as Senior Editor at Penthouse Variations, hosts and curates the In The Flesh Erotic Reading Series and wrote the popular Lusty Lady column for the *Village Voice.* Her website is www.rachelkramerbussel.com.

AMIE M. EVANS is a widely published creative nonfiction and literary erotica writer and author of the online column "Two Girls Kissing." Evans is also an editor, experienced workshop provider, and a retired burlesque and high-femme drag performer. She is on the board of directors for Saints & Sinners LGBTQ literary festival and graduated magna cum laude from the University of Pittsburgh with a BA in literature. She is currently working on her MLA at Harvard and her first novel.

ADAM GREENWAY is one personality among dozens inside one of queerotica's most lyrical authors. A poet, writer, and quiet enigma, Adam has published work in numerous anthologies and online venues, wearing alternate guises to experiment with sexuality, gender, and style. Although his name is fictitious, the events depicted in "Threeway" are not.

MARILYN JAYE LEWIS is the founder of the Erotic Authors Association, the first international writers organization to honor literary merit in erotica writing and publishing. She is the award-winning author of *Neptune & Surf,* a trio of erotic novellas, and the co-editor of the international best-selling erotic art book *The Mammoth Book of Erotic Photography.* She has received many citations and awards for her erotic fiction, including being named finalist in the William Faulkner Creative Writing Competition and winner in the New Century Writers Awards for her novel *Curse of our Profound Disorder.* Her short stories and novellas have been published worldwide and translated into French, Italian, and Japanese. *Lust: Bisexual Erotica* (Alyson, 2004) represents her collected erotic short fiction from 1997 to 2003. Other anthologies she has edited include *Hot Women's Erotica, That's Amore!, Stirring Up a Storm, Zowie! It's Yaoi!,* and the upcoming *Ribbon of Darkness: Collected Stories of Marilyn Jaye Lewis.* Her popular erotic romance novels include *When Hearts Collide* and *When the Night Stood Still.* Upcoming novels include *Freak Parade, A Killing on Mercy Road, We're Still All That,* and *Twilight of the Immortal.* Visit her website, www.marilyn-jayelewis.com.

IAN PHILIPS is the mama bear, or editor-in-chief, of Suspect Thoughts Press. He loves this job because he gets to work with brilliant word wantons, including Patrick Califia and Rob Stephenson and Amie Evans and Adam Greenway, and he gets to fuck the publisher, Greg Wharton, whom he's been happily fucking since 2001, and to whom he has been also very happily married since the 2004 Winter of Love in San Francisco. He knows his way around a porn story or two. He's written two collections' worth, and one of them even won a Lambda Literary Award. And he's even coedited a thick handful of erotic anthologies, again, all with Greg Wharton. What's with these two, are they joined at the hip? Close. Visit his web-site, www.ianphilips.com.

ROB STEPHENSON's writing and artwork appear in likely and unlikely online and print locations under many names, including Rob Stephenson. His CD, *dog*, composed with Mikael Karlsson, is available from PleaseMusicworks. Visit his website, www.dog-cd.com.

GREG WHARTON is the publisher of Suspect Thoughts Press (www.suspectthoughts.com). He is the author of *Johnny Was & Other Tall Tales* and the editor/coeditor of numerous anthologies, including the Lambda Literary Award–winning *I Do/I Don't: Queers on Marriage*. He lives in Oakland with his brilliant and sexy husband, Ian.